I WANT TO GO HOME

CINDY L. FREEMAN

AUTHOR OF THE DARK ROOM

HighTide
Publications, Inc.

Deltaville, Virginia

High Tide Publications, Inc.
1000 Bland Point Road
Deltaville, Virginia 23043
www.HighTidePublications.com

Publisher's Note: This is a work of fiction. Names, characters, places, and incidents are a product of the author's imagination. Locales and public names are sometimes used for atmospheric purposes. Any resemblance to actual people, living or dead, or to businesses, companies, events, institutions, or locales is completely coincidental.

Printed in the United States of America.

ISBN: 978-1-945990-27-4

First Edition: September 21, 2018

Other books by Cindy L. Freeman:

Diary in the Attic

Unrevealed.

The Dark Room

Chapter 1

I suppose there were signs leading up to that fateful evening, but, at fifteen, I was too busy being a self-absorbed teenager to notice. Mom called a family meeting after dinner. Although it was twelve years ago, I can still recall every detail. Leaving the dirty dishes on the dining room table, Mom ushered us into the family room. I remember where each of us sat, the exact expressions on my parents' faces, and even how our family room smelled: the lingering odor of Mom's beef stew mixed with Glade Plug-ins, which she used religiously, and my little brothers' sweaty, blond heads.

Mom started the meeting by assigning seats. Dad, who seemed tired, took his regular seat in his brown recliner and Mom sat in the antique rocker that had once been her mother's.

My brothers, Pete and Joey—who could never occupy the same room without wrestling—were separated on the leather sofa by me, to prevent them from clobbering each other. Usually, I could hold their heads apart, so they ended up punching the air, but at six and four years old, they were already getting too strong for me.

"Come on, boys. Settle down," Mom said. "Dad and I need to tell you something, and it won't be easy to hear." I remember thinking, why can't grown-ups just come out with it? Why must they prepare their kids for bad news by building the suspense and, consequently, the feeling of dread?

"I knew it," Pete said before Mom even got started. "You're getting a divorce." I was holding my breath as he blathered on. "Ryan's parents are getting a divorce, but they fight all the time." Now Joey started crying. Mom tried to calm both boys, but Pete wouldn't give her the chance. "You can't get divorced. What about us kids?" I think I was still holding my breath when four-year-old Joey wiped his tears and runny nose on my sleeve.

"Hold on, you two," Mom said. "Let me finish. We're not getting a divorce." I exhaled, and my brothers let out huge sighs. But our relief was premature. Dad squirmed uncomfortably in his recliner, avoiding eye-contact. Mom sucked in a long, slow breath of pine-scented air, and I could tell she was working to hold back tears. I wanted to run away—to fly up the stairs to my girly, pink room, climb into my soft, inviting bed with the flowered comforter and cover my head with a pillow. I could tell the announcement was not going to be good. But what could be worse than Mom and Dad getting a divorce?

"Your dad is... sick," Mom began, her voice barely audible. I looked at Dad who was staring at his sturdy hands—those hands that, for me, had always represented security. For the first time, I noticed his skin was pale, his eyes hollow.

"How sick?" I asked, not wanting to hear the answer. I was relieved when Pete interrupted.

"We'll be good and quiet, so he can rest and get better," he said.

"Yeah," said Joey, who liked to parrot his older brother. "Good and quiet."

"I'll bring you ginger ale, Daddy, and your newspaper," Pete added.

"Me, too, Daddy," chimed Joey. "And you can borrow my bunny rabbit. Bunny always makes me feel better when I'm sick." Now, as liberal tears rolled down Mom's cheeks faster than she could wipe them away, I realized I already knew the answer to my question. Dad was dying.

The remainder of the meeting became a blur as I retreated inside my head to imagine surviving chemistry without my dad, graduating from high school without Dad, going to college and leaving Mom alone to raise my brothers, and getting married without my father to walk me down the aisle. I heard only bits and pieces of the conversation that followed: Mom and Dad trying to be optimistic, Pete and Joey asking endless, unanswerable questions, words like "fight," "battle" and "never give up." Finally, the five of us hugged, and even my strong, invincible dad had tears in his eyes. He told us how much he loved us and asked us kids to help Mom.

You see, until the summer of my fifteenth year, life for Abigail Elizabeth Jordan had been ordinary. Mine was your typical American family: one mom, one dad, three kids, and Bella, a mixed-breed dog adopted from the humane society. We lived in a green and white, colonial-style house on a cul-de-sac in a middle-class neighborhood of James City County, Virginia. That's near Colonial Williamsburg, the famous living museum representing the eighteenth century when Williamsburg was the capital of Virginia.

Our only other relatives were Grandma Jordan in California, her sister, Great Aunt Mavis, and Mom's brother, Uncle George, who lived in France with his second wife, Simone. Mom's parents had passed away when I was younger, and Dad was an only child.

It was a gradual process, spanning two long years, that took my father's life. First it sapped his strength, his personality, his savings, then ultimately, his hope. Mom had never worked outside the home, not since having us kids, anyway. She was content, even proud, to be a stay-at-home mom. She always said her most important job was raising her family, and Dad agreed.

As a professor at the College of William and Mary, Dad earned enough to sustain our lifestyle, or so I thought. He had a retirement fund and stock market investments. Never, in a million years, could I have imagined that my family—the Jordans of James City County, Virginia—would end up homeless.

Chapter 2

Ayear or so before Dad's illness, I heard him and Mom talking about a recession. I knew what the word meant because we had discussed it in social studies class. But I never thought the recession would touch my family. My dad was smart. Even after losing all his stock market investments, he assured us we'd be fine. Then he got sick, and our lives began to whirl around us like a crushing tornado with ever-increasing destruction along its path.

Soon I was taking care of my brothers while Mom essentially lived at the hospital. When she was home, she spent most of her time on the phone with the college administrators or the health insurance people or buried in paperwork—whenever she wasn't cooking, cleaning, driving us to activities or doing piles of laundry, that is.

I didn't notice it at the time, but looking back, I realize Mom was becoming more and more isolated from her friends. She dropped her book club, church activities and aerobics class at the gym. It was obvious the whole situation was getting to her, but in my adolescent mind, because she was a perfect mother, she could handle anything.

All us kids had chores, but, let's face it, jobs assigned to four-

and six-year-olds are designed more for teaching responsibility than for relieving the adults' workloads. Despite a ton of homework and daily band practice, I tried to help as much as possible—watching the boys after school, packing lunches, folding clothes, and cleaning bathrooms. I delayed getting my driver's permit and trying out for cheerleading. Now it seemed I'd accomplish neither of those goals any time soon.

Mom was looking tired and acting stressed all the time, and I noticed she was growing short-tempered. The boys seemed extra whiney and out-of-control, but she didn't have the energy to deal with them. Mostly she yelled. It wasn't like her at all.

Approaching my sophomore year, I needed my mom, but she needed me more. It felt like our roles were reversing. I was missing out on being a teenager. I wasn't ready to be the parent, and I resented the responsibility being placed upon me. Then I felt guilty about resenting it. As much as I knew my attitude was wrong and selfish, sometimes I resented Dad for getting sick. Then I felt guilty for feeling that way. When life stinks and there's no one to blame, the anger festers like a huge, infected boil.

Sometime during my junior year, Dad was moved to the Medical College of Virginia in Richmond. After numerous surgeries and rounds of chemotherapy failed, he participated in a clinical trial at the hospital. That didn't work either. Dad looked like he had lost half his body weight. He was hooked up to oxygen and morphine all the time, and he was so weak that Mom had to feed him. I couldn't bear to see my strong, masculine father reduced to jutting bones and hanging flesh, but Mom insisted we kids go to MCV every weekend.

At each visit, I'd approach Dad's hospital bed hesitantly, not sure what to expect, wondering if his appearance would be more shocking than it had been the previous week. At first, we'd chat for a few minutes while Mom talked to Reuben Gray, the social worker assigned to our family. Dad always wanted to hear about school. He would encourage me to never give up on my life's goals, especially college. "With your grades, honey, you can apply for scholarships. I have confidence in you."

Then, one weekend, the conversations ended. Dad was too weak to talk, and I couldn't look at him as he wasted away in a morphine-induced stupor. Weeks before, his friends and colleagues had stopped making the one-hour trip to Richmond. Now our only visitors were Hospice volunteers and Reuben.

My mother grew more exhausted and depressed by the day. I wanted to help, but I couldn't even help myself deal with all my confusing emotions. Mom was too sad and stressed to talk about the situation. The boys were horrid, chasing each other around the hospital room, yelling like banshees, and hitting each other until Mom would make me take them to the lobby and try to keep them entertained. As Dad's condition worsened, I welcomed the chance to leave the room, to escape the putrid odor of impending death.

I remember not being surprised that day, in the spring of my junior year, when Mom announced we wouldn't be going to the hospital anymore.

Chapter 3

Dad's memorial service happened on a Tuesday, and my closest friends, Mindy and Alyssa, were excused from school to attend. Mindy sat with my family in the red-cushioned front pew. She and I had been best friends since kindergarten, which made her more like a sister, although the resemblance was not physical. Where I had reddish blonde, curly hair, Mindy's was straight and brown. I was tall and slim like my mom with fair skin and blue eyes. Mindy was five-foot two with brown eyes and a fuller figure.

Alyssa and her family sat directly behind us, and some of Dad's colleagues from his department occupied the pew across the aisle from us. Our wonderful neighbors, the Rigbys and the Johnsons were there, too.

Strangely, I didn't feel like crying. I just felt numb and sort of relieved. I had done most of my crying when I first found out Dad was sick, and I was cried-out. Bright sunlight streaming through the tall windows on the west side of the large sanctuary fell across my shoulders providing warmth but no comfort.

As usual, Mom expected me to oversee Pete and Joey who were now seven and five. It was my job to make sure they didn't talk during the service. I took the boys' hand-held games with the volume set on "mute." I couldn't take a chance they might grow restless and create a disturbance. I remember thinking that little kids don't understand how solemn such occasions are meant to be. Mom and I tried our best to prepare them, but Joey still didn't have the greatest self-control.

Mom and Grandma Jordan, Dad's mom, sat at the end of the front pew, embracing each other and weeping silently. I wanted to be the one hugging Mom and sharing her grief. I wanted to feel her arms around me, assuring me we were going to be okay.

Next to Grandma was Pete, then me, Joey, Mindy, and Mindy's parents and brother, Brendan. Grandma flew in from California for the service. She acted all lovey-dovey with us kids, but I felt like I barely knew her. When Grandpa was still alive, they traveled a lot, taking cruises and such. After he passed away, she came to visit us maybe once every other year and we talked on the phone monthly. I remember flying to California one time when Pete was a baby but after that, the trip was just too expensive for a family of five.

Uncle George couldn't attend the service, but he and Aunt Simone sent a gigantic bouquet of red and white flowers, roses and chrysanthemums adorned with a huge, white bow. It seemed pretentious to me, like Uncle George was flaunting his new continental lifestyle since divorcing my real aunt. I suppose losing my dad felt so wrong that it colored all my perceptions. I was sad, but I was also angry, intensely, selfishly angry at the injustice of it.

The pipe organ music sounded somber but soothing. I recognized the familiar hymns, but I couldn't sing. My voice was stuck somewhere deep inside, and no amount of air could push it through my vocal cords.

The minister kept speaking words about Dad that didn't seem like the person I knew. Sure, he was "intelligent, dedicated to higher education, and a good citizen who gave back to his community." But, to his family, he was so much more than platitudes. He was our rock, our solid footing. With his unconditional love for each of us, he provided the stability needed by every growing child. He always made me feel special, not ordinary. Strangely, I knew my brothers felt just as singular to Dad. He had a way of identifying and extolling each of our best qualities.

I remember thinking the pastor was pretending to know my dad. It wasn't his fault. The church was large, and our attendance had been sporadic. I wondered if he applied a standard eulogy to every memorial service, one in which he could insert the person's name, age, job, and a few characteristic qualities. I wanted to bolt upright and scream, "Terry Jordan was my father and he loved me!"

I recalled the day I fell off my bike and scraped my entire left side on the pavement. Dad carried me into the house and carefully removed the embedded cinders from my thigh and arm. Gently, he washed and dressed my wounds and held me until my tears abated.

I was only eight when my first dog, Snuggles, died. Trying to comfort me, Mom said, "Abby, don't worry. We'll get another dog, and you'll fall in love all over again." Of course, she was right, but her statement, regardless of its truth, did nothing to alleviate a little girl's grief. Dad helped me wrap my beloved pet in his favorite blue blanket and, together, we carried Snuggles to the back yard. Dad dug a grave in the same corner where Snuggles liked to nuzzle under the fence and share canine gossip with the Rigby's dog, Ike. As I dropped Snuggles' favorite ball into the grave beside him, Dad offered a simple prayer. Then, he held me and let me shed my tears of grief all over his favorite golf shirt.

Later that year, Pete came along and changed our family dynamic. I gained a sweet baby brother, whom I adored, but I worried about losing the special focus of my father's love and attention. I needn't have worried. Dad found a way to share the love he had showered on me without allowing its intensity to diminish.

As the memorial service droned on, I wanted to look behind me to see which of my friends had come, but I didn't think it would be appropriate to turn around. I decided to wait and read the guest book later.

I had attended the funerals of my maternal grandparents, barbaric affairs that they were. I remember being shocked by the open-casket custom. I wanted to scream that they didn't even look like my Grandma and Grandpa. Fortunately, Dad had been cremated, so at least we were spared the torture of viewing his emaciated remains.

Instead there was a picture of him—before he got sick—displayed beside the urn containing his ashes. He looked handsome, healthy, and confident. I wondered how such a vibrant man could be gone, reduced to ashes and memories.

Usually, during church services, even as a young child, I could feel God's presence surrounding me. It was like intuition, I suppose, but real and comforting. At times, the Holy Spirit seemed to infuse my human spirit, holding it upright as quantifiably as my spine held my physical body erect. Especially when we sang the old, familiar hymns, I sensed a deep connection to the hymn writers and the generations of worshipers who had gone before me. But at a time when I needed God's presence more than ever, there was nothing... only a black hole of emptiness.

After the service, a shorter ceremony took place at the cemetery where Dad's urn was placed in a niche at the mausoleum. Pete and Joey sat entranced in the big, black limousine, escorted by police cars. I suppose it distracted them from the intensity of the occasion. At one point, Joey asked, "Where's Daddy?" which made Mom and Grandma burst into tears. "Oh, I forgot," he said, staring at his hands.

The worst part of that day was after we returned home. I had planned to take Mindy and Alyssa upstairs to my room where we could speak frankly about the whole miserable situation. I needed to talk about it, to release the pressure that sat on my chest like an anvil. But the house began to fill with people. A few ladies from church milled about the kitchen, helping Mrs. Rigby and Mrs. Trent (Mindy's mom) uncover and carry platter after platter of food to the dining room. My stomach felt hungry, yet the thought of eating left me nauseated.

Friends, neighbors, and Dad's colleagues from the college arrived and began smothering us with hugs and typical words of condolence. When Pete and Joey made a beeline for the desserts, instinctively, I knew it was my job to keep them under control. Mindy and Alyssa helped me by suggesting board games and taking my brothers and their's to the backyard a couple times to toss a ball or play with Bella.

Finally, the long day ended, plunging the Jordan family into its new "normal." In some ways, it was easier for me. Clearly, Mom was not herself, but now it was her job to oversee the family, and I didn't have as much responsibility for my brothers. I was lonely, though. Mom spent a lot of time in her room with the door closed; and all those friends, except Mindy, who had attended the memorial service pretty much ignored me. As an adult, I understand they weren't sure what to say, and decided it would be simpler to avoid me, but at the time, I felt abandoned.

I resolved to focus my energy on schoolwork and college plans, hoping it would help me forget the previous two years and move forward with my life. What I didn't know, at the time, was that my mom, the model wife, mother, and homemaker, was headed toward destruction.

C3&0

A few weeks after the memorial service, I was upstairs in my room straightening my long, blonde "frizzies," when Mom called another of her dreaded family meetings. If I thought the conference a year earlier was life-changing, this one topped even the news that Dad was sick. Mom announced she would have to get a job. But that wasn't all. I'll never forget her next words. She looked at me with cheerless eyes and said, "I'm afraid you're going to have to put off going to college. We just don't have the money, and besides, I'll need you here to help with your brothers when I go to work." In stunned silence, I had stopped listening at the word "college." Not go to college? I had been planning this important milestone for four years or more. What was she saying? That I couldn't pursue my dream of becoming a documentary film-maker? I had narrowed my choices to either New York Film Academy or Los Angeles Film School.

"What about my future?" I asked through hot tears. I didn't want to cry, but I couldn't help myself. I was so disappointed.

"Please try to understand, Sweetheart. We haven't had any income for two years, and our health insurance paid less than half of your father's medical expenses. I couldn't keep up with the premiums any more, so I had to cancel it."

"How could it get this bad so quickly? I thought Reuben, that case worker at the hospital, was helping?"

"Reuben has suggested resources, including Medicare, but with all my time wrapped up in your father's care, I haven't been able to stay on top of the finances or the paperwork. I've already depleted your dad's retirement fund and maxed out two credit cards. I just don't see any way you can go to college next year. Maybe after I work for a while and get caught up on the bills we can think about it again."

I hadn't seen that bombshell coming. How could I not go to college? It was inconceivable. I had known what I wanted to do with my life since the seventh grade and had meticulously planned my whole career. I had to leave the room before I said something I couldn't take back. Anger, disappointment, and confusion swirled together in my brain, threatening to explode in words I knew I would regret. I stood, turned, and retreated up the stairs, leaving Mom to deal with my brothers who always cried when they saw me crying.

"Please, Abby! Try to understand!" I heard her call, but I didn't have one ounce of tolerance or empathy left in me. Once I accepted the reality that my father was dying, I assumed life would finally return to normal after it happened. Mom would be the parent again, instead of me. I would go off to college and come home for holidays. It was the natural order of things.

Chapter 4

Mom spent the first week of our summer vacation filling out applications and scheduling job interviews. She clipped coupons like crazy, and discontinued the newspaper, landline telephone, cable television, and internet. Months before, she had canceled her gym membership, which she hadn't used since Dad's illness, anyway. Mom and I still had our cell phones, but only for phone calls and limited texting. Internet access was not included in our plan. She sold Dad's old Prius, which was originally supposed to become my car, but she got only enough to cover one mortgage installment. Now, we were eating a steady diet of pasta and beans, but still she couldn't keep up with the bills.

Finally, Mom landed a minimum-wage job at the Food Lion near our neighborhood, pricing groceries and stocking shelves. Her new boss promised that, since she had completed two years of college, she'd soon get a promotion to checker. Now everything was about money. Money, or the lack of it, was all we ever talked about, it seemed. Mom tried to reassure us kids, but she wasn't very convincing. I grew more worried by the day, and it was obvious my brothers shared my concern.

"What'll happen when the money runs out, Abby?" Pete asked one June morning as I prepared breakfast.

"Yeah, what will happen?" parroted Joey. Still wearing pajamas, he had climbed up to the kitchen bar beside his brother.

"We'll be fine. Mom has a job now and, besides, Dad had life insurance." I was beginning to realize we weren't going to be fine, but there was no reason to share the truth with two little boys who should be enjoying a care-free childhood. "You don't need to worry. Eat your peanut butter toast, and then you can go outside to play." I had a ton of chores to do before Mom got home that afternoon, and I needed my brothers out of my hair for a couple hours.

"It's too hot to play outside," said Pete, his mouth dripping with gooey peanut butter. "Can we go to the pool?"

"Yeah, can we go to the pool?" asked Joey.

"Pete, do you have to chew with your mouth open? It's disgusting." Handing him a napkin, I added, "We don't have a pool membership this year."

"What? No pool?" They both asked at once.

"What are we supposed to do all summer?" asked Pete. I was as disappointed as they were.

"I'm sorry, guys, but we can't afford the pool this year. You'll have to find other things to do."

"It's not fair! Ryan and Justin and Luke all belong to the pool. Now I'll never see 'em!" Pete was yelling now and getting Joey worked up, too.

"Not fair!" yelled Joey. "I was gonna learn the breast stroke."

"I know. I can't see my friends much, either. But Mom's doing the best she can. It's hard without Dad's paycheck. We all need to work as a team and help her out. Hey, I have an idea. Let's go on an adventure. We've never ridden the Williamsburg Trolley, right?"

"What's that?" Joey asked.

"You know, dummy," said Pete. "It's that old-fashioned bus with the green top." It wasn't a real trolley. Rather it was a small red-and-green bus with wooden seats made to look like an old-fashioned trolley car. It provided easy and inexpensive service from the William and Mary campus to some of the outlying shopping areas.

"I never did that," said Joey. "Let's go. Hey, don't call me dummy. You're the dummy."

"No name-calling," I said for what seemed like the hundredth time that week. "Why don't we pack a picnic lunch and ride the trolley to the library? We'll have to walk to the shopping center to catch it, but you guys are tough, right?"

"Right!" They chimed.

"Can Bella go?" Joey asked.

"No, stupid, they don't let dogs on the bus," said Pete.

"I said no name-calling."

"Sorry, I forgot."

"Did not!" said Joey.

"Okay, enough! Now, I need to clean up the kitchen and start a load of laundry. You two get dressed and brush your teeth. Then, come downstairs with your backpacks and help me make some sandwiches."

"I want peanut butter!" Pete yelled, as he headed for the stairs.

"Me, too," said Joey, following on his brother's heels.

"You had peanut butter for breakf... oh, never mind," I said, and began loading the dishes in the dishwasher with one hand while holding my toast in the other. Since Mom started working, I had learned to multitask like a real mother... not that my life's goals had ever included becoming a mother... or a housewife, for that matter.

Between bites, I texted Mom to let her know where we would be. As usual, she was too busy to respond, but she still wanted me to check in several times a day. Next, I called Alyssa, who lived in the next neighborhood, to see if she wanted to join us, but she had other plans. I knew Mindy was spending the day with her grandparents.

At least I had averted the potential tantrums. Now, I needed to succeed in making this so-called adventure fun. Otherwise, it was going to be a long summer.

When we left the house at ten a.m., the temperature had already reached eighty-five. I tried to convince Pete and Joey that our half-mile trek was an adventurous hike and that we were explorers. We searched for "grizzly bears," "tigers," "savages," "trolls" and any other creatures I could conjure, but after fifteen minutes in the intense heat, my brothers were having none of it. When we reached the shopping center, they were hot, thirsty, and tired, and I was already fed up with their complaining.

"This is just a bus with uncomfortable seats," Pete said, once we climbed aboard the trolley. Silently, I agreed with him, but I reasoned that at least the boys rode for free and my fare was only a dollar. Best of all, we were out of the house for a while.

"Sit down and be quiet for five minutes," I said, growing impatient.

"I'm thirsty," said Joey.

"That's why we brought your water bottle. It's in your backpack."

"But I want juice."

"We don't have juice," I growled. "We have water."

"Okay, okay, I'll drink water." I recall wondering what these two annoying boys would be like as teenagers.

"How far is it to the library?" asked Pete.

"Let's see how high you can count, in your head, before we get there... silently."

"Me, too?" asked Joey between gulps of ice water.

"Yes, you too." Maybe that'll give me a few minutes of peace, I thought as I checked my phone. There was a text message from Mindy asking if I wanted to go shopping for bathing suits the next day. "Sorry," I texted back, "have to watch my brothers. How about Saturday?"

"Going to the beach with Alyssa's family," she answered.

"Oh. How long?"

"A week at the Outer Banks."

"Call me when you get back. Have fun." I wondered if she could sense my jealousy.

Yup, I was missing the whole summer. No friends, no pool, no parties, no dates, no beach, no sleepovers, no college tours. Just a whole summer of playing mom to two bratty, tedious little boys. I shuddered to think about my senior year of high school, especially with no hope of going to college. I wondered how I would survive it.

CʒƸᴐ

Finally, after numerous stops along the way, the trolley approached Lafayette Street near the downtown library. We got off at the bus/train station only a block from the library on Scotland Street, and headed for the modern, two-story building. Only blocks from the eighteenth-century village of Colonial Williamsburg, the building's steel and glass design had always seemed out of place to me.

"I'm hungry," said Joey as soon as his feet touched the ground.

"You just ate breakfast," I said. "Let's go inside and cool off a bit. We can read a few books and then come back out here to eat our lunch." I pointed at a shady spot that abutted the parking lot across from the library's rear entrance.

With voices dripping with apathy, they both said, "Okay." As active as my brothers were, I knew they wouldn't last long inside the library, but finding free activities to keep them entertained was essential to my sanity and our limited finances. I knew that summer would not include Busch Gardens or Water Country. There would be no movies or eating out. Mom stressed that we had no disposable income. In fact, I wouldn't even be getting paid for taking care of my brothers who drove me crazy and kept me from having a social life.

Upon entering the library, we passed the check-out counter and began to meander through the stacks. That's when I noticed a new play area toward the rear of the children's section. The boys rushed to it and played happily for a good twenty minutes while I used a computer nearby. I had to break up only one fight. Then, I managed to keep them interested in reading for a while, and even talked them into joining the summer reading program.

Soon it was lunch time. After basking in the comfort of an air-conditioned building, the outside heat felt brutal, but we headed for the vine-covered structure I had spotted on our way in. I remember thinking it was likely intended to be a pergola. It looked more like the ruins of an old building to me, but there were stone benches in the shade where we could sit and eat, also a water feature I had never noticed before.

"Can't we eat inside? It's too hot out here," Pete said.

"No. They don't allow food inside."

"Not fair. Don't they know we're famous explorers who been hiking for days and days?"

"Yeah, days and days," said Joey.

"Trudging through snake-infested jungles and swamps filled with alligators," I added, realizing it was up to me to salvage this so-called "adventure." Continuing to embellish our story, we settled in for a picnic lunch.

The boys wolfed down their sandwiches and carrot sticks like they hadn't eaten in days. "Be sure to save some of your water for the trip home," I reminded them.

"The library has a water fountain," said Pete. "Can't we refill our bottles?"

"Of course. Good idea, Pete." Despite the heat, the boys got involved in a rousing game of pirates, complete with pretend sword-fights and treasure-hunting. Watching to make sure they didn't get wet in the inviting waterfall, I texted Mom to let her know we'd be heading home on the two-p.m. trolley. Then, we went back inside to cool off, refill our water bottles, and check out some books.

Soon it was time to go home so I could finish the laundry, vacuum the floors, and start cooking dinner. I decided the only way I would catch up on my chores was to allow the boys an afternoon of "vegging" in front of Nickelodeon. Oh, yes! It was going to be a long, boring summer.

At the time, I couldn't have known how much I would soon yearn for those mind-numbing days filled with cooking, cleaning, washing clothes, and entertaining my needy, energetic, quarrelsome brothers.

Chapter 5

It was a long summer, all right. By July, our weekly trips to the library had become mundane, and we had worn out the Monopoly game and Legos. I could hardly wait to return to school and see my friends.

Typically, Mom would take us shopping for school clothes in August. Each of us would get a new pair of shoes and a few outfits. The boys were growing so fast their pant-bottoms now hugged their knees instead of their ankles. Joey inherited a whole wardrobe from Pete, but Pete and I would have been out of luck if we hadn't discovered the Goodwill store. All together, we spent little more than twenty dollars for our entire wardrobes, and I was feeling proud of my frugality. New shoes were out of the question, though. Mom said we'd have to wait until she paid down her credit card balances. With her pathetic income from the grocery store, I didn't see how that would ever happen.

"Maybe Grandma can help," I suggested one day, as Mom was fretting over the mounting pile of unpaid bills.

"I thought about asking her," she said, "but she's been paying for around-the-clock care for her sister since Aunt Mavis had that stroke. It's very expensive, and your grandmother is on a fixed income now."

"Oh. I always thought Grandma Jordan was rich. I mean, she sends us those Visa cards every year for Christmas."

"Abby, don't mention our situation to her when she calls. Losing her only son has been hard on her, and she would be devastated to hear about our financial problems. Besides, I should be getting a promotion soon."

Instead of getting a promotion, Mom lost her job. She told me she got laid off, but one day I overheard her talking on the phone to Jill, one of her co-workers from the store. Since I could hear only one side of the conversation through her closed bedroom door, I wasn't sure what had prompted the heated discussion. But I could tell Mom was complaining about "unfair treatment." Then, I heard her say she didn't deserve to get fired.

"Jill, you know I never did it on the job," she continued, "well, except that one time." Never did what? She talked about "a second chance" and having "kids to support."

I decided to confront her. I opened the door and walked in without knocking, something we kids had never been allowed to do. She was sitting on the edge of the bed, talking on her cell phone. As soon as I entered, she turned to me, and looking shocked, hid something behind her back.

"Mom, what's going on?"

"Get out of here, Abby!"

"You got fired? Why?"

"It's none of your business. This is a private conversation."

"Oh, so you can tell Jill you got fired, but you can't tell your daughter the truth? What did you do to get fired?"

"Jus' leave. I'll talk to you later." It sounded like she was slurring her words. "Jill, I gotta go," she said.

"What's that behind you? What are you hiding?" I approached the bed and tried to see what she was concealing. When I spotted the wine bottle, my insides tightened with fear. Mom had told me about her father's drinking and how it had ruined her childhood. She suspected her brother, my Uncle George, had a problem with alcohol, too. Repeatedly, she had warned me not to start drinking because of her family history. It was the last thing I ever expected her to do. "What are you doing?" I asked, incredulous. "It's ten in the morning and you're guzzling wine? You don't even drink!"

"Leave me alone, Abby. Jus' go."

"Mom, you're actually drunk! Are you kidding me?"

"It's jus' a little wine. It helps me relax."

"Oh, it helps you? And how does it help your children?" I was so angry. I couldn't believe my teetotaling mother was drunk. "How could you let this happen? Don't we have enough to deal with?" When I tried to grab the bottle from her, I spilled some of its deep-red contents on her shirt and across the light blue bedspread. Her phone dropped to the floor.

"No!" she yelled. "Now look what you've done." She pulled the bottle from me and held it to her bosom like it was a precious baby. The sight of it made my stomach lurch. Our mom was all we had, and now she was risking her children's well-being. How dare she be so selfish!

I grabbed the bottle, and before she could stop me, I rushed to her bathroom sink and poured the remaining contents down the drain.

"No, Abby. Stop!" But when she tried to stand up, she fell backward on the bed and lay there, staring at the ceiling with glassy eyes. As I approached, she turned toward the wall, curled into a ball and pretended to be asleep. I was thankful Pete and Joey were playing outside and hadn't seen our mother in that condition. Her final words before I stormed out of the room were, "Sorry, Abby. So sorry."

Chapter 6

By September, Mom had fallen three months behind on the mortgage payments, and we were hounded constantly by collection agencies for unpaid bills. Then, Pete got strep throat—at least that's what Mom thought it was—and we couldn't afford to take him to a doctor. The poor kid stayed home from school for a whole week with a fever. I was worried he would develop scarlet fever. I had learned about it in health class and knew he could suffer lasting effects from the disease. I begged Mom to take him to the doctor, but she said we didn't have enough money to pay for it.

"What about that free place Reuben told you about?"

"What free place?"

"Town-something."

"Olde Towne Medical Center? That's not for us. It's for poor people; people with no insurance."

"Our health insurance was canceled, remember? You stopped paying the premiums."

"Oh, I forgot. Well, it wasn't doing us much good, anyway. I have a whole pile of bills to pay from your father's illness." It was like she was trying to deny reality or something, like our problems would disappear magically if she ignored them.

Mom kept Joey and me away from Pete, so we wouldn't get sick. She controlled his fever with cool baths and helped him gargle with salt water every hour to relieve his throat pain. It was shocking to see my normally energetic brother sprawled on the sofa day after day acting lethargic and looking like a ghost.

Finally, after three days with no improvement, I took matters into my own hands and called Reuben. Immediately, he made an appointment for us at Olde Towne Medical Center and urged me to take Pete that very day. Mom wasn't happy. It was as if she were afraid of being perceived as "less than." Now I understand it was shame that prevented her from getting necessary medical attention for her son. But the actual experience wasn't shaming or embarrassing at all. The medical personnel were kind and respectful. I expected the doctor to ask, "Why did you wait so long?" but he didn't. He even gave us free antibiotics for Pete.

The next day, Pete's fever broke, and he kept down a few spoonfuls of soup. He looked like he had dropped some weight, and he was weak for a few days after that. Of course, he fell behind in his school work. I tried to help him catch up, but I was taking all AP classes and had a ton of homework, myself. His teacher recommended a tutor. That sounded like the perfect solution until Mom found out there was a charge for home-bound instruction. She said she'd work with him. Somehow, he must have gotten caught up because his mid-term grades were fine.

⊗⊗

A few days after Pete's medical appointment, Reuben followed up with a house-call. I overheard him talking to Mom. They were sitting at the dining room table where he was trying to help her organize the piles of unopened mail and numerous documents that had accumulated.

"Elizabeth, I'm concerned that you're not staying on top of the bills or taking advantage of the assistance available to families like yours. There are many resources for folks in your financial situation." He was a large man with a deep, booming voice like James Earl Jones. He looked and sounded intimidating, but he was gentle and never condescending.

"I've just never had to deal with this stuff before, Reuben. Terry took care of everything: the bills, the cars, the taxes. Everything. He said my job was to keep the house and raise our children. He said it was a full-time job, and I shouldn't have to worry about all those other details, especially money.

"But, now you do, and I don't see you taking charge."

She continued without acknowledging his comment and it sounded like she was beginning to cry. "My father was the same way, but for him it was about control. He was a bully. I didn't realize it at the time, but now I know he was an alcoholic, and the drinking made him, well... unbearable. My mother was afraid of him. She didn't have any choices in her marriage. I guess I thought I didn't, either."

I remembered my grandfather being an unpleasant man who always had a beer in his hand. I knew Mom didn't have a good relationship with him, but this was the first time I heard her admit he was an alcoholic.

"It's all so new and overwhelming," she said as I remained still, hiding in the hallway beside the staircase. "Especially with the medical bills. I can't seem to keep up with the phone calls and paperwork, and I had to let our health insurance lapse."

"I can help with that, but we need to get you organized," Reuben said. If anyone could help Mom, Reuben could, I decided, feeling a measure of relief.

"I haven't even had a chance to grieve my husband's death, and now everyone wants something from me," I heard Mom say. "I feel like I'm being crushed by responsibility."

"I understand," Reuben said. "But your situation will continue to get worse if you ignore the immediate issues. You could lose your house. You could even lose your children." That got her attention. After a pause, I heard her blow her nose.

"Where do I start?" she asked.

Thank God for Reuben, I thought. During that first visit, he showed Mom how to organize the bills by their due dates. He told her she was eligible for a widow's pension. In fact, he discovered the application hiding in a pile of unopened mail and helped her complete it. He also helped her apply for Medicaid and informed her about food stamps and other services that could get us back on our feet. But acquiring all those services would require masses of paperwork, plus phone calls, and vigilant follow-up.

Now, as I recall that frightening period in our lives, I wonder if Mom followed through with any of Reuben's suggestions. Dad had always handled the finances and Mom was out of her depth. She had been a devoted wife and a loving, nurturing mother, but it seemed she was incapable of handling the day-to-day issues, especially concerning money. It struck me as odd that a woman who could plan and execute a perfectly stupendous birthday party, didn't have a clue how to support her family.

CRSO

One day, we came home from school to find there was no air conditioning in the house. With a substantial Indian summer heat-wave, the outside temperature had reached ninety-two degrees, and it seemed even hotter inside.

That night we ate cold Vienna sausage sandwiches for dinner because Mom was determined not to use the stove. We did our homework on the deck by candlelight while fighting off swarms of mosquitoes. After a while, Mom remembered a small fan that was stored in the attic. She retrieved it and plugged it into the deck outlet. It didn't provide much in the way of cooling, but at least it moved the air enough to keep the mosquitoes from devouring us.

The next day, Mom called a repair company that, three days later, sent someone to give her an estimate. When he informed her that the entire heat pump would need to be replaced at a cost of five thousand dollars, I thought she was going to swallow her tongue. But she had no choice. The heat pump also controlled the furnace. As uncomfortable as Virginia summers were without air conditioning, we couldn't survive a whole winter without heat.

As if our family hadn't experienced enough drama, a couple days later, Mom and I entered the family room from the deck and heard water running upstairs—a lot of water. "Now what?" she asked. "Where're the boys? Oh, no!" When the lights flickered, she took off running up the stairs. Within seconds, I heard a blood-curdling scream. Pete and Joey had decided to cool off in the bathtub but left the water running until the tub overflowed. Somehow the water traveled between the walls and found its way to the breaker box in the garage. Now we had no air conditioning, no electricity, and extensive water damage.

It took seven hot, humid days and nights to restore the electricity and replace the breaker box. It took another two days to replace the air conditioning unit and two weeks after that to repair the water damage. During that time, tension and tempers ran high in the Jordan household. Our nextdoor neighbors, the Rigbys, let us take showers at their house; and when the Johnsons found out we had no electricity, they invited us over for dinner a couple of evenings. They made it clear we were welcome, but I could tell Mom felt embarrassed to keep relying on our neighbors.

Mom maxed out another credit card to pay for the repairs which ended up costing nine thousand dollars instead of five. In the meantime, she claimed to be trying to find another job, but according to her, no one was hiring.

"We're going to have to sell the house, Abby," she said one day. Mom and I were having a private meeting at the kitchen island because she didn't want the boys to know how serious our situation had become. I thought I saw her hands shaking but convinced myself it was just my imagination. "And I think we should try to sell as many of our possessions as possible, especially the valuables. Do you know how to use Craigslist?"

"I think I can figure it out, but it requires internet access. Have you talked to Reuben about selling the house? Does he think it's a good idea?"

Now she was pacing back and forth in the kitchen, where she could finally cook again, waving a wooden spoon like a drum major marching down the football field. She stopped and threw her hands in the air. "Well, I can't pay the mortgage or keep up with the other bills, so what choice do we have?"

I couldn't answer that question, so I just kept listening as she resumed her pacing. "I'll make a list of all our saleable assets," she continued, now stirring whatever was cooking in the pot, "and you can take pictures of them. Could you use the computer at the library and post them on Craigslist?"

Now panic gripped me. "Mom, are we really that desperate?"

"I'm afraid so, at least until I start drawing my widow's pension. But that could take months." Yes, she was trembling, not just her hands, but her whole body. I worried she might be having a nervous breakdown.

"How did it get this bad? I thought Dad had a retirement plan and investments. What happened, besides the recession, I mean? What about his life insurance?" Mom explained that Dad had lost nearly all his investments during the recession, and that during his illness, she had been forced to deplete the remainder of his retirement fund to keep up the mortgage payments. She said his life insurance was only enough to cover his final expenses.

"I didn't want to worry you, so I didn't tell you everything. We owe thousands in medical expenses from your father's illness, and I'm way behind on the mortgage again. I can't seem to catch up."

"What about our health insurance, until you stopped paying the premiums, I mean? I thought the college gave us great coverage."

"It did, but our policy didn't cover the experimental drugs that were our last hope. When a loved-one is dying, you'll do anything to keep that hope alive. Reuben helped me apply for Medicaid, but I haven't heard anything yet." The more she talked, the more her voice quivered. "I haven't heard about the widow's pension, either, since I sent in the application almost a month ago. Every time I call about it, I get put on hold for an eternity. Then someone transfers me, and it becomes an endless cycle. It's a full-time job trying to keep up with the bills and mounting paperwork." Suddenly, she excused herself to the powder room. I wondered if she were going to vomit. "I'll be right back," she said. "Watch the sauce so it doesn't burn."

Within minutes she returned and, oddly, acted like nothing had happened. With steady hands, she poured the sauce into a Mason jar and stored it in the refrigerator. "I know this has been hardest on you, Abby," she said, running water into the pot to let it soak. "I know how much you wanted to go to college." We hugged for a few minutes, and I noticed the strange tremors were gone.

"Don't worry, Mom," I said, trying to sound confident. "We'll figure this out. I mean, how do other people do it? There must be resources for families like us, right?"

"I don't know. Oh, Abby! What are we going to do?"

"Just stay calm," I said. I grasped her shoulders, as if I could keep the trembling from returning. "I'll spend Saturday at the library doing research. What about church? Maybe our church can help. Maybe Uncle George can help."

"But it's so embarrassing. I don't want our friends and family to know we're destitute. Besides, George lost a bundle in his divorce. Simone is wealthy, but she's not even family, not really. I feel like a failure, like I've failed you and the boys."

"Listen, Mom, you haven't failed anybody. You've tried your best to support us, but you couldn't have predicted the recession. You couldn't have known Dad would die. We thought our future was secure. Now we have to admit we need help and ask for it." At the risk of creating more tension, I added, "and drinking will only make matters worse."

"I know. I've stopped," she said. But had she really stopped or was she just getting better at hiding it? Foolishly, I decided to believe her. "I planned to go back to work as soon as Joey started kindergarten, but then your dad got sick. Besides, no one will hire me without experience. How am I supposed to gain experience without a job?" She was beginning to cry, and I felt completely helpless. "I couldn't even hold onto a minimum-wage job. I'm so sorry, Abby. I've failed you."

"Stop saying that, Mom. I know you did the best you could." But it was true. She had failed us, and I was resentful. Somehow, though, I felt responsible. At the time, I didn't realize how much responsibility I was taking upon myself. It seemed like it was my job to keep Mom from falling apart and to hold our family together. "I'll take a year off after graduation, earn some money, and then go to college on student loans. Maybe I can even get a scholarship." I tried to sound cheerful and optimistic to keep her from losing hope. "Right now, we need to accept what's happened and figure out how to move forward. Upstairs, there are two little boys who need us, so let's get a good night's sleep."

"What would I do without you, Abby? When did you get so grown up and wise?"

"I had a good role model. Now let's go to bed." We climbed the stairs arm-in-arm with Bella trailing behind. I was trying to boost Mom's confidence, to help her believe in herself, but truthfully, I was terrified.

Chapter 7

I spent most of the next Saturday at the library searching the internet for local services. At first, I couldn't find much of anything closer than Richmond, Norfolk, or Virginia Beach, but I kept "Googling" until I discovered a site, Williamsburg Homeless Shelters and Services for the Needy. Thinking of the Jordan family as "needy" was a hard pill to swallow, but the sooner I accepted the reality of our situation, the sooner we'd have a place to live.

At last, I found all sorts of applications for financial assistance and low-income housing, but as I navigated the sites, I realized I didn't have enough information to complete the on-line forms. Mom would have to gather Dad's records and accompany me to the library. My priority was to find an apartment we could afford... someplace in our current school district, of course. I was determined not to change schools in the middle of my senior year.

I moved to my next task and started uploading the photos I had taken of our valuables and posting them on Craigslist, even my trumpet and the silver bracelet Mee-maw had given me for my seventh birthday. When Mom agreed to sell her diamond engagement ring and Mee-maw's antiques, I realized just how desperate our finances must be. I managed reluctantly to post most of the big items like bikes, lawn equipment, and some furniture—things we couldn't take with us to an apartment. Next, I listed objects I knew would bring the highest price, like Mom's fine jewelry and her set of sterling silverware that we used only at Thanksgiving and Easter. Of course, I'd have to return every day after school to check the responses, a task that would be easier if I had a driver's license. At least we still had a car. That day, I vowed to take my driving test as soon as possible.

I stayed at the library all day, except for a quick walk to Aroma's, the coffee shop on Prince George Street. Around one p.m. I realized I was ravenous. Only two blocks from the historic area, the sidewalks were teeming with tourists and college students. Some were seated at the outside tables, chatting away like they didn't have a care in the world.

After reserving the bus fare home, I had only enough change for a cup of coffee. I maneuvered through the crowd and worked my way up to the counter where I ordered a cup of coffee. I doctored it generously with cream and sugar, hoping to staunch my growling stomach.

As I sat at a corner table, watching the steady stream of students come and go, talking and laughing like they didn't have a care, I saw a couple of familiar professors enter. I averted my face. I wasn't in the mood to make small-talk with Dad's colleagues or to hear how sorry they were about his passing. I couldn't have stomached even a hint of pity from people who had so casually returned to their normal lives after Dad's service. Besides, watching everyone around me eating enormous sandwiches and luscious desserts made my stomach complain even louder. I stood, and weaving through the crowd, managed to slip out unnoticed.

I had started to walk back to the library when I remembered The Peanut Shop across the street. My stomach fluttered in eagerness as I recalled that free samples were offered throughout the store with its old-world charm. I could slip easily through the rear entrance and act nonchalant like a normal, paying customer, pretending to be one of hundreds of tourists who passed through the store daily. A few samples of various flavored peanuts would tide me over until supper, I decided.

Feeling guilty, but not enough to abort my mission, I crossed the street and entered the quaint shop that Mom had used as her main source of Christmas gifts for many years. We had sent the famous Virginia-grown peanuts to Grandma and Grandpa Jordan and Aunt Mavis in California, also Uncle George in France. We had given them to our neighbors on the cul-de-sac and to Dad's associates at the college. I reasoned that the Jordans had made enough purchases to justify a few free samples.

The store filled with barrels and tins of peanuts was crowded with tourists, most of whom were sampling myriad flavors displayed in bowls on the wooden shelves that edged the inside perimeter. No one seemed to notice me as I made the rounds. A few minutes later, having temporarily abated my stomach rumbles, I exited and returned to the library.

By four-thirty, my weary eyes rebelled against staring at a computer screen. I walked to the bus station and boarded the bus for home, remembering I hadn't even started the English paper that was due Monday morning.

As usual, an enthusiastic Bella greeted me at the front door, tail wagging and oblivious to the constant worries that plagued Mom and me. Bella led me through the dining room and family room to the rear, sliding door where I found Mom standing on the deck at the gas grill. That's one more item to post on Craigslist, I reminded myself. She was heating tomato soup in a saucepan and toasting slices of bread over the open flame.

"I thought the electricity was fixed," I said.

"It was. It is," she said, looking sheepish.

"Then why..." As soon as I started to ask the question, I understood that our service had been canceled because of nonpayment.

"Oh, Mom..."

"Come on, boys," she called toward the treehouse, ignoring the issue. "Your sister's home. Let's eat."

"Good. I'm starved," said Pete as he descended the ladder with his brother following behind.

"Me, too," Joey said. I sank heavily onto a deck chair, struck by how much my brothers would miss their treehouse and our spacious backyard after we moved.

"Go wash your hands," Mom instructed the boys, "and remember to turn off the water." As soon as they were out of ear-shot she started firing questions at me. "What did you find? Are there any apartments we can afford? How about Craigslist? Were you able to post everything? How will we know if somebody wants to buy something?"

"Slow down. I can only answer one question at a time."

"Sorry. I don't want your brothers to hear."

I told her I took lots of notes, but I needed more information to apply for assistance. "You'll have to come with me the next time. Maybe there's a school bus that can drop me off at the county library. I can do my homework while I'm waiting for a computer."

"That should work. Reuben has been helping me gather copies of our tax returns and other financial records. What about apartments?"

"There's an inexpensive complex near the high school, but it doesn't have any vacancies. So, I searched for cheap motels in case we can't find an apartment right away, and I posted most of our valuable stuff on Craigslist. I'll need to check back every day."

"Sh, the boys," she said, tipping her head toward the screen door.

"Tomato soup again?" asked Joey. "I'm tired of tomato soup."

"Just be grateful for food," Mom said. "Some children go to bed hungry, you know."

After we tucked the boys in for the night, Mom and I gathered all the pertinent documents we could find in Dad's study and agreed to meet at the library Friday afternoon.

In the meantime, without electricity or hot water in the house, the laundry was piling up and I had no clean underwear. This situation wasn't totally foreign to our family. We had survived at least three hurricanes that I could remember. After Hurricane Isabel, the electricity was interrupted for ten days. We learned to boil water on the gas grill. We and our neighbors took turns sharing food from our respective freezers to keep it from going bad. At the time, it seemed like a great adventure, one that brought the neighborhood together. I remember wondering if our family would ever experience those memorable gatherings again or would we end up in a shelter, unsure of which "neighbors" we could trust, and wondering where we might be sleeping the next night?

After washing my bras and panties in the bathtub and climbing in for a chilly bath, I went to bed feeling worried and anxious. I hadn't told Mom, but Ms. Gladstone, my guidance counselor, had called me into her office one day during lunch. She expressed concern that maybe something was "going on" at home. "I know you lost your father not long ago, Abigail. If you need to talk about it, I'm here, okay?"

"No, everything's fine," I lied, fearing she might learn we were nearly penniless. I felt humiliated by our unexpected loss of affluence and social status. I suppose I assumed I'd lose the respect of my friends and teachers if they knew. I didn't want to be pitied. "It's been hard on my mom, of course."

"Of course." She was leafing through a folder on her desk. "I haven't seen any college applications yet. It takes a while to complete them, so don't wait until the last minute. I can help you with that, too, if you need it."

"Thanks, but, um, I've decided to wait a year." I knew she wouldn't be happy with that announcement.

"Oh? But Abigail, with your grades… is there a financial concern? Because you can apply for scholarships and student loans, you know."

"I know, but my mom and brothers really need me right now."

"I understand, but let's talk again before you make your final decision. I'd like to chat with your mother, too."

I was already heading out the door. "Sure, but the bell rang for first period. I'd better go." Ms. Gladstone was nice enough. I could tell she really cared about us students, but I wasn't interested in talking to anyone about my dad or college or anything. My brain was too full of worry to think past the next day.

CR&D

For several reasons, we had stopped going to church. First, we had run out of clean clothes. Then, there were the sad memories associated with Dad's memorial service. But, as I reflect, I think the main reason was Mom's overwhelming shame about our financial situation.

Most folks in our church were well-to-do. Many would even be considered wealthy. It was located near the campus, which meant some of Dad's co-workers and students attended services there. Mom never mentioned it aloud again, but I knew she was afraid they would discover our secret. At the time, I didn't know she was protecting another secret, too.

Instead of attending church, we spent our next Sabbath in a laundromat. Mom had managed to save a supply of quarters for the machines. But first—after serving us a breakfast of dry Cheerios and lukewarm water—she instructed us to sort our belongings into piles of "keep," "sell," "give-away," and "throw-away." My brothers required a good deal of supervision with this task, but without TV to distract them, they managed to pare down a little. Mom prompted us to think in terms of practical-versus-frivolous, resulting in more than a few tantrums.

The worst outburst occurred when she told Pete and Joey they could keep only one stuffed animal apiece. After a heated argument, she finally convinced them that their cast-offs would help children who couldn't afford any stuffed animals. "Think of it this way," she said. "You aren't discarding your furry friends. You're giving them new homes with children who need them more than you do."

"Why do we have to move anyway?" Pete screamed from across the hall. We were busy in our respective bedrooms, but I could clearly hear the conversation as it increased in volume.

"Yeah, why?" asked Joey. "I don't want to move!"

"I don't want to move, either, but we have to!" Mom yelled from her bedroom. "Just do what I asked you to do!" I could tell she was starting to cry. Yelling and crying had become her normal responses.

"I'm still hungry," Pete said.

"We'll have lunch soon. Drink another glass of water."

"I don't want water. I want milk."

"Me, too!" shouted Joey. "I want milk, too! Why can't we have milk?"

Silence. Frightening, hovering silence. Mom's bedroom door slammed, and, through the wall, I heard her weeping. I ran to the boys' room, and with a little quick thinking, distracted them with a game of tossing toys and balled-up clothes into boxes to earn points.

A few minutes later Mom emerged from her room, acting like nothing happened. With a strained smile on her face and mouthwash-smelling breath, she hugged me and whispered, "Thank you."

"Hey, guys," Mom said, too cheerfully, "I think there's one more strawberry yogurt left in the cooler. Why don't you two split it?" Off they ran down the steps, pushing and shoving to be first to reach the bottom. "Be careful and remember the rule!" she called after them. The Jordan family's rule was that whoever divided something must give the other first choice of pieces. It worked like a charm to ensure a perfectly even split every time.

Now, Mom and I were left facing each other with unspoken words hanging in the space between us. I wanted to scream about how life wasn't fair, but what good would come from whining and complaining? We both knew our only choice was to get busy and do whatever we could to hold our family together and find an affordable place to live.

"Come on. Let's get our dirty clothes to the laundromat and figure out what we can feed those growing boys for lunch," Mom said, with unconvincing optimism.

"I'll take my iPad. Maybe the laundromat will have Wi-Fi, and I can check our Craigslist progress. Duh! Why didn't I think of that before? I don't have to wait for a computer at the library. I can use my iPad anywhere with internet access."

"See? You don't need a college education," Mom said. "You're already brilliant." I knew she was trying to cheer me up, but I struggled to find either cheer or wit in her words.

We stuffed our dirty clothes into large, plastic garbage bags, then piled into the car and headed for the laundromat. It was a new and exciting adventure for Pete and Joey who had never seen the inside of a laundromat. Mom got them busy sorting the clothes into whites and colors, loading and unloading the washers and dryers, and arguing over whose turn it was to put coins in the slots. Between their duties, they played Nerf football in the aisles, engaging another little boy who was there with his mother.

As I had hoped, a sign on the door said, "Free Wi-Fi." I set my iPad on one of the folding tables near an electrical outlet and immediately logged onto Craigslist. I yelled to be heard over the whirring washers and rumbling dryers to tell Mom we had received numerous offers.

"Really? Wow!" She moved closer and glanced over my shoulder to see that we had multiple bids.

"I knew your grandma's antiques would sell," she said. "They weren't my style anyway." I could tell she was feigning bravery for my benefit. I knew she loved those antiques. "What do we do next?" she asked, her voice quivering.

"Now we contact the highest bidders and arrange for payment and pick-up."

"That sounds great. Can you handle it?"

"Listen, Mom. I have a paper due tomorrow, and I need to finish the research."

"Oh. Okay, then, you work on your paper while I finish the laundry. I think I can scare up enough change to take the boys to McDonald's for lunch. You know, the one near our house with the indoor playground. We can work on the iPad while they play."

"It's a deal."

Chapter 8

We spent the next two weeks selling, donating, or tossing the bulk of our possessions, keeping only the essential items. In the sweltering, sweaty heat, it was exhausting work, especially before the air conditioning was fixed. The boys were grumpy, fighting constantly, and arguing with Mom about which items to keep and which to let go. A huge eruption occurred when she said they had to sell their iPads.

"No more video games? You're the meanest mom in the whole world. I hate you!" Pete yelled from the top of the stairs. Mom stopped her packing, sank into a livingroom chair and just sat there staring out the front window, suffering etched on her face. I was packing Dad's huge collection of books into a box. When I stood to approach her, she got up and ran to the powder room. I remember the relief that washed over me when she left the room. I didn't have the energy to comfort her.

Reuben had contacted a real estate agent who promised to list our house as soon as we installed the new heat pump and completed the repairs to the structure from water damage. Just in time for the first open house, some eight thousand dollars in expenses restored the electricity and air conditioning and repaired the water damage. Mom maxed out her last credit card, confident she'd be able to pay off all the charges as soon as the house sold. In the meantime, the interest fees skyrocketed.

When Francine, our realtor, announced that Mom owed more on the house than it would sell for, Mom was shocked and devastated. She had counted on making thousands on the sale to pay off our debts and rent an apartment, but it turned out she had absolutely no equity. Francine called it an upside-down loan. In fact, Mom discovered that a couple years before the recession, Dad had taken out a second mortgage to replace the windows, roof, and siding. If Reuben hadn't intervened, we would have ended up living on the street.

Reuben helped Mom apply for a housing voucher. Then, through a local agency, he found us a motel in Williamsburg that housed at-risk families. Unfortunately, they didn't allow dogs. We asked Mindy's parents if they'd be willing to keep Bella for us until we could locate permanent housing. They agreed. As I nuzzled Bella good-bye, I tried not to cry, but I couldn't help it. I would miss her so much, her unconditional love, the way she climbed on the sofa and laid her head on my lap as I watched TV, the way she greeted me at the door after school, the way her tiny tail wagged her whole body, and the way her warm fur wrapped around my feet at night.

"You can come for a visit any time you want to," Mrs. Trent said. "She's still your dog, and as soon as you're settled in your new home, she'll be with you again." Of course, Bella had no clue what was happening, and the boys accepted the arrangement only because we convinced them it was temporary, but my gut told me Bella would never live with us again. It broke my heart.

I made Mindy pinky-swear that she wouldn't tell anyone, even her parents, about how we lost our house, that it wasn't a choice to move, especially to a ratty motel. It was just so humiliating.

Normally, I was an outgoing kid. Not that I had a lot of friends, but I tried to act friendly toward everyone. Between classes, I would say, "hi" to others as I passed them in the halls or saw them in the cafeteria, but now I found myself looking down a lot, trying to avoid eye-contact. I didn't want any of my school friends or teachers to know what had happened to my family. They would ask uncomfortable questions, and they might discover I had been forced to move and now attended my school illegally. I suppose they thought I was still depressed over my dad's death. My unintentional strategy to avoid unwanted attention worked, but it also made me isolated and lonely.

As moving day approached, the boys complained a lot, and I was terrified. I kept thinking, this must be a nightmare. Surely, we'll wake up tomorrow and everything will be fine, not like before Dad got sick, but at least ordinary. We'll live in a decent apartment that doesn't stink, one where I'll have my own room again. It'll be in a complex that allows pets, so Bella can live with us, and it'll be in our school district. Most importantly, Mom will be herself again, loving, nurturing, and free of her growing stress.

As competent as our mother had been in raising us, and as organized as she had been in maintaining our home and our schedules, she wasn't equipped to be the head of our household. It took a while for me to realize how ill-prepared she was. After Dad died, I assumed she'd step into her dual role with ease. After all, she was the adult. I expected her to make everything okay.

But everything wasn't okay. We had already lost most of our belongings, and now, we were losing our home. The only good news was that we had made nearly ten thousand dollars from selling our possessions.

Chapter 9

No moving van appeared in our driveway that day. There was no need. We had sold, donated, or thrown away all but a carload of our possessions.

It was an emotional day, especially for my brothers. Mom and I couldn't make them understand why we had to leave and why they couldn't take their bikes or skateboards or most of their toys, for that matter. What do little kids know about upside-down loans, delayed social services, and maxed-out credit cards? Childhood is supposed to be carefree, filled with play and imagination, not riddled with senseless deprivation and worry. Not that I was thrilled about leaving the only home I had ever known, but, as miserable as I felt, I was old enough to realize we had no choice. Mom needed me to be strong for her and to help Pete and Joey handle our upsetting reality.

Our favorite neighbors, the Rigbys and the Johnsons, stopped in to say good-bye, and Mrs. Rigby brought us a plate of brownies. I knew I would miss Mr. and Mrs. Rigby, because they were like surrogate grandparents to us kids. They didn't have any grandchildren of their own and often brought us cookies or invited us over to watch movies. Somehow, I knew we might not see them again, despite relocating only a few miles from our neighborhood. We might as well have been moving to Mars.

"Elizabeth," said Mr. Rigby, as we stood in the driveway. "You should have told us you were downsizing. We could have stored some of your furniture in our basement until you found a permanent place."

"That's very kind, Sal, but most of my pieces were just too big for a smaller place," Mom lied.

Other than these two couples who still worked, we had few friends living near us. Ours was a subdivision of retired "snowbirds." On our cul-de-sac, alone, there were three houses that remained unoccupied for six months out of the year. Of course, the boys and I had friends on some of the other streets, but we saw them mostly at school. After Dad's death, Mom didn't like us inviting friends over.

"Well, be sure to stop by for a visit every now and then," said Mrs. Rigby. "And send us your address as soon as you're settled. We need to see those kids before they get all grown up."

When I hugged her good-bye, she had tears in her eyes, and I could tell she really cared about us. I wanted to scream, "We're in trouble! We need help!" To this day, I wonder why I didn't reach out to those wonderful, caring neighbors.

Mom's pride metastasized like a cancerous cell, its black tendrils invading every part of our lives. She would never have admitted to our middle-class neighbors that we had been forced to sell our house at a loss, that we were, for all intents and purposes, homeless, not on-the-street homeless, but that we had been forced to give up our beautiful house with its big yard. The pervasive attitude among my middle-class peers was that homeless people were dirty, lazy, worthless freeloaders, sucking the system dry like so many ticks on a dog. "No one needs to know our business," Mom said. "Besides, our housing situation is temporary. We'll be back on our feet before you know it."

The motel that became our new home was a blue and white two-story, concrete structure with multiple layers of paint peeling off the rusty, metal railings. Far from opulent, its only saving grace was its location a few blocks from the historic area, convenient to the post office, library, and bus/train station. The room, an efficiency unit, included a kitchenette with a small refrigerator, microwave, and two-burner stove. It was stocked with a few pots, pans, and utensils. With our housing voucher, the rent was only four hundred a month.

When Mom unlocked the door to room 206, an unforgettable odor accosted my sinuses, a stench that would never have been tolerated in our house. Despite someone's obvious efforts to clean for our arrival, the room smelled of musty carpet, stale cigarette smoke, and mildew, all churning and stinking into an olfactory experience that will never leave my memory, no matter how hard I try to forget it.

We emptied our suitcases into the limited drawers and closet space, and I helped Mom cover the stained mattresses with fresh sheets. Nothing else about the room was fresh, however. The gold, shag carpet was straight out of the eighties and coordinated with beige grass-cloth wallpaper and faded, gold, ribbed bedspreads. Beside the door, a large window, shrouded with heavy gold draperies overlooked the second-story deck and parking lot below. Closing the opaque draperies meant shutting out every ray of natural light.

In the corner, next to the window, a worn, upholstered chair squeezed between the radiator and the first of two double beds. Between the beds, a built-in night stand held a single lamp. As my eyes continued to scan the uninviting space, I spotted the l-shaped kitchenette and tiny bathroom opposite. To my right, the wall supported a built-in desk, flanked by dressers with foggy mirrors and one closet the size of our broom closet at home. With scarcely enough space to move between or past the beds, I wondered how I could ever think of this horrid place as "home."

Mom announced that we needed a trip to the supermarket. I think all of us were anxious to vacate the premises for a while and breathe some fresh air, but mostly, we were excited to help Mom fill a grocery cart with the most food we had seen in weeks. Finally, we could afford to buy meat, milk, and some fresh fruits and vegetables.

That evening, having no recourse, the four of us settled into our humble quarters. Mom cooked a one-dish concoction that tasted as scrumptious as it smelled, especially when compared to tomato soup heated on the grill. In a frying pan, she sautéed ground beef with onions, carrots, and potatoes. Then, she added a bit of beef broth and some salt. As hungrily as Dickens' orphans, we gobbled every morsel. The boys asked for milk, but Mom said we needed to save it for breakfast.

Clean-up was easy. We threw our cheap, thin paper plates in the trash, and Mom washed the pan and utensils in the small sink. It was like camping, minus the tranquility of sleeping under the stars and roasting marshmallows over a campfire.

After supper, we watched TV. Even the old-fashioned TV with its twenty-inch screen was a treat after nearly a week of deprivation. Then, we took refreshing, *warm* showers, and climbed into strange beds. Never again would I take for granted such conveniences as electricity and hot water or the comfortable mattress I had tossed and the down-filled comforter I had sold.

Mom assigned Pete and Joey to the bed closest to the bathroom. She and I would share the other, she said. I missed Bella, who normally slept at my feet and woke me each morning with a sloppy kiss. Bella had been my dog since before Pete was born. She was just a puppy when I chose her from the litter of a rescue-dog. I had trained her, named her, and for nine years, had walked her, fed her, slept with her, and loved her. In return, I received constant, unconditional love and loyalty. That first night was the hardest. I drenched my pillow with silent, salty tears as I realized my furry best friend might never share my bed again.

Chapter 10

Adjusting to motel living meant learning to subsist in about three hundred square feet of space instead of a sprawling four-bedroom house on a half-acre lot. But at least there was no lawn to maintain. Since I turned twelve, mowing the grass had been one of my assigned chores, and I awaited eagerly the day when Pete would be old enough to assume this odious task, especially during the summer months when Virginia's temperatures soared into the nineties.

It didn't take more than a day to realize that privacy was virtually nonexistent in this one-room hovel, and bathroom time was at a premium. To maintain my sanity in such a confined space, I took frequent walks. Since the motel was centrally located, I could easily access the historic area for a stroll down Duke of Gloucester Street or head in the opposite direction to the college campus. Fearing that sad memories would extract fresh pangs of grief, I took care to avoid passing Dad's building, especially whenever I let Pete and Joey tag along. Occasionally, we'd run into someone we knew, a professor or student from Dad's department. My go-to response to "How is your family doing?" was "Just fine, thanks. Have a nice day."

Of paramount concern with our displacement was that now we lived beyond our school district. Mom promised to drive us to our respective schools, though, and said we were not to mention to anyone that we had moved outside the district.

Often, throughout the ensuing years, I questioned my automatic acceptance of Mom's self-imposed isolation. Eventually, I realized my response was perfectly natural. Because I was still a kid, I trusted her instincts. I suppose it was akin to living in a commune where the cult leader is so convincing as to not be challenged. Now, I realize there were many people who could have supported us, both financially and emotionally during that difficult period, but we never reached out because Mom felt the need to protect our secret and did so scrupulously. Somehow, she convinced us that the system/ community was our enemy.

I had finally earned my driver's license, but now we were a one-car family, and Mom needed the car to spend her days job-hunting. Ten thousand dollars might seem like a lot of money, but I knew it wouldn't last long after paying for rent, utilities, groceries, and gas for the car. Of course, Mom's credit card debt far exceeded that amount. Rather than trying to make payments, though, she expended her energy avoiding the collection agencies that located us eventually.

It was impossible to deny that the Jordans were poor, that we had quickly fallen from our middle-class pedestal, where money and prestige erected an invisible fortress. Now we faced degrading, repulsive poverty, a condition in which one cannot help but notice one's inferior societal station.

Less obvious was my mother's gradual incapacity to cope with all the changes. At first the signs were subtle, allowing me the temporary luxury of denial. She started to forget things. She even forgot to pick me up after school one day, claiming to have been in a long job interview. But I knew she forgot. She was, again, becoming short-tempered with the boys, and I noticed she was acting secretive. Once, I caught her hiding something in the car. When I confronted her about it, she was jumpy and evasive. "I dropped an earring," she said, but I wasn't convinced. Then, quickly, she diverted the attention to me. "Why are you so suspicious, anyway? I'm an adult, and I don't need to report my actions to my teenaged daughter."

Until her personality began to change, Mom and I had enjoyed a reasonably honest relationship. Of course, we didn't tell each other everything, but, even as a teenager, I felt I could confide in her when it came to important matters. Now, I found myself holding back because I knew she couldn't handle any more stress.

Soon, I was catching Mom in frequent lies. Some evenings she would disappear for hours at a time, leaving me to cook supper, help the boys with their homework, and tuck them in for the night. When she finally returned, her eyes seemed weirdly vacant, and she acted bizarre, stuttering and stumbling until she had to hold onto furniture to maintain her balance. Was she sick or had she started drinking again? Was she taking drugs? Surely not! My mom was a teetotaler who always cautioned me against drinking and "using." She never even drank a glass of wine with dinner. She said that since alcoholism ran in her side of the family, it was safest to avoid addictive substances altogether. No. She couldn't be drinking again. I convinced myself it was my imagination. Surely, she wouldn't risk her children's well-being or waste what little money we had on expensive booze.

Mom had always been an early riser, but now I was having to wake her. One morning, I found her difficult to rouse. I wondered if she were getting sick like Dad. At night, after everyone was asleep, I would pray, Please, God! Don't take my mom, too. I've had to give up everything else. What would I do without my mother? How would I survive? How would I take care of my brothers? It was a wholly selfish prayer, typical of a wholly self-centered teenager.

At first, out of fear, I dismissed the signs. Because I couldn't face another life-altering trauma, I refused to believe anything serious could be wrong with Mom. She was just tired and discouraged by our situation. She was grief-stricken at losing her husband, ashamed of losing her job, and overwhelmed by debt. Who wouldn't act strangely? Surely, she would snap out of it soon.

I talked to Mindy about Mom's bewildering, broken behavior, and she said Mom was probably depressed. "After all, she lost her husband, her home, her neighborhood, her whole identity. She's probably feeling helpless."

"But aren't those reasons that people start drinking or taking drugs?"

"Sure. In some cases, but your mom wouldn't put her children at risk like that." I hadn't told Mindy about catching Mom with a bottle of wine at ten in the morning. "Maybe she just needs to let off some steam. Give her a little time. She'll be herself again soon."

"I hope you're right."

But Mindy wasn't right. The terrible truth was that my mom was an alcoholic, and I was powerless to stop her passage to destruction.

CRSO

Within a month of living in the motel, Mom and I started arguing regularly. Not that we hadn't ever locked horns before, but now there were multiple disputes every day. Her justifications for her words and behavior were ludicrous. It was clear my mother no longer resembled the Elizabeth Jordan of my childhood. It was frightening.

One day, I tried delicately to suggest that maybe she was becoming dependent on alcohol, that maybe she needed help. But she wouldn't listen. She screamed at me and accused me of not appreciating all she had done to keep our family together. She denied any hint of addiction and said I resented her for a situation that was out of her control. My loving, nurturing mother was becoming impossible. Gripped by ever-increasing fear, I didn't know where to turn without betraying the unspoken promise of silence she required of me.

One evening our conflict erupted like a lanced boil. Joey was watching his favorite TV show. When Mom told him to get ready for bed, he said he would as soon as his show ended. Without warning, she jumped up, turned off the TV and yelled at him like a shrew, "I said now!" As any six-year-old would do, he flew into a tantrum, jumping on the bed and screaming about how it wasn't fair. As Joey lunged for the remote to switch the TV back on, I sat in shocked horror as she grabbed him and slapped his face. Mom had never touched one of us in anger. She had always been patient with us kids and handled discipline calmly. The Elizabeth Jordan of my childhood had elevated parenting to an art form. The shrieking, abusive woman standing before me was not the woman who raised me. Finally, I could no longer deny that something was very wrong. At first, Joey stood motionless, stunned, his hand covering the offended cheek. Then, he crumpled into a fetal position on the bed and sobbed like his heart was shattered. Livid, I sprang from my chair, seized Mom's forearms and glared at her.

"Mom!" I yelled. "What is wrong with you?" Pete climbed on the bed, trying to comfort Joey, who was sucking his thumb for the first time in years. Now, Mom collapsed in my arms and burst into tears.

"Oh, Abby," she sobbed, her face contorted with self-hatred. "What have I done? What have I done to my baby?" Her helpless plea terrified me. I wanted to run away and hide. Instead, I held her, rocked her, and tried to provide for her the strength I knew she couldn't muster. "I'm in trouble, Abby," she whispered. "I'm in trouble."

"I know," was all I could manage to say. I led her to her side of our bed, tucked her under the covers, and massaged the tense muscles in her neck and shoulders. By the time she fell asleep, Joey had stopped crying and succumbed to fitful slumber, but Pete was huddled in the corner, shaking like a baby rabbit snatched from under a bush. I went to him and held him. "Mom is sick, Petey. She didn't mean it," I said, as he buried his tear-drenched face in my chest. I hadn't called him Petey since he was three.

"Is Mommy going to die?" he asked weakly.

"No. She's not going to die. She needs help, and we're going to help her, okay?"

"I'm scared."

"I know, buddy. I'm scared, too, but everything's going to be okay." I didn't believe everything was going to be okay, but what else could I say? "Let's get you into bed. Go brush your teeth, and I'll tuck you in." I sat with him until ten-thirty when he finally slept.

I had no idea how to help my mother. I couldn't even get her to admit she had a problem... until that night. Maybe it was a first step. Feeling alone and adrift, I climbed into bed beside her, wondering if she'd remember the evening's incident the next morning. Sleep eluded me for hours. My brain was on fire. I thought about the past year and how drastically our lives had changed. Staring into the blackness, I worried about the future. I wished I could talk to my dad. He'd know what to do. I wished I could hug my precious Bella. I missed her more than ever. Maybe I should quit school and get a job, I thought. But I had only a few months remaining until graduation. If I didn't graduate, I'd never be able to go to college. Around two, I drifted off for a bit, but my hyperactive brain kept waking me up.

A few hours later, Joey awoke, urine-soaked and crying. He hadn't wet the bed since he was a toddler. Mom stirred and moaned but didn't waken. I walked Joey to the bathroom and changed him from his wet clothes into clean pajamas. Then, I placed a bath towel over the puddle on the bed and laid him on it. "Why does Mommy hate me, Sissy?" he asked in his sleepy-voice. He seemed so tiny and fragile.

"She doesn't hate you, Joe-Joe. Mommy's sick, and her sickness is making her act crazy. She didn't mean to hurt you."

"I'm sorry for being bad. Tomorrow I'll tell her sorry."

"She's sorry for hitting you. Everything'll be better tomorrow. You'll see. Now go back to sleep and try to have sweet dreams." I kissed his forehead and tucked him under the covers.

"I wanna go home, Sissy. I wanna sleep in my own bed."

"I know, Joey. Me, too." Half-awake and blinded by tears, I went to the bathroom and rinsed Joey's pungent pajamas in the sink, wringing out as much wetness as I could. I hung them over the shower bar to dry. Then, I sat on the floor, my back against the tub, and wept until I ran out of tears.

Chapter 11

Mom and Dad had never had to force me to go to bed even when I was Joey's age. At sleepovers, promptly at 10 p.m., I would say good-night and conk out amid the laughing and screeching of my friends. In the seventh grade, we named each other after the seven dwarfs from Snow White. My reputation earned me the dwarf-name, "Sleepy." So, the morning after Mom's outburst, when my alarm rang at six-thirty, I shut it off and went back to sleep.

Soon Pete was shaking me. "Get up, Abby. Mommy said you have to take us to school." I was so tired, both physically and emotionally, I wanted to stay in bed and pretend my life wasn't falling apart. I didn't want to deal with Mom or my brothers or anybody.

"Go away," I said. "I need sleep." I turned over and realized Mom wasn't in the bed. "Where is she?" I asked.

"I don't know. She left."

I sat upright. "What do you mean she left?" Joey was still asleep, making slurping noises as he sucked his thumb.

"She said she had to go for a walk and you should drive me and

Joey to school."

"I can't do that. I have to be at school before you. Besides, I don't have permission to drive to school. She knows that. What the he... what is she up to?" I looked at my phone and saw it was past eight o'clock. I had already missed the first bell. "Pete, wake up Joey, then you two hop in the shower. I'll fix breakfast and figure out what to do."

"The bed's wet. I think Joey peed in it last night."

"Yeah, I know. Don't tease him about it, okay? Just hurry and get ready for school."

I went to the kitchen sink and splashed cold water on my face. I made two bologna sandwiches and threw them into brown lunch bags. After adding an apple to each bag, I made coffee and scrambled the last two eggs in the carton. While the boys were showering, I decided the only practical solution was for me to stay home from school. I was exhausted anyway and knew I wouldn't be able to concentrate. I could drive the boys to school, then come back to the motel and sleep for a while.

I had no idea where Mom had gone or when she'd show her face again. It wasn't like her to take off without telling us anything or at least leaving a note. Until lately. Maybe she realized we needed to talk about last night and she couldn't face it. Maybe she just went for a walk to clear her head. Thankfully, she had left the car keys on the dresser.

I buttered the last two slices of bread and poured two glasses of milk for my little brothers. "Hurry up, guys," I called through the bathroom door. "You're going to be late for school." We had forty minutes before they were supposed to be in their classrooms, and it took almost thirty minutes to drive to their school on Jolly Pond Road. I pulled clothes out of the drawer for each of them and laid them on their bed. Pete was first to come out of the bathroom.

"I don't want to wear that shirt," he said.

"Just get dressed and eat your breakfast. We need to hurry, or you'll be late."

"But I wanna wear the red one."

"Pete, I don't have time to argue with you. Come on. Just cooperate. We're leaving in ten minutes. Hurry up, Joey! I need to use the bathroom, too." Pete had thrown the blue shirt on the floor and pulled his red one out of the dirty-clothes bag. I didn't care. He could wear a stinky, stained shirt to school and get teased if he wanted to.

Finally, Joey appeared. He was stark-naked and his wet hair, which had grown too long, was dripping all over the floor.

"Geez, Joey, at least cover your privates," said Pete.

"There aren't any dry towels."

"Oh, great!" I said. "What am I supposed to use?" The pandemonium continued for another ten minutes until I wanted to scream. I decided to skip the shower.

"Where's Mommy?" Joey asked, as we piled into the car.

"She had to go out. Fasten your seatbelts."

"Is she still mad at me?" Joey asked.

"She's not mad at you."

"I want Mommy to kiss me good-bye. Mommy always kisses me good-bye and says, 'Have a super-duper day'."

"You'll see her when you get home."

"That's not home." Pete said. "It's just a stupid motel."

"It's our home now. So, you'd better get used to it," I said, growing more impatient by the minute. I was too tired to address Pete's adjustment issues. I just wanted to drop my brothers at school and drive back to take a nap. I'd deal with Mom whenever she decided to show up.

The boys were grumpy and complaining when I left them with the car-line monitor. I felt sorry—but only momentarily—for their teachers who would have to cope with their sour tempers all day. Mostly, I was thinking about how tired I was and wondering how I'd catch up in calculus, advanced English, and chemistry.

When I got back to the motel, Mom was there, and no explanation was necessary. She was sitting on the steps near our second-story room, wringing her hands and mumbling nonsense. I could tell she was out-of-her-mind drunk. Her hair was a mess, her face devoid of makeup. Elizabeth Jordan never went anywhere without makeup.

"For Pete's sake, Mom! At least go inside! Must you share our problems with the whole world?"

"No key, Abby," she said, looking at me and then past me.

"Where're my boys? Have to tell Joey I din' mean it. Din' mean to hit my baby."

"I took them to school. Come inside," I said irritably. She tried to stand and nearly fell backward down the stairs. I lunged and grabbed her sleeve just in time. "Oh, Mom. What are you doing?"

I got her into the room and onto the bed. "Be a good girl and help me to the bathroom," she said. I felt like I would collapse from fatigue and worry, but I managed to pull her upright and, together, we staggered to the bathroom. Once I squeezed us both through the door, I had to help her pull down her panties and balance on the toilet. She was weaving in all directions. I couldn't believe this pathetic drunkard could be my mother, the mother who sacrificed a career willingly to raise her children. My mom was always waiting for us when we got home from school. She was always first to volunteer as class parent for each of us. She was active in PTA for both Blayton Elementary and Lafayette High School and served on the Band Boosters my freshman year. How would I ever explain this mother to her two little boys? I needed to get her sobered up before they came home.

I walked her to our bed where both of us collapsed and slept until after noon. When I woke up, Mom was clanging around in the kitchen trying to make coffee. "Well, good afternoon, sleepyhead," she said, her greeting devoid of cheer. "Where're the coffee filters?" Bloodshot eyes darted here and there, trying to see around wild, matted strands of hair that refused to stay where she swept them. Instead of tying the sash of her robe, she resorted to twitching her shoulders like that would keep it from falling to the floor. "Your school called. I told 'em you were sick," she said through her obvious haze.

"I'll make the coffee."

"Fine." She slammed the coffee can on the counter and returned to our bed where she sat, wringing her hands and pouting like a toddler.

"Mom, we need to talk."

"I know. Coffee first. We're out of milk."

When the coffee finished brewing, I carried two mismatched mugs to the bed, handed one to her, and set the other on the night stand. Still in my underwear, I climbed on the bed next to her, propped a pillow behind me and tried to figure out how to start the conversation. Mom took two sips of the welcome brew and sighed deeply before she spoke.

"Abby, you know I love you, right?" Her tone, lacking her usual affection, didn't match her words.

"Of course."

"You know I wouldn't hurt our family intens... intensh... intentionally, right?" There it was. My chance.

"But you are hurting our family. We need you, Mom. I need you. Why did you start drinking again? You knew it was dangerous." She took another, longer sip. I could tell she was choosing her next words carefully, working to sound calm.

"When your dad was so sick, the doctor gave me Valium to help my nerves. After he died I had trouble sleeping, so the doctor prescribed a sedative. When the prescriptions ran out, I couldn't afford to renew them." She was speaking in slow motion, hugging her mug with two hands like it held the power to rescue her from the hell she had created. I stared into mine, hoping the swirling brew would somehow hold my anger in check. "With all the medical bills from your father's illness," she continued, "I couldn't even afford to go back to the doctor. I needed something. It was just too hard to cope. I started with a glass of wine before bed... just one glass, to calm my nerves and help me sleep."

"I never noticed, not after that one time in your bedroom."

"I kept one bottle hidden in that useless cabinet above the fridge and another bottle in my bedroom closet. I knew it would upset you. After all my warnings to you, I knew you'd be ashamed of me."

"How did it get so out of control? Why didn't you stop when you saw you were growing dependent?"

"You just answered your own question. I was hooked at the first drop. I tried to stop again and again, but I couldn't. I'd pour that stuff down the drain, sure I could manage without it. Every time, I'd resist for a day, but the next day it took even more booze to convince me I could make it. Right this minute, I feel like I'll die if I don't have a drink."

"Oh, Mom. What are we going to do?" Suddenly, it occurred to me that her addiction must be expensive. "How much money do we have left?"

"I don't know."

"What do you mean, you don't know? It's in a bank account. Right?"

"Yeah."

"Well, where's the latest statement?" I asked, wondering why it was always up to me to be the adult.

"I haven't been to the post office lately." Just before we moved, Reuben had advised her to rent a post office box.

"We'll go this afternoon," I said. "We're almost out of food, and the car is running on fumes. How much money do you have in your purse?"

"About twenty dollars."

Then, looking directly into her bloodshot eyes, I asked, "Have you been trying to get a job?" Like a child who had been caught in the act of misbehaving, she hesitated, lowering her eyes, before answering.

"I tried for a few weeks... when we first moved here. But I can't even handle an interview without a couple of drinks." As her voice escalated in volume, she began trembling visibly, and it seemed like she might explode. "How can I hold down a job? Who would have me, anyway? I'm just a worn out, washed up housewife with no skills and a drinking problem. Oh, Abby! I'm so sorry. I've failed you, and I've failed the boys." I had heard it before. The more distraught she became, the icier my heart grew.

"I hit my baby, Abby! I'm supposed to be taking care of you, but now you're taking care of me." As much as I knew she wasn't ruining our lives on purpose, I was too furious to feel any pity. I jumped from the bed, slammed my empty mug on the night stand, nearly shattering it, pulled on my robe, and started pacing in the tiny aisle between the beds.

"There's no time to feel sorry yourself. We need a plan. Listen, Mom," I said, now facing her. "You have to stop drinking. You have to!" I was screaming. I knew it wasn't helping, but I needed to vent. "You have two little boys who need you, and I'm tired of being their mother. You must pull yourself together!"

"I can't, Abby. Don't you understand? I can't." She stood and collapsed in my arms, sobbing, but I was unmoved. I just wanted to shake some sense into her and make her be the adult again.

"Do you think you can take a shower without a drink?" I asked, my voice dripping with sarcasm. I surprised myself with an uncontrollable fury I had never experienced. "Because you stink! You stink like sweat and booze and vomit!" I couldn't stop my tirade. "How could you let this happen? Weren't our lives messed up enough already? You stink like a drunken whore!"

"Abigail Elizabeth! How dare you! I'm still your mother," she screamed, red-faced, her body rigid, with tears flooding her cheeks and dotting her nightgown.

"Then act like it!"

She jumped up, grabbed her coat and purse, and wearing her nightclothes, stormed out of the room, slamming the door. Someone in the next room banged on the wall. It was Mr. Pennell who worked nights.

"Hey, hold it down in there!" I heard through the wall. I didn't care if Mr. Pennell couldn't sleep. I didn't care if we were disturbing the entire planet. I ran to the door, jerked it open and shrieked after my mother.

"That's right! Run away! Go find some booze and numb yourself instead of thinking about your children! I hate you!" At that moment, I wanted to give up on everybody and everything, especially my mother. At seventeen, it was all too much to handle. I slammed the door and threw myself on the bed where I sobbed and sobbed. Finally, when my stomach ached from bawling, I got up and took a shower. Then, I cried again because there still wasn't a dry towel.

⋈

I knew Mom would come back eventually. How far could she go in her nightclothes, with only twenty dollars and a nearly-empty gas tank? Her credit cards had been discontinued weeks before. But, I worried she wouldn't return in time for me to pick up the boys at school. I knew she'd be drunk.

She was drunk, all right. Around three p.m. I heard her stumble up the steps outside our room, mumbling obscenities. Mom had never sworn before. I was surprised she even knew the words that were flying from her mouth. I parted the old, faded draperies just in time to see her crash-land at the top of the flight. Crap! I thought. Has she been driving in that condition? How did she even find her way back to the motel? She lay there, holding her skinned knee, looking like a heap of yesterday's trash. My mother, an attractive woman who always took pride in her appearance, was bombed, filthy, and barely recognizable.

I opened the door and pulled her inside. Immediately, she gagged and retched all over the carpet. Then she lost her balance and sat in her vomit. "Oh, Mom," I said, defeated. "What are you doing to yourself? What are you doing to us?" I couldn't stand the stench. It reeked like nothing I had ever smelled before. Worse than sewage or skunk or rotten meat. I opened the door to take a deep breath of clean air and helped her stand. For the first time, I noticed she had lost weight. She seemed no heavier than Pete. Together, we stumbled to the bathroom. She threw up again, but this time I managed to aim her toward the toilet. When it seemed there could be nothing left in her stomach but bitter bile, I lifted her into the bathtub and turned on the faucet. She sat in the lukewarm water, swaying and sobbing while I washed her hair and bathed her, still in her nightgown. I was dreading the thought of cleaning up the disgusting mess in the other room. The urine-soaked sheets on the boys' bed needed attention, too.

"Sorry, Abby. So sorry," she said, as I removed her wet clothes and dried her boney body with a damp towel.

"I know, Mom." I wrapped her in my robe and led her to our bed, hoping she had emptied her stomach of its revolting fluids. Then, gagging, I tried to clean the carpet. Later, I'd ask the front desk clerk for something stronger than dishwashing liquid and water, but now it was time to pick up my brothers from school. I prayed that Mom would be sober by the time we returned.

Chapter 12

"I got in trouble at school today," said Pete. I had just picked up my brothers, and we were headed for the post office.

"What do you mean you got in trouble? What happened?" I already knew about the incident because Pete's teacher had called only moments before I left the motel. When I saw the number for the elementary school come up on Mom's phone, I answered in case one of the boys was sick or hurt. Pretending to be Mom, I told Mrs. Foster I would talk to Pete, and I set up an appointment for Mom to meet with her about Pete's "uncharacteristic behavior."

"Justin said we're poor and I punched him," Pete explained. "Are we poor, Abby?"

"Well..."

"He said we had to move out of our house cause we're poor and he made fun of my dirty shirt."

I wanted to say, "I told you so," about the shirt, but decided it would only make matters worse. "We use our words, not our fists, remember? Besides, there's no shame in being poor." As I heard myself

speak those words aloud, I recognized that I had been experiencing
shame and embarrassment about our situation. Surely no one chooses
to be poor, especially children, for whom there are no choices at all.
Right then, I vowed to work on adjusting my attitude.

"Are we poor because Daddy died?" Joey asked.

"Yes, I guess so. You see, Dad couldn't work anymore after he got
sick, and Mom didn't have a job, except to take care of us."

"Mommies don't get paid, do they, Sissy?" said Joey.

"No, mommies don't get paid... but they should. Pete, did you
apologize to Justin?"

"Yeah. Mrs. Foster made me say 'sorry' and I had to get a red
card."

"What's a red card?" Joey asked.

"That's when you break the rules. You get a red card. If you get
two red cards, you go to the principal. If you get three, they send you
home, and your parents have to come to the school."

"I don't never wanna get a red card," Joey said.

"Then make sure you don't hit anybody," I warned. "That goes
for you, too, Pete. No more hitting, okay? Remember to use your
words."

"Okay. Where's Mommy?"

"Yeah, where's Mommy? Why didn't she pick us up?" Eventually,
I'd have to tell my brothers the truth about Mom. They needed to
understand how their childhoods just happened to intersect her
drinking problem, how it wasn't their fault or within their control.
But how do you bring up the subject of your mother's alcoholism
without going ballistic? I remember thinking that somehow, I must
find a way to resolve the blinding anger within myself, to calm my
raging emotions before talking to the boys.

"Mommy's not feeling well. She's resting at the motel. How about
a Wendy's Frosty for a snack?"

"Yeah!" they both said. When I placed my order at Wendy's drive-
thru window, I realized I had only enough money for one Frosty. To
my brothers' disappointment, I asked for an extra cup and split it
between them. Then, we drove to the post office to retrieve the mail
that had been forwarded from our house.

We arrived at the motel to find Mom sober, but grumpy and

jittery. I wasn't sure which Mom was harder to deal with, Sloshed-Mom or Sober-Mom. At least she had brushed her hair, and I noticed she had changed the boys' stinky sheets.

Pete and Joey were excited to see Mom and tell her about their day, like they had always done after school. She managed to hug them and feign interest. At least she was making the effort, but I could tell she was starting to get the shakes. She had trouble concentrating on their words, her puffy eyes darting about the room like she expected someone to jump out from a hiding place. Soon she'd need a drink. I had to decide how I was going to handle her craving without upsetting my brothers. Somehow, I needed to distract them, so I could deal with Mom. She and I needed to have a serious talk while she was sober, and I was reasonably composed, but I didn't have a clue how to keep any conversation private in such tight quarters.

I got an idea. Mom had never allowed us to watch TV until after our homework was finished. Pete and Joey would consider TV before homework a special privilege, and it just might keep them occupied for a while. "Hey, kiddos," I said. "How about some popcorn? You can watch Dexter's Laboratory before you start your homework." I knew it was their favorite show.

"Sure!" said Pete.

"Yeah!" said Joey. Mom looked at me like she was about to object, but I didn't give her the chance. I picked up her jeans and sweatshirt from the chair, where she had thrown them the previous day and shoved them at her.

"Here, Mom. Get dressed, and we'll go out for some fresh air." It was a command, not a request. As she headed for the bathroom, she looked annoyed, but she obliged. I could tell she suspected what was coming.

"You gonna leave us alone?" Joey asked as I started to make the popcorn. We couldn't afford microwave popcorn, but I remembered how Dad used to pop corn in the fireplace. I heated a burner and poured a little oil into a saucepan. I figured if I kept the pan moving like he had, the kernels wouldn't burn.

"Don't worry, Joey. We'll be right outside if you need us. No fighting, okay?"

"Yeah, Joey. No fighting," Pete said as he punched Joey's arm. Of course, Joey had to reciprocate because that's how brothers roll.

"Come on, guys. Do you want popcorn, or don't you? Pete, be nice to your brother."

"Yeah, be nice to me," Joey said, as he tried to push Pete off the bed. I remember thinking, I am never going to have kids.

"I mean it, you two. Stop or there'll be no TV or popcorn. Joey, move to the other bed."

"Can we have hot chocolate?" he asked, leaping onto our bed.

"No. We don't have any. Besides, if you spilled it on the bed it would make a terrible mess. And you already had a Frosty."

"Don't you mean half a Frosty?" Pete said.

"How about no after-school snack? Would that be better? I asked, as every ounce of patience drained from my sisterly being.

"Just shut up, Pete," Joey said, under his breath. Finally, I got the boys settled in front of the TV, and Mom and I stepped outside.

"Do you want to walk or sit?" I asked.

"Either way, I'm going to get a lecture, so what does it matter?" I ignored her cynical tone and proceeded to the steps a few feet from our room.

"How about here?" I asked, pointing to the top step. My insides felt like all my organs had melted together into one throbbing lump, and were trying to escape through every orifice.

"Fine," Mom said. It was a chilly October afternoon, and I was glad I had grabbed a jacket. As we sat on the landing, I sucked in a deep breath of cold, crisp air, hoping to boost my courage and calm my raging insides. I laid my head on her shoulder.

"Mom," I began, trying to sound gentle and loving. "Mom, I love you." I clasped her icy hands. I could feel her shaking.

"But," she said, bristling.

"But, we have a problem."

"You mean I have a problem."

"Yes, but we're a family. Your problem affects all of us."

"I don't know what to do, Abby," she said, now melting into the crook of my neck. "I don't know how to stop." She raised her head, and as suddenly as she had yielded, her demeanor transformed. At that time, her moods changed too unexpectedly to anticipate, throwing me off-guard and leaving my raw nerves defenseless. "Maybe I should just go away. You and your brothers would be better off without me."

"Come on. You know that's not the answer. We need you. I want us to be a family again."

"I can't. I can't do this anymore. It's too hard."

"I know. We'll do it together. But you have to trust me and not get mad when I try to help."

"I don't mean to get mad. Really, I don't. I don't want to hurt my kids. I can't seem to control myself. I've turned into somebody I don't recognize."

"It's part of the disease, Mom. It's called alcoholism, and you can't control it or stop it by yourself. You need help."

Whenever I could find Wi-Fi access, I had been researching alcoholism. One day, my online investigation led me to an organization called Alateen. I registered for a chat room with a counselor named Ellen. I didn't know if that was her real name, but we started "chatting" online a couple times a week. I was learning a lot about Mom's condition and how to disengage from her words and behavior. Ellen recommended that I join a local Alateen group, but I knew I'd never be able to get away for meetings.

Mom continued, "Who can help? I'm so ashamed. I don't want anybody to know. Oh, God, Abby! I need a drink so bad! What have I done?" She was trembling more noticeably now, and I held her tightly, thinking I should be able to stop her shaking through sheer will. I was scared out of my mind, but I knew I had to be strong for her. This was my chance, maybe my only chance. She might explode, but at the risk of her yelling or even hitting me, I had to try. Ellen had advised me to speak "tenderly but firmly."

"Remember all those AA groups that met at our church?" I began. "They still do."

"AA? No. I can't." Her eyes widened with panic.

"Just listen, okay?" I touched her arm gently and tried to connect with her downcast eyes. "I checked, and there's one that meets at noon every day. I'll go with you while the boys are in school."

"I can't. What if somebody recognizes me?"

"That's why it's called Alcoholics Anonymous. They use first names only, and they take a pledge to keep each other's comments private. I've done some research and I've heard it really works."

"Wait. How can you go with me? You have school."

"I'll take some time off... just till you feel comfortable going alone."

"What if I fail? What if I can't do it?" Just then, breaking the spell of my carefully chosen words, Joey opened the door of room 206 and found us sitting on the step.

"Pete won't let me watch my show, Mommy. He keeps changing the channel."

"Work it out!" I growled through clenched teeth.

"I'm not talking to you. I'm talking to Mommy," he said. I stood and rushed toward Joey, grabbed his arm, and turned him toward the room. I looked back to see Mom hugging her knees, and I heard her heavy sigh.

"Can't we have five minutes to talk without being interrupted?" I hissed.

"Ow! Mommy, Abby's hurting my arm," he cried in his fake, I'm-pitiful voice.

"Just be quiet and get back inside," I said, pushing him into the room. After a few minutes of refereeing, I managed to get the boys to compromise. "Fifteen more minutes of TV. Then, you need to start your homework. If you keep arguing, I'll switch it off, and there'll be no more TV for the rest of week. Got it?"

"You're mean, Abby."

"Shut up, Joey," Pete said. Do you want to lose TV for a whole week?"

"Okay, okay. Can I have more popcorn?"

I grabbed the pot and slammed it on the bed. "Here, knock yourself out."

"Hey, save some for me," Pete said, as he moved from the other bed. Another scuffle ensued, which I decided to ignore. They could kill each other for all I cared. I went back outside to rejoin Mom, but she was gone.

I walked down the steps and looked in every direction. She was nowhere to be seen. I circled the motel and ran through the parking lot, zig-zagging between cars. Since she didn't have her purse, I knew she couldn't get far. I thought I saw some movement in the front seat of our car, still parked where I had left it. Maybe it was just the setting sun reflecting off the metal surface. There it was again. I approached the car cautiously, and that's when I saw Mom hunkered in the passenger seat. She was searching through the glove box. When she spotted me, she tried to lock the door, but I beat her to it. I pulled the door open just in time to spot the bottle. "Mom, no. Give it to me. You don't want to do this." I reached for the bottle, but she was hugging it to her chest and scrambling for the driver's side.

"I need it, Abby. Please! I need it." I noticed it was something other than wine this time. Maybe whiskey. It didn't matter. Whatever it was, I had to take it from her.

"Give it to me, Mom!" Now we were engaged in a full-blown tussle. Forgetting every strategy from Alateen, the only thing on my mind was pulling the odious liquid from her grasp, but she was just as determined to keep it. With ever-increasing fear, I noticed her crazed eyes and uncharacteristic strength. For a moment, I wondered if she might be desperate enough to kill me. We were wild animals, brawling, clawing, pushing, and pulling each other. She tried to exit the driver's side, but I grabbed her sweat shirt and pulled her toward me. Finally, I wrested the bottle from her and backed out of the car. She lunged at me, pawing like an angry tiger, and nearly landed head-first on the pavement.

"No!" she screamed, jumped up and ran after me. With all my strength, I heaved that bottle of liquor toward the wooded area. "No!" she screamed again. I was afraid the boys—or worse, our neighbors—would hear her tirade. When the bottle landed on the edge of the paved surface, it broke into tiny shards. Mom dropped to the ground, and like a bratty little kid, pounded her thighs and cried, "No, no, no!" Then, realizing she had lost the battle, she curled into a ball and mewed like a kitten. It was a sickening sight.

"I can't, Abby. I just can't," she cried.

"Yes, you can. One day at a time." I sat beside her on the hard, cold asphalt and held her as she sobbed. "We'll do it together."

"I'm sorry, Abby."

"I know. Come on, let's go inside. You can take a warm bath, and I'll cook supper." Feeling wobbly, myself, I helped her to her feet and kicked the car door shut. With one arm around her tiny waist, I walked her toward the motel.

Chapter 13

Not only could I not leave my brothers alone, but I had to babysit my mother. I thought if I bolstered her through the worst of her withdrawal, she could attend AA meetings. I took off the entire week from school, sending a note to the attendance office claiming that an intestinal virus had left me dehydrated. Mom signed it and Mindy, again sworn to secrecy, delivered it for me. I also called Pete's teacher, Mrs. Foster, pretending to be Mom. I said I couldn't make our appointment, but that I had talked to Pete and he promised not to get into any more fights.

"I'm concerned about Peter, Mrs. Jordan. He hasn't been himself lately," she said.

"Yes, well, as you know, he lost his father a few months ago. I'm sure he's still dealing with that trauma."

"How would you feel about him talking to a counselor? We have a wonderful psychologist here."

"I'm sure that would be helpful."

"Great. I'll schedule some sessions."

"Thank you. Will these sessions be during the school day?"

"It can be arranged, if that's your preference."

"Yes, perfect. Thank you." It seemed that my lowered voice and formal speech had convinced Mrs. Foster she was speaking to my mother.

CRBO

Besides Ellen, Mindy was the only person I could confide in, yet I seldom saw her now that I was tied down with Mom. Of course, we texted and talked on the phone. Even so, I felt trapped and isolated. Whenever I drove Pete and Joey to and from school, I made Mom go with me. Wherever I went, she went. I couldn't risk her finding a way to buy alcohol. Withdrawal had made her volatile. I decided it was time to tell Pete and Joey the truth. The next time I chatted with Ellen, I asked for advice about how to tell them without scaring them.

"Abby, they know something's wrong and have already imagined the worst. The truth will ease their concerns. You mentioned a social worker. Could you get him to help you talk to your brothers?"

"Maybe." We hadn't seen Reuben for a while, and he wasn't aware of how serious Mom's addiction had become.

"It's important for your brothers to know that your mother's alcoholism is not their fault and that it's not their job to take care of her. Help them understand how alcohol has affected your mom's brain. Abby, you are being very brave, but it is not your job to be their mother. You need to reach out to another adult for help, someone in your local community, like a teacher or your guidance counselor."

"Okay. I'll think about it." I said the words, knowing I fully intended to protect our privacy.

One evening, as Mom showered, I turned on the TV and sat the boys down as far away as possible from the bathroom... only a few feet. We were on the floor with our backs resting against my bed. "Hey, guys. I need to tell you something." I sounded like Mom used to at the beginning of our family meetings... when we were still a family. But, unlike her, I made a point of not saying, "It's going to be hard to hear."

"You've noticed Mom isn't herself."

"Yeah. She's mean," Joey said.

"Why is she mad at us all the time?" asked Pete.

"She's not. She's mad at herself."

"Then, why does she yell at us?"

"She can't help it because she's sick. Her brain is sick."

"Why doesn't she go to the doctor and get some medicine?" Joey asked.

"Well, that's part of the problem. After Daddy died, she was very sad. The doctor tried to help her, but he gave her too much medicine. Then, when she had to give up our house and all our things, she just couldn't cope."

"What's 'cope'?" asked Joey.

"You know," said Pete. "She couldn't handle it. Like she was too sad."

"That's right, Pete. She was depressed, and she started drinking bad stuff to try to feel better."

"You mean beer?" asked Pete. "Tyrone told me when his Dad drinks beer he yells at Tyrone and his mom and sisters."

"Yes. Beer is a type of alcohol, but Mom feels better when she drinks, at least for a little while. It's when she stops that she gets mean and grumpy."

"Well, let's get her some beer, then," Joey said. I wanted to laugh at Joey's concrete thinking, but I knew he hadn't intended to be funny.

"No," I explained. "She's addicted, which means she'll keep needing more and more alcohol to feel better, and she'll get even sicker. What we have to do is help her stop drinking." I noticed the shower had stopped and looked behind us to make sure the bathroom door was still closed.

"So, don't buy any of that alcohol stuff," Pete said.

"It's not that easy." I was whispering now. "Some people can drink a little and stop, but addicts can't stop, and they feel terrible when they try. It's like when you want to eat all your Halloween candy at once. You can't stop unless Mom hides it and lets you eat only one or two pieces a day. When you eat too much sugar, you get all crazy and hyper."

"Yeah," they both said at once, their eyes brightening with comprehension.

"Later, when the sugar-high wears off, you feel tired and grumpy. Do you understand?"

"Yeah."

"I'm trying to get Mom some help, but it's going to take time. She won't get better right away. We need to be patient with her, even when she's mean. Can you do that?"

"Like let her hit us and stuff?" asked Joey.

"Of course not. I won't let her hit you again, but just try to understand when she says mean things and acts crazy, it's not really our mom. It's the disease messing with her brain."

The bathroom door opened. "Sh! She's coming. Take this book." I grabbed a spelling book and handed it to Joey. Mom shuffled out of the bathroom looking dreadful. Her eyes were sunken and ringed with dark shadows. Her skin was pale, and her gray roots had grown a couple inches long. She had aged ten years in the last month, it seemed. I wanted to treat her to a day at the spa, but, on our budget, such a luxury was out of the question.

I had checked her bank statement and found that the balance had dipped to less than six thousand dollars. We had been living in the motel for only two months and nearly half our savings was gone. With no income and thousands in outstanding bills to pay off, we'd be on the street in no time. I stood, met her halfway, and led her to our shared bed.

"Lie down, Mom," I said, patting the bed. "Turn over and I'll give you a nice back rub."

"I need a drink, Abby," she whispered. "I'm in bad shape."

"I know, but you can do this," I said quietly, trying to remain calm. The boys had stood and were staring at her like she was a circus-act gone wrong.

"Turn off the TV, Pete, and you two finish your homework. I'll fix supper soon." For the first time, they obeyed me without argument.

Chapter 14

I grew worried that I wouldn't be able to catch up with my school work, but I simply couldn't leave Mom alone. I did the best I could to keep up without going to classes. Mindy sent me her notes from the classes we shared, but by Thursday, I was totally lost in calculus. My other friends kept calling or texting, and Mrs. Gladstone called twice. Remembering an episode from Grey's Anatomy, I made up a story about how I had gotten food poisoning and ended up dehydrated. "I feel sure I'll be well enough to return Monday," I said in a weak voice and thanked her for her concern.

Alyssa wanted to stop by to see me, but she didn't know I had moved. "No, no." I said. "I'm not supposed to have visitors. The doctor wants me to rest."

Sometimes Mom was verbally abusive; other times she cried and begged me to get her a drink, "just one," of course. I had to keep telling myself what I had told my brothers: it's the addiction talking. I was determined to get her through one week without alcohol, and I was just as determined to get her started in AA. In the meantime, my online work with Ellen had equipped me with some helpful strategies. It wasn't long before Mom gave me the opportunity to exercise them.

One night, around midnight, I awoke to the sounds of Mom trying to sneak out. I had hidden the car keys, and she was rummaging through my purse. When I caught her, she acted indignant, saying she thought it was her purse. "I was just looking for a cough drop. How dare you accuse me!" Soon we were engaged in a whispering argument that increased in volume with each word. When one of the boys began to stir, I grabbed our coats and the room key and dragged Mom outside. It was bitterly cold and, while she had put on socks and shoes to "search for a cough drop," I was bare-footed.

"Oh crap! It's freezing out here. Don't move," I said, as I held her robe with one hand and, with the other, reached inside the room for my slippers. "Come on, let's take a walk." I was sleepy, cold, and exasperated. I wondered how long it would take to get my mother back.

"You don't trust me," she said, as I pulled her around the periphery of the parking lot, not once releasing her arm.

"That's right," I said, remembering one of the tools from Alateen. "I don't trust you." Ellen called the technique "mirroring."

"You're nothing but an ungrateful brat!"

"I'm an ungrateful brat."

"You treat your own mother like a child."

"I treat you like a child." I had learned that arguing wouldn't get me anywhere with this facsimile of a mother. It just increased her agitation and verbal abuse. Inside I was seething, but I kept agreeing with everything she said.

"All I need is one drink, one lousy drink! I'm an adult, for Crissake! How dare you..." It went on through the night, with her shouting and swearing at me, while I led her, dressed in pajamas and slippers, in a big circle in the loneliest parking lot in the world.

A car pulled into the lot and a young couple emerged. As they proceeded toward the motel, they gave us a wide berth, never taking their eyes off us. It was like they expected us to jump them. I couldn't blame them for being suspicious. We probably looked like two crazed escapees from a mental institution.

After a while, I could tell Mom was getting tired, but I kept pulling her forward, trying to wear her out so she would sleep. The next day, I'd take her to the AA meeting. If I could just keep her sober until then, all would be well. I couldn't endure much more of that twenty-four-hour prison-guard duty.

Finally, we climbed the steps, went inside, removed our coats and slippers, and crawled under the warm, welcoming covers. I rubbed Mom's back while she mumbled, "You're a good girl, Abby. You take such good care of me. What would I do without you?" Finally, she fell asleep.

I, on the other hand, was wide awake. I got up, wrapped myself in the faded bedspread, sat at the built-in desk, and tried to do some schoolwork by flashlight. With the draperies closed, our room was as black as a coal mine. My flashlight cast eerie shadows on the walls and ghost-like reflections in the mirror. But I wasn't spooked. I remember thinking that ghosts, goblins, and even vampires couldn't possibly be scarier than the reality of my life. Finally, I was too drowsy to think. Sometime after three-thirty, I fell into bed and succumbed to exhaustion.

It was nearly five when Mom awoke with a jerk. She was drenched in sweat and shaking violently. I thought she might be having a seizure. She started swatting at something invisible and repeating over and over, "Get 'em off me." I tried to hold her, but she resisted my embrace, flinging her arms wildly. "Have. To. Have. A. Drink. Please, Abby. Just. One. Drink." I pinned her flailing arms and held her firmly, shushing her, stroking her hair, and trying desperately to soothe her so she wouldn't wake the boys.

"You're doing great, Mom," I said, working to sound calm, but I heard my own voice quivering against her skull. "You're almost there. You can do this."

"No, Abby, I can't. I can't do it."

Pete stirred, mumbling sleepily, "What's going on? What time is it?"

"It's okay. Go back to sleep," I whispered in the dark. "Mom had a nightmare. That's all." Then, I murmured softly, "Sh, Mom. You'll wake Joey."

Somewhere I had heard or read that warm milk was a remedy for insomnia. As soon as Mom stopped swatting, I tucked her under the covers, and went to the kitchen, tripping over things in the dark. I switched on the small light above the stove and heated some milk.

"Hey," said Pete as he rolled away from the light source, and pulled the covers over his head. Joey slept on.

When the milk was warm, I poured it into a mug, grabbed a towel, and took it to Mom. "Here," I whispered, as I helped her sit up. "Drink this." She took a sip and spat it out. Fortunately, the towel caught most of the tepid liquid before it soaked the bed covers.

"What is that?" she asked.

"It's warm milk. It'll help you sleep."

"Yuck," she said, but I induced her to drink most of it. Surprisingly, it did calm her agitation, and she stopped shaking. I climbed into bed and held her and stroked her hair until we both fell asleep.

With four people living in one room, I had learned to place my phone under my pillow so only I could hear the alarm. When it rang at 7:00 a.m., I felt like I had just gone to sleep. I shut it off quickly, so I could shower before anyone else woke up. No one stirred, not even Mom. I grabbed the clothes I had set out the previous night and tip-toed to the bathroom. After using the toilet without flushing, I turned on the shower and checked to make sure the noise hadn't aroused anyone. I had no idea what kind of mood to expect from Mom, and I needed to be fully awake to deal with anything she might dish out.

While I was showering, I promised myself that, at noon, Mom and I would be at the church for her first meeting. I hoped it wasn't a closed meeting because if I weren't allowed to accompany her, she would never stay.

"Hurry up, Abby!" Pete called through the door. "I gotta pee!"

"Here we go," I said, my cynicism bouncing off the bathroom tiles. "Hold your horses. I'm almost done." The next hour was chaotic as I brewed coffee, cooked breakfast, packed lunches, readied the boys for school, gathered the dirty clothes, and tried to keep Mom from "losing it." Finally, the four of us, and our dirty laundry, piled into the car.

After Mom and I dropped the boys off at school, we went to the laundromat. I kept her busy folding clothes, but I could tell she was jumpy. Every time a dryer buzzed, or a toddler squealed, it startled her. By eleven, the laundry was done, giving us just enough time to eat our packed lunches, stop at the post office, and get to the church for the AA meeting.

As we pulled into the church's parking lot, Mom acted as nervous as I felt. I decided we'd enter through the rear door instead of the main entrance where we risked being seen by the office staff or clergy. We had never joined the parish officially but had attended services often enough to be recognized.

I knew exactly where the meeting was held. As we walked along the rear hallway, Mom tried repeatedly to convince me to change my mind.

"I can do this on my own, Abby," she said, sounding like an angry three-year-old. As we reached the narrow corridor leading to the meeting room her level of agitation increased. "You'll see. I won't take another drink. Please, Abby. I promise." I ignored her attempts to avert me from my singular mission. Holding her arm firmly, I kept my eyes focused forward, and continued walking.

We entered a large room awash in an annoying, florescent glow. It smelled of coffee and stale cigarettes. A friendly, bearded man greeted us and invited us to pour a cup of coffee from a huge, old-fashioned urn. I thanked him and fixed a cup for each of us. Fortunately, we didn't see anyone we knew. It seemed like nearly a hundred people were gathered there. I couldn't believe it! I knew the church hosted evening meetings, too, and wondered how so many people in a community like Williamsburg could be addicts.

As I led Mom to the back row of chairs, I noticed she was trembling again. "Don't make me do this, Abby," she whispered, fidgeting with her gloves. "These people are drunks. I'm not a drunk. I can quit anytime I want to."

I remember thinking, Sure, Mom. That's why I can't let you out of my sight. But, recalling Ellen's advice, I set our coffee cups on the floor and helped Mom remove her coat, refusing to engage in words that would surely escalate into an argument. As she tried to pull away from me, I pressed her onto a chair and sat beside her. That's when I saw Ginny Hanson's dad seated near the front. He hadn't spotted us and probably wouldn't recognize me if he had. Mr. Hanson was a successful attorney who lived in a nicer neighborhood than ours, in a bigger, finer house. I never expected to see somebody like him at an AA meeting. I think that's the moment I first understood that alcoholism is no respecter of persons or positions. Scanning the room, I noticed a wide range of ages and races. Feeling a little less isolated and slightly more hopeful, I reckoned that if all these people could conquer their addictions, maybe Mom could, too.

Seated at the front, facing the group, was a tough-looking man with gray hair, multiple tattoos, leathery skin and faded blue jeans. His freshly-pressed, white shirt and tie seemed out-of-place. Promptly at noon, he took charge of the meeting. "Hello," he said loudly as he stood. "My name is Walt and I'm an alcoholic."

As if they had rehearsed it, everyone in the room responded, "Hi, Walt."

"Welcome to this open meeting of Alcoholics Anonymous. Please join me in the Serenity Prayer."

Mom and I listened as nearly everyone else recited the comforting words:

God, grant me the serenity to accept the things I cannot change; courage to change the things I can; and the wisdom to know the difference. Amen

Next, Walt read the Twelve Steps upon which the AA program is based. After that, several people stood, one-by-one and identified themselves by their given names. Each speaker was greeted by the entire group. Each told a unique, yet similar story that no one interrupted.

One young man—I think his name was Andrew—appeared no older than I was at the time. He divulged that his driver's license had been revoked because of repeated DUIs. He explained that his eventual arrest was the best thing that could have happened to him. "That was more than a year ago," he said. "And now I wouldn't consider missing a meeting. I've been sober for six months." Everyone applauded.

The next speaker was a well-dressed woman who seemed to be

around Mom's age. She introduced herself as Rhonda. When she started to speak, Mom leaned forward in her seat. "I slipped up this week," Rhonda said. "The stress at work got to me, and I ended up at a bar. Instead of using The Steps or calling my sponsor, I blocked everything. It felt like I zoned out, like I had no conscious control over myself or my choices." Mom was nodding her head slightly as if she could relate to Rhonda's story.

"After three months sober," Rhonda continued, "I guess I was feeling like I could have one little drink and stop, but of course, I couldn't. Four shots later, it hit me that I had messed up big-time. I called my sponsor who picked me up and drove me home. I felt like such a loser until she told me how many times she had failed before committing to the program for life. She said she still had to work The Steps every single day, even after five years of sobriety. That gave me the courage to start over. So, today, I'm happy to say I've been sober four whole days." Again, everyone applauded.

A few more people stood and shared their stories of failure, hope, more failure, and finally, success. Walt closed the meeting by inviting the attendees to stand and join in reciting The Lord's Prayer. This time Mom and I were able to participate. I squeezed her hand and told her how proud I was of her for coming. "But I still need a drink," she whispered. "I thought this was supposed to help."

"You have to keep coming, Mom. One meeting isn't going to cure you. We'll come back tomorrow and the next day and the next day. Let's pick up one of those pamphlets about the Twelve Steps. We can read them together every day." I noticed some books on the table, too.

As people were filing out to return to their respective lives and jobs, we approached the table. "Hi," Walt said, cheerfully. "You ladies are new, aren't you?"

With downcast eyes, Mom looked like she wanted to melt into the floor, but I held her hand and responded, "Yes. Hi, Walt. I'm Abby and this is, uh, Liz." I asked if the books were available to borrow.

"Absolutely. Take whatever you want, and welcome. Will we see you tomorrow?"

"Yes," I said. "We'll be here."

"Great. You're welcome to bring your lunches and eat during the meeting." He gestured about the room. "As you can see, lots of folks do."

"Thanks," I said. I found a book that I thought might be helpful for Mom and picked up a pamphlet listing the Twelve Steps. We left and drove back to the motel. I felt encouraged and I thought Mom did, too. I'd need to keep reminding her that her sobriety wouldn't happen overnight. She'd have to continue working The Steps, one day at a time.

CR‏⋈

Back at the motel, as I started putting the clean clothes away, I asked Mom if she felt like going to the grocery store. She had already settled into the chair by the window.

"I think I'll stay here and read," she said, leafing through the book entitled, A.A. How It Works.

"Okay. We're out of almost everything, but I guess it can wait until tomorrow."

"You go ahead without me."

That was not going to happen, but I didn't want to risk destroying our new positive vibe by telling her I didn't trust her to be alone. Instead, I said, "I need to do some school work, anyway. Maybe we can get a few things after we pick up the boys."

"Okay."

"What did you think about the meeting, Mom?"

She looked up. "It was fine, but I don't think I need to go anymore. I'm feeling much stronger."

"That's great. But let's finish out the week and see how it goes after that. We have to return the book anyway." I was determined she would return the next day and the day after that. I'd make sure of it. It took all my self-control to refrain from arguing about it.

"Right," she said. She was already engrossed in the book. So, I sat at the desk and tried to decipher my calculus homework.

Chapter 15

By Sunday, the Jordan family's life had returned to normal—as normal as life can be when you're living in a tiny motel room with no income and a mother who could revert to drinking any moment. I had survived a tough week, and now I needed to get back to school. I was nervous about leaving Mom alone and terrified to return to classes where I knew my friends would have a million questions about my absence, and where I had fallen behind in every subject.

Mom mentioned that my guidance counselor had called a couple times and left messages which I already knew. She said Ms. Gladstone was concerned about my extended absence. I would need to prepare a convincing story and go to her office first thing Monday morning. Maybe I'd tell her the truth and ask for her help like Ellen, my on-line counselor, had suggested. Sunday evening, as I laid out my clothes for the next day, I conducted a mental rehearsal of my explanation for missing a week of school.

Mom and I had already discussed some strategies for dealing with her urge to drink, everything from working The Steps to snapping a rubber band on her wrist. She and I had attended the lunch-time meeting faithfully every day that week, and she felt confident she was ready to go alone. She had borrowed and read two books about the Twelve Step program, including The Big Book recommended by Walt. I knew she hadn't had a drink because she hadn't been out of my sight, but I could tell she was still struggling against the craving. She would jump up and head for the door, then turn suddenly like someone had punched her. Every few minutes, she would move from the bed to the chair and back again. She had developed noticeable ticks, too, like shoulder twitching or spells of rapid blinking. Several times a day, she went to the bathroom and splashed cold water on her face. I figured these habits were signs of withdrawal.

"Hey, Mom," I suggested as she was preparing breakfast Monday morning. "Why don't you get your hair done today?"

"Yeah, Mom," Pete said. "Your hair looks old."

"We can't afford it," Mom said, ignoring Pete's unintended insult.

"But, when you start job-hunting again, you'll need to look your best."

"That's right. Maybe I should. I'll see if I can get an appointment." As she ran her fingers through her straggly hair, a pang of fear shot through me when I noticed the telltale trembling. She caught me watching, grabbed the offending hand and pushed it resolutely to her lap.

"You won't forget your meeting, will you?"

"Of course not. Now don't worry about me. Just have a super-duper day at school."

"Okay," I said, wrapping her boney body in my embrace, but I knew I would worry all day.

"Me, too, Mommy?" asked Joey.

"Yes, you too, Joe-Joe," she said as she scooped him up and gave him a big hug and kiss. Pete jumped from the bed to get in on the action, too. It was great to see Mom trying to act like our mother again. I wondered how long it would take to expel all traces of alcohol from her system. As much as I wanted to bask in relief, I feared what I might find waiting for me after school.

We piled into the car, and without preamble, Pete said, "I want to be a Stormtrooper for Halloween."

"Me too," said Joey, predictably.

"Oh, my goodness! I forgot about Halloween," Mom said. "It's next weekend, isn't it?"

"Can we go trick-or-treating in our old neighborhood?" asked Pete.

"Of course. Oh, Abby. What are we going to do about costumes for the boys? We can't afford..." Every little decision, to her, was a major hurdle. Despite Ellen's advice, I remember thinking it was my responsibility to spare her any distress that might cause her to backslide. Yet, often I wanted to grab her shoulders and shake her into reason.

"Don't worry," I interrupted. "We'll figure out something." I had no idea what we'd do, but I was afraid to let Mom concern herself with anything other than her recovery.

In my mind, it was important for Pete and Joey to participate in Halloween as they always had. It was one of those traditions that represented normalcy. Because nothing else about their life was normal, I was determined to help my little brothers feel like ordinary kids. I was the poster child for co-dependency—a new term Ellen had taught me.

Despite my lingering resentment about our circumstances, I was old enough to understand how we had gotten to that point. My little brothers weren't. I could hear Ellen's words ringing in my head, "Abby, you must be careful not to become your mother's caretaker. She needs to learn how to function without dependence on alcohol or her teenage daughter."

Of course, Ellen was right. I was guilty of trying to rescue Mom and to "mother" my little brothers, but someone had to protect them. They had lost their father, their home, their toys, and their pet. They had also lost some of their friends who now bullied them about being poor. I could imagine how the bullying might escalate if their friends found out their mother was a drunk. Somebody had to make sure they didn't lose their entire childhoods.

When Mom picked me up after school that afternoon, I felt a rush of relief because she seemed sober. She had made it through a whole day without me. I knew she still had a long way to go before she would look and act like her old self, but she was excited to tell me about Diana, her new sponsor at AA. Diana had told Mom to call her any time she needed help or encouragement.

"Diana's been sober for almost four years," she said with a child-like lilt to her voice. "She started drinking when her marriage was falling apart. Like me, she had never touched a drop before. She thought a glass of wine in the evening would calm her nerves. But, she couldn't stop at one glass. I related to her immediately, and I think we can become good friends."

With cautious optimism, I said, "That's wonderful." Mainly, I was hoping Diana might take some of the pressure off me.

"Abby, I can never thank you enough."

"For what?"

"For putting up with my moods, for making me go to AA and..."

"Mom, you're doing all the hard work," I interrupted, embarrassed by her gushing.

"No, Abby. Let me finish." As she drove toward the boys' school, she said, "Sweetheart, you've been through hell with me, and you've had to be there for your brothers when I wasn't a fit mother. I love you so much, and I appreciate everything you've done for our family."

Wanting to let my hopes soar, but fearing disappointment, I responded simply, "You're welcome."

She smiled and changed the subject. "I withdrew a hundred dollars from our bank account this morning. It has to cover groceries and costumes for the boys."

"What about your hair?"

"That can wait. Maybe I'll let it go completely gray. Then, I won't have to worry about all those drunks at AA hitting on me." We both laughed at her joke because we understood that now she included herself in the category of "drunks." It was a healthy admission.

"Oh, Mom," I said, as I took her right hand off the steering wheel and held it for a moment. "I'm so proud of you." Feeling her warm, steady hand filled me with optimism.

"Thanks, sweetie." Her voice was steady, too. Did I dare feel hopeful?

Suddenly, I remembered something. "Hey, wasn't Brendan a Star Wars-something last Halloween?" Brendan was Mindy's younger brother. "I think he had a light saber and everything."

"Hmm. Yes. I think he went as Luke Skywalker."

"Let's see if we can borrow his costume," I said. Then, we can check out the Goodwill store for Pete's. Immediately, I texted Mindy. She confirmed that Brendan had dressed as Luke Skywalker and said Joey could borrow the costume. After picking up the boys, I suggested we stop by Mindy's house.

"Yeah! We can see Bella!" the boys shouted from the back seat.

"No, wait," Mom said, displaying anxiety.

"What's wrong?" I asked.

"Um, nothing. It's just that, well... the Trents live in that nice house and Lisa always looks so put-together, and... I mean, they don't know why we moved, do they?" Her voice was starting to quiver, and she kept looking at herself in the rearview mirror, running one hand through her graying, stringy hair and trying to smooth the puffiness that lingered under her eyes.

"No, Mom. Mrs. Trent doesn't know anything except that we moved to another part of town." Suddenly, I felt nervous, too, about how I'd react to being in Mindy's spacious, beautiful house again, but I really wanted to see Bella. "Come on," I said. "It'll be okay." I was encouraging myself as much as her. Reluctantly, she agreed.

∝≬∾

When we got there, Mrs. Trent greeted us at the front door. I noticed she looked startled when she saw Mom, but she didn't say anything except, "Well, hello Jordans! It's so good to see you."

Mom was right. Mrs. Trent did always look flawless with her perfectly styled hair and manicured hands. Whatever the occasion, whether casual or elegant, she looked sophisticated in a smart wardrobe that draped her tall, slender figure just right. With a long face and aquiline nose, she wasn't what most people would describe as pretty, but her smiling eyes were kind and sincere. From the time Mindy and I were five years old, Mrs. Trent had made me feel welcome in her home, and I loved going there.

As soon as Bella spotted us, she rushed to the foyer, her tail wagging furiously, and she barked her happy-bark. I felt like I would burst into tears at the sight of her. I knelt to nuzzle her and realized how much I had missed her familiar doggy-smell, and the feel of her soft coat against my cheek. Pete and Joey went crazy with delight, allowing Bella to attack them with her sloppy kisses. Mrs. Trent barely got the door closed before they were lying on the floor and giggling convulsively while they let Bella lick their faces.

"Can we play with Bella in the backyard?" asked Pete.

"Yeah, can we?" Joey asked.

"Of course," Mindy's mom said. "She's your dog. Brendan's already out there."

"Yay! Come on, Bella!"

Once the boys were out of ear-shot, the conversation turned more serious. I could read concern on Mrs. Trent's face. She invited Mom and me into the formal living room, and motioning for us to sit, asked Mom how we were doing. I had been in Mindy's house hundreds of times through the years, but this was the first time I felt uneasy.

"We're fine, Lisa," Mom said, staring holes in the colorful Persian rug beneath our feet. Just then, Mindy came bounding down the stairs.

"Hi, Abby. Hi, Mrs. Jordan," she said, and sat next to me on the sofa. Mrs. Trent poured coffee into her best China cups and offered us some delicious-looking pastries that she had laid out on the coffee table.

"Have you found a permanent place to live, Liz?" she asked Mom, handing her a cup of coffee.

"Not yet, but soon, I hope," Mom answered, pulling her hair over one cheek like she was trying to hide behind it.

"Thanks for taking care of Bella," I said to Mrs. Trent as I tried to push away the envy and stem the tears that threatened to spill. I hadn't realized how hard it would be to see my beloved dog again or to face my best friend's mom after losing everything.

"It's no trouble at all. She's a sweet dog, and Mindy has been doing all the care. Then, turning to Mom she asked, "Is there anything else we can do?"

"No, but thanks," Mom said stiffly. I could tell she was struggling to keep her eyes from darting about the room. She looked like she was going to jump out of her skin. I needed to get us out of there as quickly as possible.

"You seem thin, Liz. Are you feeling okay?"

The look of sympathy on Mrs. Trent's face led me to suspect Mindy had betrayed my confidence. I glanced accusingly at her, but she shrugged her shoulders and shook her head subtly as if to say, "I haven't told her anything."

"I'm fine," Mom said. "It's nothing that two or three of these pastries won't cure." Her laugh was strained, and she studied the coffee in her cup like she was willing it to suck her into its swirling vortex.

"That's for sure," I said, helping myself.

"There're plenty more in the kitchen. So, don't be shy," said Mrs. Trent. I was thinking, when was the last time we had plenty of anything? As I glanced around Mindy's elegantly appointed, spacious house, I couldn't help but compare it to our dingy, disgusting motel room. "Mindy, take some goodies outside to the boys, please. There's lemonade in the refrigerator or milk if they prefer it."

"Okay. Come on, Abby. Will you help me?"

"Sure," I said, but I hesitated to leave Mom alone with Mrs. Trent. I could tell she was terribly uncomfortable and couldn't wait to get out of there.

Less than an hour later, with the costume in hand, we made our exit. Saying good-bye to Bella was even tougher than it had been the first time. I wanted to scoop her up and run. I sniffed her fur, memorizing its scent, and kissed her cold, wet nose. Then, wiping my eyes furiously, I turned, said a quick "thank you," and walked away.

I dreaded returning to our substandard room, and I knew Mom had been making her own silent comparisons. How could I ever invite Mindy or Alyssa or any other friends to my horrid, cramped hovel? I want to go home, I thought longingly, to my real home.

Chapter 16

As soon as we had managed Halloween successfully, the whole world, it seemed, focused on Christmas. We scarcely acknowledged Thanksgiving except for splurging on a turkey breast. My brothers were growing more excited by the day, but Mom was displaying ever-increasing anxiety about the impending holiday. She had been attending her meetings every day and working The Steps faithfully. I was sure she hadn't touched a drop in more than a month.

"How will I give the boys a Merry Christmas, Abby?" she asked one day in November. "I submitted applications all over town for temporary holiday work, but I haven't gotten any responses."

"Did you try the outlets? Surely they're hiring."

"Yes. I applied at five or six stores. I must have started looking too late in the season. I just don't know how these things work." As much as Ellen had cautioned me to avoid taking care of Mom—she referred to it as being the adult-child—I felt compelled to ease Mom's holiday stress. At last, our lives were relatively calm, and I couldn't risk a dangerous relapse. Ellen had also mentioned that kids are more resilient than we give them credit for. She encouraged me to be honest with the boys about our financial situation, explaining that they shouldn't expect a lot of presents.

"Listen, Mom. Maybe it's time we told the boys the truth."

"But, I just can't bring myself to ruin their Christmas."

"Maybe I should get a job."

"No. Absolutely not. School is your job, and you have only a few months until graduation. Besides you just got caught up from babysitting me for a week. Maybe I'll get a call tomorrow." She was beginning to sound like my mother, the real Elizabeth Jordan, and I noticed she was looking better. She had started to wear makeup again. She had even trimmed and styled her hair.

Two days later, Mom did get a call. Kmart wanted her to start as soon as possible. The job paid only minimum wage, but even temporary employees were eligible for a discount on merchandise.

"What'll you do about your meetings, and how will we get to school?" I asked one Saturday as we were cleaning our room.

"I requested evenings and weekends, and the manager said that's exactly what she needs. I know it'll be hard on you, Abby, but it's only until January."

"Don't worry. We'll be fine," I said, trying to sound confident. Then, under my breath, I added, "I have no social life anyway." I had a ton of homework, and now I would be tied down with my brothers again. Knowing I had no time for a boyfriend, I rebuffed any guys who asked me out.

I had stopped chatting with Ellen. I missed her wise counsel, but I couldn't access Wi-Fi often enough to maintain our sessions.

Mindy was busy preparing for mid-terms and planning for college, and now had a steady boyfriend who monopolized her weekends, but she came whenever she could get away. Not once during her occasional visits did my dear friend utter a disparaging word about our humble living-quarters. She never made me feel inferior. Often, she would bring something, like homemade cookies or a small toy or game for the boys, but her kindness never felt like pity. She would say, "Brendan doesn't play with this anymore. I thought Pete and Joey might like it."

We were fine for a while. I even managed to get caught up with my school work. Mom met with Pete's and Joey's teachers who reported that the boys were doing better in school, and Mrs. Foster was pleased to tell her that Pete had stopped fighting with other kids. Mom also talked with Mrs. Gladstone who supplied her with a stack of college catalogues and scholarship applications for me.

Without a car at my disposal, it was challenging to vary our surroundings when the boys grew too bored to entertain themselves. We had to restrict our weekend activities to anything within walking distance, like the library, post office, and train station. Sometimes we'd walk to the historic area where the boys could run around on the Palace Green or visit the sheep and horses.

Pete's new friend, Ian from two doors down, attended Matthew Whaley School, which wasn't far from the motel. Ian knew how to get us into the school's playground on weekends. But there was the constant problem of keeping the boys' stomachs full. The more they played, the more they ate. It helped that Mom could buy most of our groceries at Kmart. There were no desserts and no snack foods, only the essentials. With the help of food stamps and her employee discount, we were managing, but Mom's job would end the second week in January. Every few days there was something new to worry about, it seemed.

Chapter 17

Christmas day was nothing like the ones we had spent in the past, but Mom tried to make it festive. She bought a small table-top tree from Kmart. It was already adorned with lights and ornaments, so there was nothing to decorate. She placed it on the built-in desk and surrounded it with gifts she had bought and wrapped at the store. Gift-wrapping was one of her tasks as a holiday temp, and her supervisor said she could wrap her own presents during lulls.

Pete and Joey received one small toy each from Santa, but mostly they got much-needed clothes and new sneakers. I was proud of them for not complaining. Maybe for them, like me, it was enough to have their mom back or maybe Ellen was right about kids being resilient when we tell them the truth.

For Mom's gift, I helped my brothers make coupon books which we decorated with markers and stickers. She could redeem coupons for extra hugs, cleaning the bathroom or a whole day without arguing. We had fun making them, and Mom said she loved them. I managed to sneak into the grocery cart a bag of her favorite coffee and some chocolate biscotti, too. She gave me a compilation of stories by one of my favorite authors, Jane Austen, and some warm flannel pajamas.

I gave my brothers matching Star Wars pajamas and balls—a football for Pete and a soccer ball for Joey. Technically, all the gifts were from Mom—since she gave us the money to buy them—and all were purchased at Kmart with her employee discount.

My brothers gave me a warm hat-scarf-gloves set in my favorite shade of lavender, which, to their delight, I modeled for them immediately.

All-in-all we did okay for a nearly homeless family. Mom even splurged on dinner at Golden Corral. It was the only restaurant we could find open on Christmas day. Pete and Joey returned to the buffet again and again, filling their plates to overflowing until I worried they might be sick. Unexpectedly, after downing his second helping of soft ice cream, Joey lowered his head and said sadly, "I miss Daddy."

"I know, Joe-Joe. I do, too," Mom said. I could tell she was trying to hold back tears, and, suddenly, I was teetering on the edge of a melt-down.

"Mom, can we go to the cemetery after lunch?" I asked. "We haven't been there since Dad's memorial service."

"Yeah, can we go tell Daddy 'Merry Christmas'?" Joey asked through his new front teeth. Pete remained silent, staring at his plate.

"I think that's a great idea," Mom said, wiping her eyes with her napkin. "That is, if you two 'Hungry, Hungry Hippos' can pull yourselves away from the dessert buffet."

CЗВD

With hearts as full as our bellies, we left the restaurant and drove to the cemetery. It was a cold, blustery day. Mom parked as close to the mausoleum as possible, but we had to walk the few remaining yards along a paved path. I recalled more than one Virginia Christmas when the temperature had been balmy, like a spring day. That December twenty-fifth was not one of them. Wondering if it might snow, I was thankful to be wearing my new hat, scarf, and gloves. As we approached the entrance to the crypt, I lifted the scarf to cover my mouth and nose and sprinted the remaining distance, pulling Joey with me.

"Hurry, it's freezing!" I shouted back to Mom and Pete. The inside temperature wasn't much warmer, but at least we were sheltered from the biting wind. Not one other soul had braved the frigid weather to visit their dearly departed on Christmas Day. Only the Jordan family stood facing rows and rows of niches. Since Dad's nook was too high for Joey to see, I lifted him enough that he could rest his feet on my thighs.

"How does he fit in there?" Joey wanted to know. I lowered him to the marble floor. Mom tried to explain the process of cremation, but when Joey became visibly disturbed by her description, she reminded him that Dad was in heaven where he couldn't feel pain or sadness.

"Only his ashes are in the urn," I heard her say as I turned toward the exit. That's when I saw Pete, leaning against the opposite wall, looking forlorn. I approached him and knelt to his eye-level.

"Are you okay, buddy? I asked, placing my hand on his shoulder. He didn't respond. He was staring at the floor and biting his lower lip. "This is hard, isn't it?" Something about Christmas made me feel an extra measure of affection for my annoying brothers. Remaining mute, he nodded, his eyes focused on the marble floor. "Do you want to come closer?" He shook his head. "Sometimes it feels better when we look. Then we can say a proper good-bye."

"I don't want to say good-bye," he muttered. "I want him to come back and live with us."

"I know. I do, too. We miss him, don't we, especially at Christmas?" His head nodded slightly. I drew him into my arms and now let my own tears fall freely, assuring him it was okay for big boys to cry. I vowed silently, that no matter what the future held, I would keep our family together. I would make sure my little brothers were okay.

Gently, with the end of my scarf, I wiped Pete's tear-stained cheeks. I smiled at him, grasped his hand and stood. Then, the four of us ran back to the car through cold raindrops spitting from a gray sky that threatened sleet.

During the drive back to our motel, the inside of our car

remained as soundless as the empty streets we traveled. I think each of us was lost in our own thoughts of Christmases past... Christmases that included Dad and Bella. I remembered how Bella would lick my face and whimper to wake me; how Dad was always the first one up, sitting in his recliner with a cup of coffee in his "World's Greatest Dad" mug; how he would tease us, pretending we had to wait until after breakfast before diving into the massive pile of gifts that spilled from under the tree.

Life would never be the same, but for now, we were okay. We had a place to live, enough food, warm pajamas...and a sober mother. That evening, with ice pelting against the windows of the tiny room we called "home," I allowed myself to feel almost peaceful. I could never have predicted that the worst was yet to come.

Chapter 18

Our family's next trial began in January—on the day Mom was laid off from Kmart. Since mid-October, she had been going to her meetings daily and working The Steps. I was so proud of her for the progress she had made. It seemed like she was on solid footing toward a lifelong journey of sobriety. My brothers and I were thrilled to have our mother back.

I should have seen it coming. Within a couple of weeks, Mom was, again, showing signs of stress. Collection agencies called constantly, hounding her to pay off the outstanding medical bills and credit-card bills. Since working, she had been trying to pay the minimum amounts on three maxed-out credit cards, as Reuben had advised her, but it wasn't enough to keep the interest charges from accruing steadily. I knew that, without an income, by March, she wouldn't be able to cover our rent.

The day her job ended was the second day she failed to pick me up at school. I waited on the front steps for twenty minutes. Fortunately, Mom had insisted that, no matter how poor we became, she and I would keep our cell phones. I called hers and left numerous messages. Nothing. I texted her. No response. Soon it would be time to get the boys. She simply couldn't be late picking them up. I had to act.

I called Mindy who had just pulled into her driveway. "I'm sorry to ask this, but do you think you could come back to school?"

"What's going on?" she asked.

"It's Mom. She hasn't shown up, and it's almost time to pick up Pete and Joey. I'm really worried."

"Hey, no problem. I'll be right there."

"You're a life-saver. Thanks." Mindy turned around immediately and drove back to school.

Mindy's car was last in the carpool line at the boys' school, but, thankfully, we weren't late. At first, the monitor wouldn't release them to us. I had to go to the main office and show my driver's license. Fortunately, I was listed as one of their approved drivers.

As Mindy took us to the motel, I began to feel panicky about what I might find. Mom wouldn't have left us stranded unless she had fallen "off the wagon." But she had been doing so well. She had stayed sober for nearly two months. How could she let this happen? I wondered. How would I shield my brothers from seeing Mom in a drunken stupor? Should I ask Mindy to take the boys to her house? Should I call Diana or Reuben and have one of them meet us at the motel? In my panicked state, I wasn't sure what to do.

Approaching the railroad tracks that ran perpendicular to the motel, we could see flashing red and blue lights casting an eerie, purple glow over the parking lot. "What's going on?" Pete asked, leaning forward in his seat.

"Look," said Joey. "A fire engine at our motel." My heart was pounding, and I felt like I couldn't catch my breath. Could the motel—our home—be on fire? Mindy rounded the corner and started to enter the parking lot only to find the entrance blocked by a fire truck, an ambulance, and two police cruisers. As the boys chattered excitedly in the back seat about the emergency vehicles, Mindy and I shared a private look of fear.

"Park here," I said, motioning to a spot on the street. She pulled over and, with my most authoritative voice, I told my brothers to stay in the car. "Mindy, make sure they do." I opened the passenger-side door and stepped out. I began walking toward the parking lot, my legs heavy and my heart thumping like I had just finished a ten-K.

Then I saw it. The door to our room was open. No, please, no. I knew something terrible had happened. I broke into a run. Thoughts of the scene awaiting me were too horrible to imagine. I tried to dismiss them as I worked through the crowd that had gathered in the parking lot. Finally, I reached the stairs, but when I tried to climb to the second floor, a police officer blocked me. "You can't go up there," he said. "Please stay back."

"But, that's my room!" I shouted. "My mom! Where is she?" My head was spinning. I grabbed the metal railing for support. This can't be real.

"Mom!" I shouted, trying to move past the cop. But he held me in place. "What's happened? Just tell me what's happened."

"What's your name?" he asked.

"What?"

"Who are you?"

"Abby. Abigail Jordan. My mom is Elizabeth Jordan, and we live there. Please tell me what's going on."

"There's been an accident."

"What do you mean? What kind of accident?"

"That's all I know, but you can't go up." Two EMTs emerged from our room with a gurney. "No! Mom!" I cried. It couldn't be. But I knew it was.

When the gurney reached the ground level, I saw her lying there still and ashen with an oxygen mask covering her nose and mouth. An IV bag dangled above her. "Mom? Oh, God! Is she dead?" I asked through scalding tears.

"This is her daughter," I heard the cop say.

"She's unconscious, but she's alive," one attendant said. I followed them to the ambulance.

"She seems to have overdosed," the EMT added. "Do you want to ride in the ambulance?"

"Yes. Oh, wait! My little brothers."

"Brothers? Where are they?" asked the officer.

"Over there." I was pointing toward Mindy's car, just visible beyond the tall shrubs. I was too confused and upset to think what to do.

"You can meet us at the hospital if you prefer."

"Yeah, okay. Um... which hospital?"

"Riverside. Meet us inside the emergency entrance."

"Listen, uh, Abby," said the cop. "I'll take you and your brothers. You're in no shape to drive."

"Mindy," I said, absentmindedly as I watched Mom being lifted into the ambulance.

"What?"

"My friend can drive us."

The next few minutes were a whirlwind. I'm not sure how everything got settled, but Pete, Joey and I ended up in the back of a police car, speeding toward the hospital behind an ambulance that carried our unconscious mother. Mindy said she would call her mom and meet us at Riverside. I was trying to keep myself calm so I could soothe my brothers, who were terrified and asking questions I couldn't answer. It was a nightmare, one I wished I could wake up from. How could this be happening? What exactly was happening?

When we reached the hospital, the policeman walked us into the emergency room and took us to the reception desk. The three of us kids stood there, clinging to each other like band-aids to a wound. Then, as the EMTs whisked Mom away, I heard the officer explaining something to the receptionist. He led us to some empty chairs in the bustling waiting area. As I glanced around, I saw people of all ages awaiting treatment for ailments both obvious and invisible. An inconsolable baby wailed in the arms of its worried-looking mother; a teenager wearing a soccer uniform held an icepack on her swollen ankle; an elderly woman sat slumped in a wheelchair; a man wearing filthy coveralls and a construction hat held his hand in the air as blood soaked the gauze bandage covering his thumb.

"Can we see her?" I asked the officer. I was determined not to cry. I knew I had to be strong for my brothers, but I could feel my insides shaking. I hoped Mindy and Mrs. Trent would arrive soon.

"Stay here," the policeman said. "I'll find out."

I sucked in a breath of antiseptic air and turned to Pete and Joey. Trying to sound confident, I said, "Mom's going to be okay. She's in the hospital now where the doctors can help her."

"But, what's wrong with her?" Joey asked.

"Yeah, what happened to her?" asked Pete.

"I don't know," I lied. We just have to wait and help each other stay calm, okay?"

"Is she going to die like Daddy?" asked Joey. I hesitated before answering. His question seemed to jolt me out of my shock. I remember thinking I shouldn't lie about something like that. If I said "no" and Mom died, my brothers would never trust me again. But I didn't want to scare them unnecessarily, either. I pulled away from their embrace and knelt on the floor, so I could look directly into their anxious faces. I wished that baby would stop crying. I wished I didn't have to be the adult.

"Right now, I can't promise anything, but whatever happens, we'll be together, and we'll deal with it together, okay?" We fell into each other's arms and remained huddled for a few minutes. As far as we were concerned there was no one else in that packed waiting room. We were the Jordan kids alone in the world... waiting, waiting, waiting.

Joey broke the spell. "I'm hot," he said. That's when I realized we were still wearing our winter coats and hats.

"Of course, you are, buddy." I said, glad to have something ordinary to deal with. "Come on, let's take off these heavy clothes. Hey, I'll bet you're getting hungry, too, aren't you?"

"Kind of," said Pete.

"I think I noticed a vending machine just around the corner. Let's see how much change I have in my purse." We spread our outerwear on the chairs to save our seats and headed toward the vending machine.

Just then, the receptionist called, "Miss Jordan?"

"Here, take this and get a snack," I said, pouring loose change into my brothers' hands. "Stay where I can see you."

Guardedly, I approached the receptionist, fearing what I was about to hear. The kind policeman stood there at the desk. "Can I... may I see her?" I asked. "May I see my mom?"

"Not yet," the woman said. "She's being admitted to the ICU. Once she's settled in her room, you should be able to visit."

"Intensive Care?" I asked, incredulous. "It's that serious?"

Then the officer said, "Abby is there someone I can call for you? Your father, maybe?"

"No, thanks," I said, still trying to process how Mom could have consumed enough alcohol—assuming it was alcohol—to land her in Intensive Care. "My friend and her mother are on their way."

"Okay. Good. I need to get back on the job. Will you and your brothers be all right?"

"Yeah. We're fine. Thanks for your help, Officer..." I looked at his name tag. "Officer Petro... Petron..."

"It's Petronowich," he said. "Aleksander Petronowich."

"That's a mouth full," I laughed uncomfortably, wiping the tears that were determined to keep making an entrance.

"That's why everybody calls me Alek."

"Thanks, Alek."

"Listen, Abby, keep me posted about your mom, okay?" I nodded and tried to smile. "If you need anything, here's my number. You can call me day or night." Alek handed me his card, shook my hand, and walked out the door under the big red letters that spelled, "Emergency Entrance." I thanked the receptionist and joined my brothers at the vending machine.

Armed with M&Ms, Snickers bars and a variety of chips, we returned to the waiting room. Without supervision, my brothers had selected the junkiest junk foods, but right then, their nutrition was the least of my concerns.

Soon, Mindy and her mother showed up. I fell into Mindy's arms, feeling limp with relief that I wasn't alone, but my emotions felt out of control, vacillating among fear, sadness, and anger. Of course, they started asking questions, wanting to know about Mom's condition, but I still didn't have any answers. All I could tell them was that she was being admitted to Intensive Care and she was unconscious.

"Let me see what I can find out," said Mrs. Trent. Since she was a nurse, I hoped she might have an inside connection. When Mrs. Trent returned, she said Mom was settled in her room, and we could visit for a few minutes. We stood and started to grab our coats when she added, "The doctor wants to talk to you before you go in. She'll meet you in the second floor waiting area. Do you want us to go with you?"

"Yes, if you don't mind," I said, feeling weak.

"Of course," Mrs. Trent answered. "We'll stay as long as you need us."

Joey, who had been noisily wadding his empty chip bag into a ball, asked, "Can we see Mommy now?"

"Yes, dummy," said Pete. "That's what she just said." I shot him a disapproving glare and he uttered an insincere, "Sorry."

"The doctor wants to talk to us first. She'll tell us about Mom's condition. Now, you two need to be on your best behavior, understand?"

"Yeah."

I rested my hands on their shoulders and we followed the nurse who had talked to Mrs. Trent. We took the elevator to the second floor and walked to the ICU waiting room, a smaller space than the ER waiting area.

"Sit over there and finish your snacks," I said to the boys, motioning toward a round table in the corner. "I'll talk to the doctor and tell you what she says."

"I'm thirsty," Joey said.

"Do you have any change left?" I asked.

"No."

"Then you'll have to wait until we can find a water fountain." Soon, the doctor entered.

"Are you Abigail?" I heard her ask Mindy.

"No, she's over there. Abby, the doctor's here."

"Sit here and be quiet," I warned my brothers. I walked across the room and shook hands with the doctor, a petite, olive-skinned woman with dark, shiny hair that she wore in a bun. She didn't look old enough to be a doctor.

Before she had a chance to say anything, I asked, "Is my mother going to be okay?"

"I'm Doctor Santos," she said. "Let's sit down, Abigail." Her serious demeanor made me anticipate the worst news. She motioned to a chair and sat beside me. Mindy and her mom sat across from us leaning forward in their seats. Pete and Joey had found a checkers game and were setting it up. I felt relieved that they might be too engrossed to hear our conversation.

"Your mother is in a coma," the doctor began. "She ingested a large amount of alcohol which poisoned her system. There may have been pills, too. We're waiting for test results."

"Oh, Mom, no," I said, resting my head in my hands. Feeling defeated, I tried not to cry. "Why?" I raised my head and a sob escaped. When the doctor placed a hand on my back, I drank in as much air as I could and wiped my tears. I explained, "She was doing so well. She was sober for nearly two months, and she was doing really well."

"So, she's an alcoholic?" the doctor asked. I saw Mrs. Trent share a look with Mindy that told me she was hearing this information for the first time.

"Yes, but she was doing great. I don't understand."

"It's very difficult for alcoholics to maintain their sobriety," Doctor Santos said, now covering my clasped hands with hers. "Addicts have to deal with the overwhelming urge every minute of every day."

"When will she come out of the coma?" I remember feeling very tired.

"I don't know. The next twelve to twenty-four hours will be critical. Her blood alcohol level was point-three-five."

Mrs. Trent gasped.

"What does that mean?" I asked.

"It's extremely high. Even before we pumped her stomach, it shut down her respiratory system. She's breathing with the help of a ventilator."

I hesitated to ask the next question, but I had to know the answer. "Doctor, do you think she did it on purpose?"

"Was she trying to kill herself? It's possible. There was a lot of alcohol in her system, but she did manage to dial nine-one-one before losing consciousness. What do you think, Abigail?"

"She's been through a rough time, but she seemed determined. She went to AA every day. I really thought she'd make it."

When I tried to stand, my legs wouldn't cooperate. Mindy and Mrs. Trent jumped up and moved closer, each supporting an elbow. Their touch was comforting. "Can we... may we see her?" I asked.

"Yes, for a few minutes," said the doctor, "but I need to prepare you. Like I said, she's in a coma, and she's hooked up to a ventilator and lots of other tubes. Your brothers might find it upsetting."

"I think they'd be more upset if they weren't allowed to go in," I said.

"All right, then. Her room is just down the hall, that way." She pointed to the right. "You and your brothers will need to sanitize your hands and wear masks." With Mindy and her mom supporting me, I straightened and motioned for Pete and Joey to join me.

"But I was winning," Joey complained.

"No, you weren't," said Pete. "You were cheating."

"Was not."

I sighed and moved toward them, like I was about to "jerk a knot in them," as Mee-maw used to say.

"We'll wait here," Mrs. Trent said.

As we approached Mom's room, I tried to prepare my brothers for what they were about to see, especially since their only other experience caused them to associate hospitals with death. They had seen Dad hooked up to tubes and monitors, and he never came home. I needed to help them understand that Mom could get well. After putting on masks and sanitizing our hands, we entered the tiny room filled with disturbing machines.

"This feels funny," said Joey, as he tried to adjust the adult-size mask that covered most of his face. I helped him by pushing it down a bit and pinching the nosepiece. Then, I repeated the process with Pete.

We stepped into the room, but both boys halted abruptly just inside the door. I had to encourage them to move closer to the bed. "Come on," I said. "It's okay." I suspected they were having the same flashbacks to Dad's hospitalization that I was. I took a hand in each of mine, and we moved cautiously toward our frail-looking mother. She seemed especially thin, almost disappearing under the sheet, and her skin was pale with reddish circles ringing her closed eyes. Tubes extended from her body and beeping monitors surrounded her motionless form.

"I'll leave you here," said Doctor Santos who had followed us in. "Don't stay more than a few minutes."

"What's wrong with her," Joey asked in a tiny voice.

"She's sick, Joey," I said. "She's in a coma, which means she's unconscious."

"Like she's asleep?" he asked.

"Yes, but she might be able to hear us."

"Can we talk to her, then?" asked Pete.

"Yes. Absolutely," I answered, trying desperately to stem the angry tears that had a stubborn will of their own.

"What should I say?" asked Pete.

"Well, you could tell her about your day at school." I sounded calm, but inside my head I was screaming at my mother, "Open your eyes! How could you be so selfish to put your children through this... this agony!"

Pete began talking about school and soon Joey joined in. With no response from Mom, they kept turning to me for approval. I didn't need that surgical mask to hide my true feelings. I had learned how to hide behind a mask of my own making, one that I could put on as quickly as lip gloss, the one I wore whenever I had to be the grown-up, whenever my brothers needed to know that someone would steady their shaky, shattering world.

"Are you sure she can hear us?" Pete asked.

"No, but it's possible. The doctor said we should talk to her even if she doesn't seem to hear us. It'll help her get better."

"Is she gonna die?" Joey asked. I wanted to lie. I wanted to tell him she would get better and come back to us, but I knew she could die. My chest felt heavy, like my lungs were caught in a vise. Light-headed, I struggled to breathe. I leaned against the bed-side cart and willed myself to keep it together.

Joey repeated his question with more urgency. "Sissy, is Mommy going to die?"

"I don't know," I said. Before he could react, I added, "We should let Mom rest. We can come back tomorrow. Give her a kiss and tell her you love her." I managed to lift Joey, so he could kiss her forehead through his mask, and Pete kissed the hand that didn't have an IV stuck in it. "We love you, Mom," I said, trying to sound light-hearted. "Hurry and get well." As the boys headed for the corridor, I lingered long enough to lean over her bed and growl, "Don't you die, Mom. Don't you dare leave us alone."

I declined Mrs. Trent's offer to take us to her house. My brothers didn't need any more changes in their routine just then. Our tiny motel room, despite its shortcomings, was familiar and held their few comforting possessions. Besides, I was anxious to see what state the room was in and whether there might be some clues as to what prompted Mom's extreme overdose.

"Okay," said Mrs. Trent. "But let's get you and those growing boys some supper first."

"That would be great," I said. "Oh, wait. I don't have any money. I gave the last of my change..."

"Don't worry. This is on me. How about Golden Corral?"

"Yeah! Golden Corral!" the boys chorused.

"It's probably the only place that can fill up these two bottomless pits." I laughed without joy.

Pete and Joey ate nearly as much as they had on Christmas Day, but, as hungry as my stomach felt, I couldn't seem to push more than a few bites past the lump in my throat.

Chapter 19

When Mrs. Trent dropped us off at the motel, it was nearly the boys' bedtime. She didn't say one word about our living situation, but she couldn't hide her shock. I read it in her eyes.

"Are you sure you kids will be okay here alone tonight? You know you're welcome to stay with us." I thanked her, and trying to sound confident, assured her we'd be fine.

"We'll do our homework and go straight to bed." She made me promise to lock the door and to call her if we needed anything.

As soon as we walked through the door, I could smell alcohol... and vomit. Two empty whiskey bottles lay on the floor between the beds. Quickly, I blocked my brothers' view and kicked the bottles under their bed. My bed was covered in vomit.

"Ew! What's that smell?" Joey asked.

"Gross!" said Pete.

"It's from Mommy's sick stomach. I'll clean it up while you do your homework." I propped the door open to air out the place and set about stripping the bed. Fortunately, the wretched puke hadn't seeped through to the sheets. Awkwardly, I emptied it into the toilet and rinsed the bedspread and blanket in the bathtub. I carried the dripping covers outside to drape them over the railing and instructed the boys to take their showers and get ready for bed.

While they showered, I called Diana. She was devastated to hear about Mom and promised to visit her the next day.

"She was making such good progress. Why didn't she call me?" Diana asked.

"I don't get it. It was her last day at Kmart. Of course, she was worried about money, but that's nothing new."

"Set-backs are normal," she said. "But what could have triggered such an extreme reaction?"

"Maybe she thought she could take one or two drinks and hide the bottle, or bottles for later, but it didn't end up that way."

"Right. It never does," she said. I mentioned the whiskey bottles I found in our room.

"I didn't know she was hitting the hard stuff. When did that start?"

"I don't know exactly."

As I was talking to Diana, I pulled the bottles from under the bed and shoved them to the bottom of the trash can.

"Will you and your brothers be okay tonight?"

"We're fine, thanks. I'll go to school late tomorrow, so I can drop off the boys first. Then I'll have to figure out what to do until Mom gets out of the hospital. Our schools don't even know we moved out of the district."

"Honey, if you need anything... Listen, I'll go see Liz tomorrow. I have to work in the morning, but I can check on her later." I thanked her and told her I'd call the nurses' station to make sure they'd let a non-family member in the ICU. That's when I noticed something wedged between the bed and the nightstand. When I realized what it was, my stomach jumped into my throat. I must have startled audibly.

"What? What is it?" Diane asked.

"I just found a prescription bottle."

"What drug, Abby? What does the bottle say?"

"Vicodin."

"Geez! What was she thinking?"

"Is that bad?" I asked.

"Yeah. It's bad. Vicodin is a narcotic. I think you should call the nurses' station and tell them what she took. Do you want me to do it?"

"No. It's okay. I'll call."

"I'm so sorry, Abby. I should've had a clue, but she seemed fine last week. Worried about money, but fine."

"I know. I thought so, too. Where could she have gotten a prescription for narcotics?"

"Look at the label. Is her name on the label?"

"No. There's no name and no doctor's name."

"Street drugs. She bought 'em on the street. They could have been laced with something else."

As soon as the boys were asleep, I took my phone in the bathroom and called the hospital. I made peanut butter sandwiches for their lunches, hauled the bedspread and blanket back inside, throwing them into the tub, and fell into bed, drained.

My plan was to wake up early and do my homework, but I pushed "snooze" so many times Pete had to wake me at seven-thirty. The sweetheart had made breakfast: Cheerios with banana slices and the last drops of milk. Fortunately, it was Friday. I'd be able to get caught up with my schoolwork over the weekend.

After I drove the boys to their school, I decided the best plan was for me to skip school. I needed to fill the gas tank, buy groceries, and go to the laundromat, but I had exactly three pennies in my wallet.

I remembered that Mom's purse was still in the motel room. I could take her driver's license and checkbook to the bank. But I wondered if the teller would release any funds to me. I was beginning to panic. I had a responsibility to Pete and Joey. How would I take care of them without money? I thought about the credit card bills and the medical bills. We had no health insurance for Mom and no income. I'd have to quit school and get a job. Even that wouldn't be enough to support us, and besides, I wouldn't be able to find work right away. My brain backflipped, and my heart beat so fast I thought I might be having a heart attack. I remember wondering if it was even possible for a healthy seventeen-year-old to have a heart attack.

I pulled into the McDonalds parking lot on Richmond Road, maneuvering around the long line of cars at the drive-thru, and parking in one of the spaces reserved for take-out customers. I had to get myself calmed down, so I could think clearly. Lowering the vanity mirror, I stared at my reflection. "Come on, Abby," I said. "You can do this. Just pull yourself together and think."

After a few minutes of coaching the girl in the mirror, I began to feel calmer. Less anxious but completely alone, I drove to the motel, where I retrieved the bags of dirty clothes and Mom's purse. I practiced her signature a few times and used her makeup, trying to look older. With her eyeliner, I even drew some subtle crow's feet around my eyes. People were always saying how much I looked like her. I put on Mom's coat and hat, wrapped her scarf around my neck, and headed for the bank, using the drive-up window farthest from the building.

I'm sure I was shaking visibly, but the teller never questioned my identity. I withdrew two hundred dollars and she said, "Thank you, Mrs. Jordan. Have a nice day."

I responded with a curt, "Thanks," and proceeded to the gas station. It wasn't until later as I waited for the clothes to wash that I noticed the bank receipt I had stuffed mindlessly into Mom's coat pocket. It showed a balance of nine hundred eighty-five dollars. "Crap!" I said aloud, realizing it was only enough to get us through another month. I knew Mom had been trying to keep the creditors at bay with minimum payments, but we needed money to live on, too.

Anxiety began to overwhelm me again when my phone rang. I didn't recognize the number. At first, I considered not answering. But what if it's the hospital? I thought after two rings. What if Mom is... I couldn't even consider the possibilities. Nervously, I answered. It was the attendance monitor at my school.

"Yes, this is Abigail," I said, trying to sound sick. "Well, you see, my mom was taken to the hospital yesterday. She's in a coma, so she couldn't call you," I said, coughing for effect. Immediately, I realized how lame my excuse sounded and added, "You can check. She's at Riverside in ICU... Yes, I should be back Monday. Probably just a cold..."

With a back seat full of clean clothes, including a freshly laundered blanket and bedspread, I headed to the motel to put them away, straighten up the room, and finish my homework. I made a quick call to the hospital and learned there was no change in Mom's condition. Then, I packed snacks and drinks for the boys, so we could go straight to the hospital after I picked them up from school.

❆

As soon as Pete climbed in the car he asked, "Abby, do we have to spend all weekend at the hospital like when Daddy was sick?"

"No. We'll just go for a short visit to see how Mom is doing."

"Okay, good. Ian asked me over to play tomorrow. Hey, guess what?"

"What?"

"Ian's house... I mean Ian's room looks just like ours."

"It does?"

"Yeah, but it's backwards."

Joey laughed, "A backwards room. That's silly. I'm hungry, Abby. Can we get snacks from the machine again?"

"No. I brought snacks. You can eat in the waiting room." Mom had tried to break us of snacking between meals, but the boys were always ravenous after school.

"You brought healthy junk, right?"

"You guessed it, Sherlock."

When we arrived at the hospital, I set up the boys in the second-floor waiting room with their apples and peanut butter and turned the TV channel to Nickelodeon. I walked the few steps to Mom's room, where I found Diana sitting beside the bed, holding Mom's hand. I knew she couldn't do anything to speed my mother's recovery, but I found her presence comforting. "How is she?" I asked.

Diana stood, gave me a hug, and said, "There's no change. She's still in a coma."

"What if she doesn't come out of it?" I asked.

"Honey don't go there unless you have to. Sometimes patients are comatose for weeks when they suddenly snap out of it."

"But the doctor said twenty-four to forty-eight hours."

"Doctors have to tell you something."

"Have you seen Doctor Santos today?" I asked.

"No, but a nurse was here when I arrived. She said something about renal failure."

"Renal failure?"

"I'm not sure what it means. Why don't I go ask a nurse if Doctor Santos can come and give us a progress report? You stay here and talk to your mom."

"Okay. I just need to check on my brothers first." When I peeked around the corner into the waiting room, Pete and Joey were totally engrossed in their show, mouths agape. I returned to Mom's room and waited for Diana.

I sat there alone beside the bed that held the silent, motionless form of my mother. I needed her to wake up and assure me everything would be okay. Suddenly, a force beyond my control overtook my body. It was an overwhelming urge to scream from the depths of my core. I wanted to tell her she was selfish and stupid and spineless. I wanted to pound her chest and will her to regain consciousness. The intensity of my hateful feelings gripped me with fear. I stood and walked to the door, fighting the urge to run away, as far away from that room and my life as my feet would take me.

Leaning against the door jamb, stretching my arms above my head, I indulged in a silent scream so powerful it strained every muscle from the tips of my fingers to my raised heels. No tears flowed. There was only anger—intense anger that shook my body like a seizure. I wanted to drop to the floor in a heap and sleep for days.

The movement of someone walking briskly past the room caught my attention, but my eyes and ears couldn't focus. I shook myself like a dog after its bath, this time with conscious effort. I couldn't let Diana see me like that. Please, God, help me.

I returned to Mom's side and confessed that I had impersonated her at the bank and forged her signature. If anything could rouse her, I thought, surely an account of her daughter's criminal behavior would. I imagined her scolding me, reminding me to set a good example for my brothers, expressing her disappointment. I would have welcomed a stern tongue-lashing, any response at all.

"Doctor Santos does her rounds in the morning," Diana said, as she reentered the room. "I talked to the nurse again, though. Are you okay? You look pale."

"Yeah, I'm fine." I wasn't fine. I was a wreck. "What did she say?"

"She mentioned the possibility of kidney failure, but otherwise there's been no change. She didn't say kidney failure is certain, only that it's possible. I'm sorry, Abby." She placed her hand on my arm. "I know this waiting must be driving you crazy."

"Yeah. It's hard," I said without emotion. "I'd better let my brothers see her." I started to leave and nearly bumped into a kind-looking woman. She was tall, dressed in black, with short, gray hair and wore glasses and a clerical collar.

"Oh, sorry," she said. "Are you Missus Jordan's daughter?"

"Yes." She introduced herself to Diana and me as Marina, the hospital chaplain and asked me if Mom was protestant. I told her we used to attend the United Methodist Church. She told us she was available whenever we needed to talk and gave me her card. Then she asked if she could say a prayer for Mom.

"Yes, please," I answered, although I was miffed at God just then. Marina drew me closer to the bed and laid her hand on Mom's shoulder. I don't remember her words, but I remember the surge that passed through me as she prayed. It felt oddly warm and comforting. Before she left, Marina promised to visit Mom again the next day and said she would continue to pray for her and for me. I thanked her and headed to the waiting room to check on the boys.

Before I had the chance, Reuben walked in, with Pete and Joey in tow. "Look who I found in the waiting room, staying out of trouble," he quipped in his bass voice. I could tell he was trying to inject levity into an otherwise serious atmosphere. It was good to see his familiar face. Reuben had a way of making you feel that everything would be okay. I greeted him with a hug and introduced him to Diana. "Let's go have a chat in the waiting room and let Liz rest," he said.

Reuben explained that a social worker would be there in the morning to meet with us. "But, you're our social worker," I said, wondering what was going on.

"I was your father's case worker, but I'm not connected with this hospital. Your mom will be assigned a new case worker, and you kids will, too."

"But, why? Why do we need a case worker at all?"

"Because you're minors, and now you're minors without a guardian. It's policy." A strange uneasiness swirled in the pit of my stomach. It was the feeling of dread you get during a scary movie when the camera zooms in.

After our visit, I drove us to the motel past streetlights that stood as silent sentinels. I reflected on the vast changes that had invaded our lives in less than a year's time. Soon we'd be approaching the anniversary of Dad's death—the date when everything began to change. Our beautiful home was being enjoyed by another family. We had lost one parent and now were in danger of losing another. Most of our belongings were gone, and we were crammed into a minuscule room with too much debt to ever recover. I had abandoned my dreams of college and a career. It looked like I'd need to drop out of high school and get a job just to keep us fed. It seemed like our situation couldn't possibly get worse.

Chapter 20

Arriving at the motel, we climbed the steps to find two women standing outside our room. They introduced themselves and flashed identification badges, but I don't remember their names.

"Are you Abigail Jordan?" the taller one asked when we reached the second floor.

"Yes."

"We're from Child Protective Services. May we come in?"

"Um. Why?" Not waiting for their answer, I unlocked the door and ushered the boys inside. "Go in and start your homework."

"But it's Friday," Pete said.

"Just go. You can watch TV for a while." I turned to the women who exuded an air of authority. "What's this about?"

"May we come inside and talk to you?" The tall, stocky one, wearing a gray coat and matching wool hat, seemed to be in charge. She did all the talking. The shorter one appeared younger and slightly less intimidating as she stood silently a step behind her imposing colleague. With gloved hands, each held her coat lapel closed against the biting wind.

"I'd rather we talked out here," I said. The long, frizzy tendrils of hair that weren't tucked under my hat blew in little tornadoes around my face and into my mouth and eyes.

"This warrant says you must let us in." No longer polite, she pulled an official-looking piece of paper from her giant handbag and showed it to me. "So, we can do this in one of two ways. Either you let us in or we call the police." As fear engulfed me, I tried not to let my eyes bulge. I needed to present myself as mature and confident, but my knees were starting to buckle. I leaned against the door jamb for support.

"Okay, but just for a few minutes." My croaking voice betrayed the terror I felt. "I need to feed my brothers and help them with their homework." As I stalled for time, I was doing a checklist in my mind: beds made? Check; dishes put away? Check; bathroom tidy? Check. Reluctantly, I opened the door and ushered the women into our tiny, tired room.

Pete and Joey had dropped their outerwear on the floor and were sitting on their bed, watching TV. I scooped up their coats, hats and gloves, quickly shoving them into the over-stuffed closet. "Sorry, there's only one chair. Um. We mostly sit on the beds." I felt compelled to apologize for everything. Out of the corner of my eye, I caught the boys glancing sideways from the TV sizing up the strangers. I worked hard to keep my back straight and my voice steady, so they wouldn't sense my fear.

"That's fine. We'll stand. We understand you've been taking care of your brothers lately." From her huge satchel, she pulled a clipboard and a pen.

"Our mother's in the hospital."

"I know. I'm sorry. How is she doing?"

"She's in a coma, but when she comes home, she'll take care of us again."

"How long have you been living here...at this motel?"

"A few months. What's this about, anyway?" She was taking notes and I wondered what she was writing.

"What if your mother doesn't come home for a while? How will you go to school and care for your brothers? What about money? How are you supporting yourselves?"

"Mom has money in the bank."

"And a job? Is there a steady income?"

"She works at Kmart," I lied.

"Do you have any relatives living nearby?"

"No, ma'am. Our grandmother lives in California and we have an uncle in France."

Now she looked up from her clipboard. "Abigail, as a seventeen-year-old, you are not eligible to serve as legal guardian for your brothers, or yourself, for that matter."

I turned my back to my brothers and spoke quietly but firmly through gritted teeth, hoping the boys wouldn't hear. "But I'm almost eighteen. I'm a senior and I'm doing just fine. As you can see, we have a place to live." I gestured about the room. "My brothers are clean and fed, and they go to school every day. Pete has even been seeing a counselor."

"And what about you?" Her blue eyes which matched the blue of her scarf, were her only attractive feature but did nothing to ease my fear. Maybe it was the authoritative manner with which she spoke or that official-looking clipboard she carried. "And what about you? Are you attending school regularly?"

"Well, I missed today, but..." She didn't let me finish.

"Listen, Abigail. I'm sure you're doing a fine job in your mother's absence, but you have no way of knowing how long she'll be incapacitated. Your responsibility is to finish high school."

"I make good grades and I plan to graduate in June." I heard myself sounding surly, but I couldn't seem to control my tone. Something about these women put me on the defensive.

"As social workers for the Commonwealth of Virginia, we are obligated to investigate your situation, especially since there has been alcohol abuse in the home. We need to take you and your brothers into protective custody until..."

"What?" I interrupted, speaking in a forceful whisper. "No. Are you serious?" My eyes glanced toward the boys, checking to see if they had heard.

"... until you turn eighteen or your mother is able to resume care for you and your brothers."

"I'm taking care of us. We're a family. Who called you, anyway? Was it Reuben? Mrs. Gladstone? They should mind their own business." I knew my nasty attitude wouldn't endear me to them or help my case, but I couldn't control it. I remembered my promise to keep our family together. I couldn't allow these strangers to separate us.

Now, the shorter, younger-looking woman brushed past me and started snooping like she was investigating a murder scene. She still hadn't spoken. My eyes followed her as she opened the closet and peered into the bathroom. When she approached the kitchen, Joey slid across the bed and came to stand at my side. He put his hand in mine and looked up at me with big, fear-filled eyes. I squeezed his hand, trying to reassure him. Pete sat like a statue pretending to watch TV. His head remained still, but his eyes followed Miss Nosey Rosey as she opened first the refrigerator, then the cupboards, one by one. I was glad I had just stocked up on groceries.

"I'd like to speak with your brothers, too."

"No," I said too forcefully, then quickly lowered my voice. "Um, they've had a hard day and they're tired and hungry."

"Abigail, we're only concerned with their welfare." She tried to touch my arm, but I withdrew it.

"I'm almost eighteen. I'm an adult and I can take care of my brothers and myself." I released Joey's hand, pushing him behind me as if the barricade of my body could keep him safe. I took off my coat and hat and threw them on the bed, instantly regretting the intensity of my action.

"I'm sure you can, but because you're underage, we need to..."

"What? Take us away? Absolutely not!" As my voice escalated again, I checked to see if Pete had heard me. I could read fear in his eyes that remained glued to the television. Joey was still hiding behind me, now holding the hem of my sweater.

"Abigail, please calm down and listen," said the tall one in a voice that sounded too sweet. "It's likely the foster homes will be a temporary arrangement."

"Homes? Plural? Like separate homes? No!" I yelled, feeling

helpless and frightened. "What's happening?" Pete asked, moving to stand next to me.

"It's nothing, Pete. Everything's fine."

Turning back to the woman with the clipboard, I said, "Please leave now. You're scaring my brothers."

I stepped to the door, pulling Joey with me, and opened it. The icy wind blew my homework papers from the desk onto the floor. I lowered my voice and tried once more to sound calm. "You can't do this," I pleaded. "My brothers have been through so much. They need me. I'm all they've got. Please."

"I'm afraid you have no choice, Abigail. It's the law. Your foster homes will be arranged by tomorrow. We'll come back in the morning. Pack your clothes and be ready by nine o'clock."

I was too stunned to respond. How could this be happening? No, it wouldn't happen! I couldn't stand by and let them place us with foster parents, total strangers. The boys would be devastated. I would be devastated. Sure, they were a pain, but as fed-up as I was with being the responsible adult, I couldn't bear the thought of losing my brothers.

Leaving the boys inside, I closed the door and stood there on the balcony in shock.

When the tall woman reached the staircase, she turned around and said, "Don't force us to involve the police, Abigail. Make sure you're ready to leave in the morning."

I watched the two uninvited strangers descend the stairs and walk to their car like they didn't care that their actions would completely disrupt the lives of my innocent brothers and me...again.

My legs gave out. I slid down the wall to the cold surface of the balcony floor with its layers of chipped paint. A powerful wave of hopelessness consumed me. Pulling my knees to my chin, I sobbed into my jeans. Pete opened the door and peeked through the crack. He rushed to me and wrapped his arms around my neck.

"What's wrong, sissy? Why are you crying?" Joey joined him.

"Sissy, who were those ladies?" he asked. "Is Mommy okay?"

I couldn't speak.

"Abby, it's cold out here," said Pete, shaking me. "Come inside." Finally, wiping my tears and dripping nose on my scratchy sweater sleeve, I stood on wobbly legs.

"You're right, Pete," I said. "It is cold and we're letting all the heat out, aren't we?" I placed my hands on my brothers' shoulders, and guided them inside, aware that I was deeply chilled.

"We'd better have some supper," I said as I stepped over the papers that littered the floor. Moving decisively toward the kitchen sink, I washed my hands too vigorously. I scrubbed and scrubbed, trying to cleanse away the disgust that remained from that frightening encounter.

"Abby, who were those mean ladies and why were you crying?" Pete asked.

"Let's fill up those empty stomachs first. Then I'll explain." I needed time to think.

"Yeah. I'm starved!" said Joey.

"You're always starved," said Pete.

"So are you. Right, sissy?"

"Right. You're both bottomless pits." I tried to laugh, hoping it would calm the boys. "How about grilled cheese and applesauce?"

"Yeah! Grilled cheese."

"Pete, switch off the TV and start your homework."

"Okay," said Pete. "But just tell me, did Mommy die?" Now, Joey climbed under the covers with his favorite stuffed rabbit and lay there, sucking his thumb.

"No, Pete. It wasn't about Mommy. I promise I'll tell you everything after dinner."

As I pulled a frying pan from the cupboard and began preparing the sandwiches, I resolved that no one would separate us. When those women showed up the next morning, the Jordan kids would be gone.

Chapter 21

After supper, I sat with my brothers on their bed. "I need to talk to you guys," I said.

"Is it about the two ladies?" asked Pete.

"Yes."

"Who were they?"

"Yeah, who were they?" asked Joey.

Wedging between them, I enfolded them in my arms. I had made an important decision, and there was no time to waste in implementing my plan. First, I had to prepare my brothers and enlist their cooperation. "Here's the deal," I started cautiously. "Those women were from Child Protective Services. They said it's against the law for me to take care of you."

"That's crazy," said Pete.

"Yeah, crazy," said Joey.

"Are we supposed to take care of ourselves? We're just little kids."

"Yeah. We can't even drive."

"Just listen, okay? They said we have to live with foster parents until..."

Pete interrupted, "What? What do you mean?" He sat up, visibly agitated, his eyes darting. I squeezed his arm and inhaled deeply.

"They're planning to come back tomorrow morning. Because I'm not eighteen yet and because Mom is an alcoholic, they might separate us and put us in foster homes. That's why I was crying."

"Take us away? No! I won't go!"

"Me neither!" shouted Joey. "They can't take us. I'll punch 'em and kick 'em!"

"Don't worry. I'm not going to let that happen. But it means we'll to have to move... tonight."

"Like run away?"

"Exactly."

"Where'll we go? Can we go home? I wanna to go home," said Joey, starting to cry.

"We can't go home. Another family lives in our house now. I don't know where we'll go, but when those women come in the morning, we can't be here. Do you understand? I won't let them separate us." I hugged them tightly.

"What about our stuff?" Pete asked.

"We'll take whatever we can fit into the car... just the important stuff, though. We may have to live in our car for a while."

"I'm scared, Abby. What if they find us?"

"They won't find us."

"But what if they do? Will they put us in jail?"

"Let's not worry about that right now. We need to leave while it's still dark outside. So, we'd better get busy. I want you to take showers... with soap. Wash your hair and brush your teeth. Put on some warm clothes. Then we'll start packing." They jumped up and complied without a fuss.

"Are we gonna sleep in our clothes?" Pete asked as he headed for the bathroom.

"Yes. We'll pack the car tonight. Then we'll sleep for a few hours. I'll wake you up early, and we'll leave while it's still dark outside."

"What about school?"

"Well, tomorrow's Saturday. So, I have a couple days to figure that out. Right now, we just need to leave so those women can't take us." While the boys were showering, I pulled our suitcases from under the beds. Once again, we wouldn't be able to take everything. I had to decide what was truly important and what we could leave behind.

In my suitcase, I packed our basic toiletries like shower gel, shampoo, toothpaste, and toilet paper, also mom's makeup. I added my warmest clothes, then folded three blankets and stuffed them into a large garbage bag. I needed to take at least some of the groceries I had just bought. That's where Mom's suitcase came in handy. In it, I packed the canned foods and dry goods. I admit to stealing a can opener and some flatware from the kitchen.

While the boys showered, I cooked most of the raw food I had just bought. With the eggs hard-boiled, I placed them in zipper bags and returned them to the refrigerator. I cut up the raw vegetables, storing them in plastic bags. Finally, I popped the remaining popcorn.

As soon as Pete and Joey completed their packing, we carried our suitcases to the car stealthily. Then, we climbed into bed, fully dressed. I set my alarm for five a.m. thinking it would give us plenty of time to make our get-away before dawn.

For a few minutes, our darkened room fell silent, but soon the sounds of restlessness—twisting, turning and sighing—began.

"Abby," said Pete. "I can't sleep."

"Me neither," said Joey.

"I know. Try taking some deep breaths. Like this. Inhale-exhale, inhale-exhale," I coached them. "Now, think about a beautiful, peaceful place."

"Like our tree house?"

"Yes, or like the beach. Remember our summer vacations at the Outer Banks? Imagine the warm sun on your skin and the waves flowing in and out, in and out." I was using my best sing-song tone, trying to lull them (and me) into a state of relaxation. Once again, the room grew quiet. But the silence didn't last.

"Sissy, can I sleep with you?"

"Me, too?"

"Come on, you two." They climbed into my bed, one on each side of me.

"Sissy, I'm scared. What if those mean ladies find us?"

"Don't worry, Joe-Joe. Those women were just doing their jobs, but I'm not going to let anybody separate us. I'll always be here for you and Pete." I remembered a prayer that Mom had taught me when I was about Joey's age. It had made me feel protected.

"Now I lay me down to sleep," I began. "I pray the Lord my soul to keep. If I should die before I wake, I pray the Lord my soul to take."

As I recited the familiar words, I realized they weren't as comforting as I had remembered. It must have been Mom's voice that made me feel secure. I tried to remember the sound of her voice—before she started drinking, that is. I couldn't hear it. No matter how hard I tried, I couldn't hear my own mother's voice. I thought of her lying there, unconscious, in the hospital bed. I wondered if I'd ever hear her voice again.

Finally, the boys drifted off to sleep. That's when I seemed to hear a different voice. The words weren't audible, but they were clear, spoken inside my head... "Be not afraid. I am with you always, even unto the ends of the earth." Both the voice and the message were soothing. The words were from a scripture I had learned in Sunday school many years before. All at once, I realized I wasn't alone. I felt a presence surrounding me, not a scary specter, like a ghost, but a warm, loving presence infusing me with peace and calming my anxious mind. Carefully, I released my sleeping brothers, got up, and crawled into their bed, where I fell into a deep sleep.

As scheduled, my phone alarm sounded at five a.m. I roused the boys. Through our sleepy haze, we emptied the contents of the refrigerator and packed them into Mom's suitcase. Then, each of us used the bathroom and put on our warmest outerwear. After a final look about the room, we made our exit quietly before sunrise. The moon hid behind a heavy cloud cover, making the parking lot black and eerie as we headed for our car.

The next part of my plan was to go to the train station and hang out in the parking lot until daylight. I knew that commuters frequently parked there overnight and hoped our car wouldn't be noticed, especially since the police station was within sight. Surely, by the time the CPS women reported us missing, the cops would assume we were long gone, not hiding under their noses. At eight o'clock we would be at the hospital to check on Mom.

I pulled the car into one of several employee parking lots that served the office buildings near the train station, choosing a space adjacent to a wooded area. Once I shut off the engine, the car's inside temperature plummeted quickly. Pulling the blankets out of the trash bag, I wrapped each of the boys in one and encouraged them to go back to sleep. Joey sprawled on the back seat and Pete reclined the front passenger seat, dozing off almost immediately. I wrapped the third blanket around me, grateful for the extra warmth, but I didn't try to sleep. I needed to plan our next move.

It was only a matter of time before the social workers would report us missing. I wasn't sure if they could trace our car right away, but the police could eventually. Maybe we should board a train or bus and travel to Richmond or even Washington, DC. In DC, I reasoned, there would be a good public transportation option, which we'd need without a car. It was likely we could find homeless shelters there, too.

As soon as I thought Mindy might be awake, I called her. I needed to tell somebody what had happened, and I needed her to keep tabs on Mom. I wouldn't mention our whereabouts. That way, if Mindy were questioned, she could say honestly that she didn't know where we had gone.

"You what?" Mindy said, disbelieving. "Abby are you crazy?"

"You would have done the same thing in my situation, and you know it."

"You're probably right, but what about school? What about your mom?"

"That's where you come in, Mindy. I need you to report on Mom's condition for me. I'll call you every few days to check in, okay?"

"What am I going to tell my mom and dad? Where will you go, anyway? You can't just live in your car. Come here. You can live with us."

"No. Your parents have done us a huge favor by taking Bella. I couldn't ask them to house and feed three extra people. Besides, your parents would be obligated to report us to CPS. If they got caught harboring us, they could get in trouble with the law." It was growing light outside, and Pete began to stir. "Don't say anything to your parents," I whispered. "I need time to decide where to go. I'll call you tomorrow."

"Who're you talking to?" Pete asked, rubbing his eyes.

"Mindy."

"What time is it?"

"Seven-fifteen. Are you hungry?"

"Yeah."

"Me, too," came a drowsy voice from the back seat.

"Let's see what we can fix. I boiled all the eggs last night. We can slice some and make egg sandwiches. There's a little orange juice left, too."

"But I want scrambled..." Joey started to say, then added, "Oh, yeah. We can't cook."

"It sure is cold in here," said Pete, shivering. "Can't you turn on the heat?"

"If I start the car, someone might notice us. Wrap up in your blanket. You'll be fine."

"I'm scared. I want Mommy," Joey said.

"We'll leave for the hospital right after breakfast." I got out and retrieved some of the food bags from the trunk, noticing it had served well as a refrigerator. We worked together to make egg sandwiches and took turns drinking from the last carton of orange juice. I couldn't help but worry what would happen when we ran out of food... and money.

We arrived at Riverside shortly after eight a.m. and went straight to the ICU, greeting familiar nurses along the way. I hoped no one knew about the CPS visit or suspected we had run away.

Mom was still comatose, but we talked to her and told her not to worry about us. I wasn't sure I could leave her behind, but I told her that Mindy and Diana would be checking on her. Pete asked her to wake up and get better. Joey did, too. We kissed her good-bye. Then, after a quick restroom stop, we were on our way... or so I thought.

As we passed the nurses' station, I heard someone say, "There they are." My instinct was to run, but caution stopped me. I knew we wouldn't get far. I had to keep my cool. I grasped my brother's shoulders and pushed them forward slowly, pretending not to have heard.

"Abigail?" I froze for a moment trying to form a plan. If it were one of the CPS women from the motel, we were screwed. I turned and, with a casual smile, greeted the speaker.

"Yes, I'm Abigail."

"Hello, Abigail," she said, looking friendly and not at all threatening. "My name is Marsha and I'm a social worker here at the hospital." She held out her hand. Before I reached for it, I squeezed my brothers' shoulders.

"Hi, Marsha." I shook her hand.

"... and you must be Peter and Joseph." The plain-looking woman with short, graying hair presented her hand to each of them, and they looked at me before shaking it. I smiled and nodded my approval. She wore a crisp, white shirt tucked into her khaki slacks. Her belt held a cell-phone holster, and she carried a Manila folder.

In a stroke of genius borne of fear, I said, "It's nice to meet you, but we already have a social worker. Maybe you know him. His name is Reuben Gray."

"Reuben Gray? No, I don't think..."

I tried to keep myself from talking too fast, but the words spilled out quicker than I could control them. "He's been our social worker since our father died last year, and he's been very helpful to our family. In fact, we're on our way to meet him right now."

"Oh. I see. I didn't notice anyone listed in your mother's file, so I thought..."

"Yeah... well... Reuben started working with our family in Richmond when our dad was at MCV. He's stayed with our case since. He found us a place to live and everything."

"Good. Yes, that's good. I'll get in touch with MCV and make sure your mother's file is updated. I'll need to have a chat with Mr. Gray." Relief flooded my racing mind when it seemed clear she hadn't been in contact with the women from CPS.

"Thanks for checking on us. We'll be back to see our mother tomorrow. We need to get going to our appointment... you know... with Reuben."

"Of course, dear. It was nice to meet all of you. I'll check on you tomorrow, and if you need anything in the meantime, here's my card."

"Okay. Thank you." I stuffed her card into my coat pocket and turned toward the elevator. Pete looked up at me with questioning eyes, but I just kept walking and propelling my brothers forward.

"Are we going to see Mister Reuben?" Pete asked when the elevator door closed.

"No. We're going to the bank."

"She seemed like a nice lady. Why did you lie to her?"

"Because she will eventually connect with the women from CPS and they'll try to separate us."

The boys sat in silence as I drove to the bank. Once more, I posed as Elizabeth Jordan at the drive-thru window and forged her signature. This time, I withdrew four hundred dollars without a problem.

Desperate for caffeine, I stopped by a convenience store. Leaving the boys with strict instructions to stay fastened in their seatbelts, I quickly purchased a cup of coffee, pocketed some extra creamers, and returned to the car.

"Can we get a snack?" asked Joey.

"No."

"Why not? We have lots of money now."

"Besides the fact that you just ate breakfast, this money has to last a long time. We can't waste it. That means no treats."

"But you got coffee," argued Pete.

"Coffee is not a treat. It's a necessity."

"Aw," said Pete, disbelieving.

"Without my morning coffee, I become very, very grouchy," I said, gradually raising my voice for effect, "and I devour annoying little boys!"

"But we're big boys," Joey said from the back seat, giggling at my Oscar-the-Grouch impersonation.

"Big boys get tortured," I growled, lunging back and tickling him. Pete reached over and pulled off my hat. When he started laughing and teasing me about how my frizzy hair made me look like a monster, I shook my fuzzy curls at him, tickling his face and snarling. It was the first normal moment we had had in days, and it felt good.

"Now, stop complaining and let's get going on our new adventure.

Here. Knock yourselves out," I said, tossing little packs of Half-and-Half in their laps.

"Where're we going?" asked Pete.

"How would you like to take a train ride?"

"Really?" asked Joey. "I never rode on a train." Glancing in the rearview mirror, I saw him wipe a creamy moustache on his coat sleeve.

"First, I have to see if we can afford it. If not, we'll ride the bus."

"Why can't you just drive us?" Pete asked.

"Once those women discover we're missing, the police will start looking for our car. When they find our car, we can't be in it."

"But where'll we go?" Pete asked. Before I could answer, he added, "Hey, I was supposed to play with Ian today. I didn't even get to say bye."

"I'm sorry, Pete, but we had to leave."

"Well, what if I don't wanna leave? What if I wanna stay?" For once Joey didn't parrot his brother. He just looked at Pete like he had lost his mind.

"Do you want to go to a foster home… with strangers?" I asked.

"Maybe I do! Who made you the boss, anyway? I can take care of myself. Maybe I'll live with Ian or Luke."

"Don't be ridiculous."

"What if Mom wakes up and we're gone? I hate this! I hate you! I hate everybody!"

Now Joey was crying. "Stop fighting! I'm scared! Just stop it!" He was yelling and kicking the back of my seat.

Pete was hysterical, yelling, "Hate, hate, hate" and unbuckling his seatbelt. I began to panic. What if he opened the door and started running? I'd never catch him. He could get hit by a car. Somehow, I had to diffuse the escalating tempers. But how?

I unbuckled my seatbelt, and nearly knocking over my coffee in the cupholder, grabbed Pete and hugged him tightly, pinning his arms against his body. I rocked him back and forth, back and forth, shushing him and crooning into his ear, "I know, Pete. It's scary. But it's going to be okay. Come on. We're going to be okay." At first, he resisted, but finally relaxed into my arms and laid his weary head on my shoulder. Joey unfastened his seatbelt and joined us in the front, squeezing between the seats. The three of us hugged and rocked. We had to stick together.

When I felt like all of us were calmer, I said, "Hey, I have an idea."

"What?" Pete mumbled into my shoulder.

"We'll stay in our car until tomorrow and see how we feel then, okay?" I released Pete and wiped Joey's tears with a napkin. "Maybe Mom will wake up." We weren't ready to leave her, and I needed to buy us some time. We still held out hope that she would regain consiousness and recover.

In the meantime, I'd check to see if we had enough money for the train fare to DC. Running away made perfect sense in my teenage mind. In many ways, I was mature for my age. I felt confident in my ability to "parent" my brothers. I had gained a lot of experience in the past year. I modeled my parenting after my own mother's style... not the alcoholic lunatic who fell apart, overdosed, and left us to fend for ourselves, but the too-perfect Stepford mother she had been while Dad was alive.

In retrospect, I realize how foolish I was to risk my little brothers' safety by going to a strange city without any concrete plans in place. I allowed fear to overshadow reason. All I could think about was how those CPS agents wanted to place us in separate foster homes.

If you've never lived in a car in the middle of winter with two energetic boys and no bathroom, you can't imagine how uncomfortable it is. It's like a cross-country trip with no heat and no motels along the way. We took restroom breaks inside the station, but sometimes I encouraged my brothers to pee in the woods next to the parking lot. I was afraid the station personnel might become suspicious if they saw us coming and going too often.

Finally, by afternoon, we were going stir-crazy. We walked to the library nearby just to stretch our legs and enjoy the indoor warmth for a while. That evening, we took advantage of its roomy restrooms to brush our teeth and refill our water bottles. Then, worried that someone might recognize us and turn us in, we headed back outside. I couldn't recall a time when Williamsburg had been that cold in January. It felt like my toes would freeze off my feet. We took off our shoes and added another layer of socks, but even that didn't help much.

Once darkness fell, we felt safer. I moved the car to another parking lot closer to the tracks, but more isolated. Keeping a close watch on the gas gauge, I ran the engine for a few minutes at a time, so we could get warm and listen to the local news. I wanted to hear if we had been reported as missing.

After a whole day and night, I decided we had pushed our luck far enough. I began to consider our options. Stupidly, I reasoned that DC was easier to navigate than Richmond and farther away from the officials who would eventually be looking for us. But, it was also farther away from Mom and Mindy and everything we knew. Whenever I thought about leaving Mom, I felt too paralyzed to act. I was furious at her, but I thought she needed me. I felt responsible for her alcoholism, for her overdose, and most importantly, for my brothers.

As an adult, I've learned that Mom and I were classic co-dependents. We had switched roles, and although Ellen, my online counselor, had tried to help me see our situation clearly, in my teenage mind, it was up to me, and me alone, to take care of our family. I thought about the series of events that had brought our lives to that point. For some reason, I equated reaching out for help with getting caught. I suppose Mom had conditioned me to be mistrustful of authority, and the visit from CPS seemed to validate her perception.

The next morning, we awoke to an ice-covered car. Ice and snow were rare in Williamsburg, but that storm was a blessing. It camouflaged our car and license plate, buying us some extra time. It seemed like we were hunkered inside an igloo. Surprisingly, the interior temperature felt warmer than it had before the ice storm.

Taking care not to disturb the thick, glassy layer, I used my feet to push open the driver's-side door. We climbed out and trudged to the library for a bathroom break, slipping and sliding along the frozen pavement. The trees sparkled with their icy limbs, making the whole area into a winter wonderland.

Except for a woman at the check-out desk, the building was nearly deserted. I smiled and waved nonchalantly as we passed.

I instructed Pete and Joey to wash up and change their shirts and underwear while I stood guard outside the boys' restroom. Before long, I heard chattering, giggling, and what Mom always referred to as "messing around." Quickly, I glanced right and left. With no one in sight, I cracked open the door. "Hurry up, boys, and be quiet," I ordered in a stage whisper. Finally, they emerged, looking disheveled, but smelling better. They held out their dirty clothes.

"What should we do with these?" Pete asked.

"Give them to me." I stuffed them into my backpack. Next, it was my turn. I sent Pete and Joey to the play area only a few feet away with strict instructions to stay there until I came for them. "... and play quietly," I added. Realizing I had gotten my "monthly," I longed to take a shower. I wished I could wash my hair, too. I took several wet, soapy paper towels into a stall and did the best I could to clean up. Thankfully, my backpack held enough personal-hygiene supplies for one cycle, but I would need a plan for the following month. I remember wondering how women living on the street managed this unavoidable inconvenience.

Just as I was getting started, someone entered the ladies' room and used the adjoining stall. I waited in silence until I heard her flush, wash her hands, and leave. Awkwardly, I manipulated the small space to wash up and change my clothes, hoping my brothers weren't drawing attention to themselves. I washed my face and brushed my teeth at the sink. Then, I pulled my blonde frizz into a ponytail and rejoined the boys.

That morning, I had inquired about the cost of train fare to Union Station in DC and learned the three of us could travel one-way for ninety dollars. I had bought our Amtrak tickets, planning to catch the nine-thirty-seven train the following morning.

We spent the day reading, playing made-up games, and eating most of the remaining food. I made Joey spell words from his spelling book and Pete had to recite his multiplication tables. Whenever they complained, I reminded them of the CPS agents. My blackmail was cruel, but it worked like a charm.

As we were settling in to sleep, I spotted the flashing lights of a police cruiser. It was headed in our direction, and I knew most of the camouflaging ice had melted off our car. I told the boys to be quiet and follow me out the driver's-side door. Quickly, I disabled the map light and we slid out, crouching low to the ground. I grabbed my brothers' hands and pulled them into the dark woods. The air was frigid, and the parking lot's lights cast eerie shadows through the trees. We crept forward until I was sure we were hidden by thick underbrush.

"What's wrong?" Pete asked. "Where're we going?"

"Sh! Be quiet and stay down," I whispered.

"Ow!" Joey exclaimed as he tripped over a tree root and landed on one knee.

Immediately, I covered his mouth with my hand and whispered, "Hush. Just keep moving." When we reached a small clearing, I ordered the boys to lie still on the cold, damp ground. "Don't make a sound. I'll be right back."

"I think my knee is bleeding," Joey whispered.

"I'll look at it later." Bending low, I inched back toward the lot through prickly branches until I could see our car. The cruiser was parked in front of the station. Wishing I hadn't left our blankets in the car, I crouched on the ground and wrapped my arms around myself. When I looked up again, the patrol car was nowhere in sight. Either the cops had turned onto Lafayette Street or they were waiting in the dark parking lot for us to return. I didn't dare go back until I was sure it would be safe.

As I lay there trembling from cold and fear, I thought about Alek, the policeman who had driven us to the hospital the night of Mom's overdose. For a moment, I considered contacting him like he suggested. Would he help us, or would he turn us over to CPS? Foolishly, I decided I couldn't take the chance that he might betray us to the authorities.

I rejoined my frightened brothers and found them shaking and sniffling into each other's coats. As the three of us clung together on the frozen ground, I tried to reassure them and keep them warm. We remained in our huddled, shivering mass for several minutes to be sure the coast was clear.

No one slept that night. After our close call, I knew it was time to make our next move, and now my brothers trusted my decision.

Chapter 22

The boys were relieved to ditch our car and excited to board the train, but I was nervous about going to a new city, one I had visited only once on a field trip. I had no idea where we'd live after we arrived in our nation's capital. Each of us took one suitcase and a backpack. We left our school books behind in favor of carrying what little food remained, and I insisted we make space for those blankets that had become indispensable when we stayed in our car. If we had to live on the street until I could locate a shelter, the blankets would be essential to our survival.

Climbing aboard, we stowed our bulging suitcases. The coach car was already packed with passengers who had boarded in Newport News. Some were sleeping; some were reading; others were using laptops or tablets. No one looked up as we entered. We were fortunate to find three seats together, two on one side and one across the aisle. Glancing around, I wondered if we were the only family relocating to a new city without a clue where we would live when we got there.

The toasty, warm railway car surrounded us with comfort. For the first time in two days, we could shed our coats, hats and gloves, and allow our fingers and toes to thaw. As we settled into our seats, Pete yawned and stretched. I showed him how to recline his window seat and close the curtain. As soon as the train was underway, he fell fast asleep. I thought Joey might be too excited by his new travel experience to sleep, but soon he, too, curled up and succumbed to fatigue.

I kept checking to make sure he wasn't leaning against the young woman in the adjoining seat. With her earbuds plugged into her laptop, she was watching a movie, oblivious to the little homeless boy sleeping soundly beside her. She appeared to be about my age, maybe a couple years older, and I found myself wondering if she appreciated her good fortune.

I began to fantasize about her persona. For no reason other than my own envious projection, I decided she was a college student who had been home for semester break. She might be returning to Richmond University or Virginia Commonwealth, maybe even GWU in DC. My imaginary scenario gave her two parents who adored her and were proud of her excellent grades. Her expensive-looking leather jacket and stylish boots were Christmas presents and her state-of-the-art laptop... Suddenly, I caught myself. Stop it, Abby. Just stop your ridiculous fantasizing and get to work. You have two little brothers who need a place to sleep tonight.

I noticed how long the boys' hair had grown and wondered how I'd manage to get haircuts for them. They were beginning to look like street urchins. I contemplated whether that was what they would become. As fear and uncertainty consumed me, I realized it was too late to change my mind and go back.

The train's rocking motion, combined with heaven-sent warmth, made me drowsy. I remember fighting against the urge to escape into sleep, but I couldn't allow myself the luxury of a nap. Determined to stay awake, I blinked and rubbed my eyes. Pulling my phone from my backpack, I set it on the seat-tray in front of me, wishing I hadn't sold my Ipad. While the boys dozed, I used Amtrak's free Wi-Fi to do some research. My goal was to find a safe place for us to live.

Logging onto Google Maps, I was heartened briefly to find numerous shelters within walking distance of Union Station. But as

I began to explore the shelters' websites, I discovered that most of the places served only indigent men. The few apartments for homeless families required a referral from a family shelter, but the family shelters were reserved for DC residents in crisis. Discovering that the process was an unending cycle, I began to have serious doubts. What have I done? I chided myself. I've uprooted my brothers and pulled them away from everything and everyone they know. They trusted me to take care of them. It occurred to me that maybe I was looking in the wrong places. Surely there were emergency shelters in a city the size of Washington.

We had boarded the train at nine thirty-seven a.m. and were due to arrive at Union Station a little after one. If I didn't find a shelter for us within the next three hours, we'd be sleeping in a cold alley that night.

Pete was first to open his eyes. "What're you doing?" he asked as he stretched and, with an unexpected jolt, returned his seat to its upright position.

"Trying to find us a place to live."

"Can't we live in a motel?"

"One or two nights in a motel would take all our money. We need to find a shelter, one that serves meals."

"Can we eat now?"

"Let's wait for Joey to wake up. It's only a little past eleven anyway."

Since moving into the motel, Mom had tried to break us of snacking. "We can't afford to eat between meals," she would say. There was always enough money to pay for her booze, though. She managed to support that habit. I felt anger rising in my throat, the same anger I had felt in Mom's hospital room when I was telling her (and convincing myself) that I loved her. Even as the words left my mouth, all I could feel was intense rage. How could I love someone who had caused our lives to be trashed? She was my mother. I was supposed to love her and respect her, but I couldn't stop hating her. What if I never saw her again?

"Where are we?" Pete asked, raising the window shade to look outside. The train lumbered slowly through a wooded area. Like the bare trees reaching for sunshine through a gray cloud cover, my mind reached in vain for clarity and calm.

"I'm not sure. Maybe Fredericksburg. Plug me in, will you? My phone's almost dead," I said, pointing to the power strip along the side of the car. Not knowing when I'd be able to recharge again, I decided to leave it plugged in for the remainder of the trip. I was thankful to still have a phone, thinking that Mom made at least one good financial decision when she set up direct-deposit payments from her checking account to Verizon. How long it would last was anyone's guess. I didn't even know how much it cost.

When Joey awoke, we opened the last of our food supply: a can of Spam and half a pack of saltine crackers. The boys wanted to buy food from the café car, but I knew it would be too expensive on our tight budget. We needed to stretch our legs. Struggling to stay upright as the train swayed and lurched, we tottered back to the food car where I told them they could split a carton of milk.

Navigating a long waiting line at the counter, I bought the milk and a bottle of water. Maybe it was my imagination, but I thought the attendant eyed us curiously. I wondered if we looked so bedraggled that she thought we were stowaways. Despite my quasi-bath at the library, I felt dirty and alien, as if my brothers and I were inferior to the other travelers.

We settled in our seats, this time with Joey at the window and Pete across the aisle. "We need to talk about something," I said, waving Pete closer.

"Uh-oh." said Pete as we huddled together. "This sounds omnibus... omnivorous... omnipo... what the heck is that word?"

"Ominous," I laughed.

"Yeah, that."

"Here's the deal," I said, speaking quietly. "When we get to DC, I think it would be best if we pretend I'm your mother."

"What? You don't look old enough to be our mother."

"I can make myself look older. Do you think you could get used to calling me mom?"

"Why?"

"Since I'm not eighteen, I can't be your legal guardian. If Social Services finds out or suspects we're runaways, they'll separate us just like those women tried to do."

"You won't let 'em take us away, right?" Joey asked.

"I wouldn't be able to stop it, Joe-Joe. We can't get into any of the shelters unless one of us is an adult. I have Mom's driver's license and Social Security card, and if you guys call me mom, I think we'll stand a better chance of finding a place to stay."

"Isn't that lying?" asked Joey.

"Let's think of it more like a game, like make-believe."

"Do me and Joey need to change our names, Ab... I mean Mom?"

"No, I think you can keep your real names."

"When can we go home, sissy?" Joey asked.

"When can we go home... who?" I asked, waiting for him to correct himself.

"Oh, yeah. When can we go home, Mommy?"

"Good job, Joey." I said patting his thigh. "You'll get used to it with a little practice. Hopefully, those women will stop looking for us once they realize we skipped town. After I turn eighteen in April, we should be able to go back to Williamsburg."

"April! That's like... three months!" Pete said, counting on his fingers.

"Sh. Keep your voice down."

He lowered his voice. "What about school? What about Mom... our real mom, I mean? What happens when she wakes up and we aren't there? Are you sure this is a good idea?"

"I'm afraid I don't have any answers. Right now, all we can do is take one day at a time. I have to find us somewhere to sleep tonight." I could tell my brothers were frightened, but I remember thinking they couldn't possibly be as scared as I was. I had no choice but to hold myself together. Two little boys depended on me, and I was determined not to let them down. I needed more time on the internet.

I convinced Joey to switch seats with me, so the boys could play some games while I searched on my phone. I pulled a spiral notebook from my backpack and taught them how to play Hangman, a game I couldn't believe they had never played. They also completed several rounds of Tic-Tac-Toe, Dots and Boxes, and a couple of made-up games. I was impressed with their resourcefulness. More impressive was the fact that they cooperated with each other rather than bickering... most of the time.

CRBO

While our destination drew closer, I wasn't any closer to finding us a place to stay. When the conductor announced, "Next stop, Alexandria!" my worry turned to unabashed terror. What do homeless families do? How do they survive, especially in the winter? Where will we go? I was beginning to wish we had stayed in our car. It was cold and cramped, but at least we were sheltered from the elements, and in Williamsburg, we knew our way around the town.

"Look, Joey! It's snowing," Pete said excitedly. As we pulled into the Alexandria station, we saw that big, fluffy flakes covered the platform. Usually, we eastern Virginians loved snow. It was a rare treat that almost always resulted in a day off school. A typical snow day in Williamsburg meant rushing outside to build a snowman and engage in snowball fights until our pants and shoes soaked through. When we were too wet and cold to continue, we would put on our flannel pajamas, warm up with hot chocolate in front of the fireplace and watch our favorite movies all afternoon. Only two days of homelessness had taught me to never again view the white stuff through Norman Rockwell glasses.

At Union Station, we exited the train underground, along with hundreds of other travelers, dragging our suitcases up the escalator to the main level. We followed the crowd to the central lobby which was filled with people rushing in all directions. After sitting for three hours, we needed to stretch our legs, so we maneuvered our rolling suitcases through the crowd until we reached The Great Hall.

For a few moments, the boys were distracted from their fear. Pointing upward at the tall, curved ceiling, Joey exclaimed, "Wow! It's huge! Look at that! It's as high as the sky!"

"What are those octagons all over the ceiling, Abby?" asked Pete.

"You mean Mom, right?" I reminded him.

"Oops. I forgot... Mom."

"To answer your question, I think they're just decorative." We walked around the hall for a while, pulling our suitcases behind us.

As awe-inspiring as the architecture was to the boys, we still needed a place to spend the night.

"Can we go in the stores?" Pete asked, taking in the massive hall with its marble floor and extravagant shops and restaurants.

"Yes. But be careful not to bump anything with your backpack or suitcase." We walked through an upscale jewelry store and a crowded souvenir shop, but it didn't take long for the boys to realize there was very little merchandise of interest, even for window shopping.

"Let's go outside and see the snow," Joey suggested.

"Yeah," said Pete. "It's hot in here."

"Okay. But first, we need to find a ladies' room," I said. "We'll take turns guarding the luggage."

"You mean we have to go in the girls' bathroom with you?" asked Pete.

"I'm afraid so."

"Embarrassing!"

"I can't let you guys out of my sight. We're not in Williamsburg anymore."

"Are there bad people here?" asked Joey.

"It's just best to be careful." After finishing our business in the crowded restroom, we found the front entrance and walked outside. It was still snowing as we passed Columbia Circle and headed north on Massachusetts Avenue. It felt good to cool off and breathe some fresh air, but I knew it wouldn't be wise to let the moisture soak through our jeans and shoes. I was thinking if we had to spend the night outside, it would be impossible to stay warm in wet clothes.

We walked west for about three blocks. The boys had fun catching snowflakes on their tongues. The snow provided another temporary distraction for them. They tried to make snowballs, but the fluffy, dry flakes refused to stick together. I spotted a shelter that I had read about on the internet. Despite a sign above the door that said, "Come unto Me," from my research I had learned that the invitation applied only to homeless men.

"Where're we going?" Pete asked.

"We're just exploring the area and getting some fresh air. See that open space up ahead? You can run and play there for a bit but keep your jeans dry." I hesitated to take them far from the station and risk getting lost, but they desperately needed some exercise.

"I think we should go back to the station," I said at last. "We might have to spend the night there."

"Where're the beds?" asked Joey.

"There aren't any beds. We'll have to sleep in chairs or on the floor." Before he could ask any more questions, I mentioned that I had seen a McDonald's near the gates. "We can have an early supper there if you promise to eat some salad with your burger... and no soda." I was really getting into my "mother" role.

"How about French fries?" Pete asked.

"No French fries."

"Aw!"

We had removed our hats, scarves, and gloves, stuffing them into the outer compartments of our suitcases, but, after waiting in line at McDonald's for twenty minutes or more in our coats, we grew uncomfortably warm again.

I ordered three cheeseburgers and a salad to split. We returned to the main lobby where we tried to find empty seats together. No luck. We improvised by stacking two suitcases to create a makeshift table. Pete and I shared one chair, and we used the third suitcase as a seat for Joey. Finally, we could relax and enjoy a hot meal for the first time in days. The food tasted even better than it smelled. Each of us could have wolfed down a second cheeseburger, but I reminded the boys we needed to conserve our money.

As we ate like wild dogs devouring their "kill," I scoped out areas of the massive lobby that might serve as a shelter for the night. Everywhere, travelers were dozing. I hoped we would blend into the crowd. If anyone questioned us, we could say we had missed our connection and were waiting for the next train.

It bothered me that deceit was becoming a normal way of life. What kind of example was I setting for my brothers? How could I teach them to be honest when they heard me telling lies? As I remembered all those Sunday school lessons from my childhood, I was filled with guilt. But my guilt was fleeting. The will to survive took precedence over any remorse I felt.

While the boys played a game of paper football in the aisle, I spent another hour on the internet with the same discouraging results as before. Then, I called Mindy to see how Mom was doing. "There's still no change. Where are you, anyway?"

"Some place safe," I said. I didn't feel safe at all, and I lacked confidence in my ability to keep my brothers from harm. I wanted to confide in Mindy. I needed a trustworthy ally. But if I withheld our location from her, she couldn't be coaxed into divulging our whereabouts.

Chapter 23

The boys' bedtime passed, compelling me to act. I figured if they were tired enough they would sleep anywhere. It seemed the most promising spot was along the wall beside my end-seat. I placed my coat on the chair to save it, praying no one would steal it. Then, we made our way to the restroom once more.

Returning to the waiting area, I found my coat undisturbed. Earlier, I had noticed that security guards monitored the lobby regularly. Not only would I need to conceal my brothers, but I couldn't risk falling asleep.

I positioned our three suitcases and backpacks to form a barricade, arranging them to look like an ordinary pile of luggage. Leaving space for people to pass between the wall and the rows of seats, I zipped the boys' coats and rolled them into make-shift pillows. I handed them their stuffed animals and instructed them to lie parallel to the wall.

"It's too bright in here. I can't sleep with all these lights on," said Joey.

"And it's too noisy with that guy announcing all the time," said

Pete.

"Well, then, I guess you'll have to stay awake all night."

"Where will you be, Mom?" Pete teased.

"Right there." I pointed to the seat I had staked out less than two feet away. "If you wake up, don't go anywhere without me. Got it?"

"Yes, Mom," they said, giggling. I tousled their hair and tickled them. Then, I had to cover their mouths to hush their laughter. It reminded me of when our dad played "tickle monster" with us at bedtime. Mom would complain that as soon as she got us settled with stories and prayers, he would undo her efforts. But we adored his antics.

"What if I have to pee?" Joey asked.

"Do not leave this spot without me."

"The floor is hard," Pete said. "Can't we use our blankets?"

"No," I whispered. "It would look like we planned to spend the night—like we were homeless tramps."

"We are, aren't we?" His smile had disappeared.

"Yes," I conceded, "but if we pretend to be passengers who missed their connection, maybe no one will bother us." I scanned the area to make sure no security guards were in sight.

A janitor dressed in a navy-blue jumpsuit was busy emptying trash cans and pushing a broom. As he moved closer, I worried he might report us. I decided I couldn't leave our prospects to chance.

"Hi," I said. "How are you this evening?" Not giving him an opening, I continued, "My boys are so tired. We missed our connection. Imagine that." I laughed for effect. "I told them they could nap until the next train comes."

"Um-um," he muttered, not bothering to remove his earbuds.

"I guess the ice and snow slowed us down and made us late."

"Um-um."

"I hope they're not in your way."

"Nope." He swept past them and went about his business.

"How many nights do we have to sleep here?" Pete asked when I breathed a sigh of relief.

"Hopefully, only one. I'm trying to find an emergency shelter. Now go to sleep." I kissed their foreheads, returned to my seat, and pulled out my phone. If necessary, I would search all night until I found a safe, warm place for us to stay.

Now, all these years later, I wonder what I was thinking by taking us to a strange city without a plan in place. All I could think about was getting far away from the CPS workers who had threatened to separate us. I thought I was making mature decisions for my brothers' sakes. I thought I was being responsible.

"Cute boys," someone said. An older woman sitting across from me, smiled. Fuzzy white hair like Grandma Jordan's peeked out from the edges of her pink, knitted hat, and she was wearing a hot-pink jogging suit.

"Thanks," I said, hoping my curt response would end the conversation. I turned back to my phone.

"How old are they?"

"Eight and six."

"I have two grandsons about that age. I'm on my way to visit them in Allentown. You look young to have an eight-year-old."

"I got married when I was eighteen," I lied, covertly switching Mindy's BFF ring to my left hand.

"You remind me of myself when I was younger. I got stuck in a bus station in Philly one night and had to sleep in the ladies' room. I was a freshman in college and hadn't traveled on my own much. I was trying to get home for the Christmas holidays and missed my connection. Didn't even have enough change to call my parents." I shifted in my seat, keeping my eyes glued to my phone. It didn't deter her. "You see in those days, we didn't have mobile phones," she continued, completely ignoring my cues. "We had to use phone booths. Well, I can't imagine how upset my parents must have been when I didn't show up. Except they told me later. I've never been so scared in all my life."

"I don't mean to be rude, but I have to get some work done while they sleep," I added, nodding at my phone.

"Oh, of course. Sorry to bother you."

Ignoring her hurt expression, I went back to searching the internet. I felt her staring at me and considered moving to another seat. A few minutes later, she was standing over me, holding a paper bag. "Here," she said. "I think your boys might enjoy these."

"What's this?"

"Just a little something I made for my grandkids. I'll take them shopping, instead."

"Oh, no, I couldn't ..."

"Take it, dear, and God bless." She placed the bag on my lap.

Gingerly, I unrolled the top and peeked inside. Before I could gather my thoughts enough to thank her, she disappeared into the crowd of travelers boarding the next train. I stood to run after her, but realizing I couldn't leave my brothers, sat again and pulled two beautiful, hand-knitted scarves from the bag, one in shades of blue, the other swirled with beige, brown and cream-colored yarn.

CXEXO

Regardless of their complaints about the lights and the noise, the boys drifted off within minutes. I Googled, "Emergency Shelters, Washington, DC." Scrolling past the ones I had already investigated, I found one called Harmony House, a shelter for single mothers and their children. "You are not alone," the website stated. "We offer emergency and support services."

It sounded perfect. I'd call in the morning. I programmed the phone number into my contact list, pocketed my phone, and tried to keep my eyes open. Fearing robbery, I had divided our money and stashed it in numerous hiding places: inside my shoes and bra and in various pockets. Inspecting the area to make sure no guards lurked near us, I rolled my coat into a ball and leaned back. My eyes grew heavy, but I managed to stay awake for a few hours.

Around two a.m., I awoke abruptly, wondering, for a moment, where I was. My back felt like a knife was stuck in it and my neck was stiff. I stood to stretch and noticed a heavy-set guard heading in our direction. The massive waiting area was nearly as busy as it had been during the day. Grabbing my coat and pretending to put it on, I stretched my arms wide to block the guard's view of my sleeping brothers. "Please, God," I uttered.

Suddenly, attending to his walky-talky, the guard turned and headed in the opposite direction. The boys twisted and shifted but slept on. I paced back and forth, keeping watch until nearly five a.m.

I was exhausted, but thankful, when Joey woke up and announced he needed to use the restroom. I had been "holding it" for at least an hour.

"My back is broken," said Pete as he stood. He bent over and rubbed his joints like a little old man with arthritis.

"I hear you, buddy," I said, still working out the kinks in my own lumbar region. "Hurry and gather your things so we can beat the restroom crowd before breakfast."

"But I gotta go now," said Joey.

We grabbed our stuff and rushed to the ladies' room. Pete, the human camel, guarded our bags as Joey and I hurried into adjoining stalls.

Saving our remaining food supply for an emergency, we stood in line at McDonald's for a hot breakfast of pancakes, eggs and sausage. I added milk for the boys and coffee for me.

"What are we going to do today, Sis... Mom?" Pete asked, syrup dripping down his chin.

"Use your napkin. Well, I think I've found a shelter."

"Hooray!" said Joey. "Does it have beds?"

"Sh. I'm sure it does, but it's too early to call. I'll wait until eight o'clock." We needed to learn our way around the city and figure out the subway system.

While the boys finished eating, I sipped the remainder of my coffee and logged onto Google Maps. It looked like we could walk to the National Mall along Delaware Avenue. I could show the boys the Capitol, the Reflecting Pool, and the presidential monuments surrounding the Mall. There would be plenty of places for them to run and release some of their endless energy. It might distract them from the seriousness of our situation. I hoped it had stopped snowing.

"Can we meet the president?" Joey asked, as we discarded our trash and put on our coats.

"No, stupid," said Pete. I shot him a look of disapproval. He tormented his brother constantly, it seemed, but I was too tired to deal with it.

"I'm not stupid! You're stupid!" Joey shouted and pushed his brother. As tired as we all were, I could envision a knock-down brawl erupting in the middle of Union Station. I inched between my brothers, and pushing them apart, said something useless.

"Hey! Do you want to go outside, or don't you?" Grabbing their arms and pushing them toward our pile of luggage, I tried to distract them with talk of seeing some famous sites.

"Is it still snowing?" Pete asked, giving Joey the stink-eye.

"I don't know, but I'm ready to stretch my legs and find out. Let's go."

Like we had before, we exited the station at Columbus Circle and found Delaware Avenue. The morning was clear and the crisp, cold air felt refreshing. Snow-covered sidewalks resembled fluffy clouds. Immediately, Joey started across the street where a car, horn blaring, came within inches of hitting him. "Joey, stop!" I yelled and grabbed his hood.

"What? You said we were going that way."

"You have to wait for the signal. See?" I explained, as I pointed to the red pedestrian sign. "You can't just walk into the street and expect cars to stop for you."

"Why?" he asked, his eyes welling with tears.

"Because we're not in Williamsburg anymore, pea brain, that's why," Pete said.

"Pete do not call your brother names!" I yelled. Suddenly, I felt rage out of proportion to the offense. "Joey didn't know!"

As I reflect on the incident, I realize I was exhausted and scared. Fatigue and stress contributed to the over-reaction that followed.

"Okay, okay," Pete said, dismissing me, but I decided I wasn't going to let it slide this time. His name-calling had to stop, and Mom had not addressed it for a long time. Furious, I was determined to put an end to it.

I dropped my suitcase in the snow and gripping Joey's hood with one hand, I told him to stay on the curb. With the other hand, I pulled Pete closer. I bent down and grabbed his chin, so I could make eye-contact. No amount of struggling could release my vise-grip. "Listen, Pete. You've made plenty of mistakes, and you need to stop bullying Joey when he messes up. Do you hear me?" My voice escalated with every word. I was no longer play-acting at being a parent. I was the parent. Whether I wanted it or not—I had slipped into this new role, rife with its obligations, worries, and self-inflicted accountability.

Pete rolled his eyes, but I ignored it. With one hand holding his chin firmly and one hand locked onto Joey's hood, I continued my lecture. "That's how we learn—by asking questions and correcting our mistakes. You and I learned that way, and now it's Joey's turn."

He tried to pull away, but I wouldn't let him.

"Ow! You're hurting me!"

"Here's the deal, Pete. If you continue to call your brother insulting names, there will be consequences." I had no idea what consequences I would devise if he challenged me, but I knew if I failed to follow through with my threat, he wouldn't listen to me in the future. His very life could depend on accepting me as the authority figure. I wondered what sort of punishment could reform the behavior of an eight-year-old boy who had already lost everything.

"Apologize to your brother right now."

"No!" I squeezed his chin.

"Sorry," he said. "Can we go now? I'm cold."

"Not until you apologize like you mean it." I remained resolved. I knew it was important. He started to roll his eyes again. I jerked his chin to show him I meant business and turned his face toward Joey.

"Ow! I'm sorry," he said.

"You're sorry for what?" I insisted.

"I'm sorry for calling you names." I inhaled the frigid air.

"He's not going to do it any more, Joey, so you can forgive him."

"I forgive you," Joey said, tears streaming down his cheeks.

"Good. Now hug each other and let's go have a nice day."

"But wait for the signal," Joey announced proudly, sniffing.

"Yes, wait for the signal." I couldn't help but smile as I wiped his tears. The boys hugged, and we crossed the street.

Chapter 24

Ineeded to give my brothers some fun, just one day where they could forget about being homeless and scared. Once we got moving, the sun came out. We enjoyed walking and visiting some of the sites I had seen on my ninth-grade field trip.

By ten o'clock, we had checked out the Jefferson and Lincoln Memorials. Pete surprised me with his interest in Thomas Jefferson. I promised to take him to Monticello one day. While Joey played hide-and-seek with a squirrel, I prompted Pete to read the words from the Declaration of Independence that were etched in the marble wall, and complimented him on a job well-done.

Next, we ascended the steps of the Lincoln Memorial. Both boys were well-informed about Abraham Lincoln and could tell me he was our sixteenth president who served during the War Between the States. With my help, Joey read the quote behind the massive sculpture, and Pete read some of the Gettysburg Address. They wanted to move on to the Washington Memorial, but I convinced them to save it for another day. I hoped we would be settled somewhere when that day came.

I found a bench next to the Reflecting Pool where I sat with our luggage while the boys ran around, enjoying the Mall's open spaces. Only a few patches of snow remained in the shaded areas. Wiping the wet bench, I sat and basked in the sun's warmth to make a couple of phone calls. I called Mindy to let her know we were okay and to see if she had checked on Mom. When she said two women from Child Protective Services had visited and questioned both her and her parents, a twinge of panic ran through me.

"Abby, you were smart not to tell me where you went. Those women were pushy, but I acted surprised about your disappearance. I just kept saying I didn't know anything and that I was worried about you."

"Thanks, Mindy."

"Are you guys okay?"

"Yeah, we're fine." We weren't anything close to fine. "How's Mom?"

Mindy told me Mom still hadn't regained consciousness, but Doctor Santos reported improvement in her respiratory system... enough to remove her breathing tube. "She's breathing on her own, Abby. Isn't that wonderful news?"

"Yeah, wonderful." I tried to sound lighthearted, but Mindy's youthful exuberance nearly made me gag. I could tell she thought I was living some exciting adventure. Within a week's time our emotional ages had grown years apart. It wasn't her fault. She had no idea how dire our situation had become. She knew only what I had told her, which was nothing.

"I miss you, Abby, and everybody at school is asking about you. Yesterday, both Ms. Gladstone and Mr. Gregory called me into their offices and asked me what I knew. I told them about your mom being in the hospital, but I said I didn't know where you were. Then, I mentioned the CPS agents, hoping they might think you guys had been taken into custody. Hey, when are you coming home?" Home. Would the boys and I ever see "home" again? I hadn't been able to think past where we might sleep that night.

"It could be April," I said.

"April! How will you ever get caught up at school?"

"Maybe Mom'll be better by then." I tried to sound confident, but I didn't have the energy to keep up my charade. I told Mindy I needed to make a couple more calls and would text her later.

As I watched Pete and Joey running, playing, and pushing each other like normal little boys, my mind bombarded me with questions that had no answers. What if Mom never regains consciousness? What if she ends up a vegetable? Is it possible for her to wake up from the coma and live a normal life? Was she trying to commit suicide? Would she try again? I could have worked myself into another panic attack. Struggling to keep my cool, I focused my efforts on finding housing.

Sitting up straight, and trying to blink away fear-filled thoughts, I called Harmony House. A woman with a warm, friendly voice answered the phone and described what sounded like the perfect shelter for a family like ours. She seemed genuinely sad to inform me there was a waiting list. "We'll take anything," I pleaded. "We'll sleep on the floor."

"I'm sorry," she explained, "but we must follow regulations, or we could be closed down."

"How many are on the list?" I was biting my lip trying not to cry.

"Three, currently. Each family unit occupies a room, and we have only eight rooms. I can add you to the waiting list. Sometimes folks move out unexpectedly or find other accommodations."

"Yes, please add me and my two br... uh, sons." She took my name, or rather my mother's name, and phone number and promised to call me as soon as a room became available. Before I hung up, she asked if I had tried the Hypothermia Hotline.

"No. What's that?"

"It's a clearing house for emergency shelter during the winter months. They might be able to help you." I took the number and thanked her.

Immediately, I dialed the hotline, only to hear, "This number is no longer in service." Before I had a chance to process anger, disappointment or any other emotion, Joey was running toward me announcing to all the world that he needed to do a "number-two." I had forgotten to scope out restrooms in the area.

"Hurry! I gotta go bad!"

"Okay, okay. Just hold on." Our daily existence had devolved into an endless series of bodily functions.

Searching in all directions, I spotted a row of portable "potties" on the opposite side of the Reflecting Pool. "Oh, great! All the way over there. Come on, Pete!" I yelled. "Grab your stuff and follow us." I picked up Joey's backpack and my own, flinging one over each shoulder, grabbed my suitcase handle, and yelled to Joey to start running.

We sprinted half the length of the Mall, around the end of the Reflecting Pool, and uphill, across an expansive lawn, determined to make it in time. The thought of an accident involving fecal matter and no running water was enough to propel me forward at warp speed. We hit the damp, grassy area, our suitcases flopping this way and that. "Don't look back, Joey. Just keep running," I yelled.

As Pete caught up to me, he wanted to know where we were headed in such a hurry. "Geez, you look like a couple of crazies," he said. I was too winded to speak in complete sentences.

"Joey... bathroom... emergency," I said, gasping for air. With the "potties" only a few yards away, Joey dropped his suitcase and ran ahead.

"Praise the Lord!" he bellowed, waving his arms at the sky and taking off like a wild stallion. The sight was so hilarious that Pete and I stopped in our tracks, bent over, and gave in to hysterics. We dropped to our knees on the damp ground, barely able to breathe, and indulged in a welcome release of tension. Life had become too serious, filled with fear and uncertainty. Unexpected, uncontrollable laughter washed our souls with a cleansing balm.

"What's wrong with you two?" Joey asked when he emerged from the "potty," letting the door slam behind him.

"You should be a comedian, Joe-Joe," I said, trying to catch my breath.

"What do you mean?" he asked, clueless as to how entertaining he had been.

"Nothing. Well, Pete, we might as well go while we're here."

CRO

After our restroom break, we headed for the nearest Metro station. It was time for us to get acquainted with the subway system. Drawing on memories from my field trip, I purchased tickets from the machine and instructed the boys how to use them. "Save your card in your coat pocket," I said. "You'll need it again." Once we reached the platform, I studied the various routes displayed on the map. I had no idea where we were going. I wished we were going home.

"Can we eat when we get on the train?" Joey asked. At the time, I didn't know eating wasn't allowed in the Metro.

"Let me figure out which train to take first." Studying the map, I instructed the boys to stand close to me. If I recalled correctly, admission to the zoo was free. It would be a perfect place to hang out for the afternoon.

The boys and I boarded the orange line, got off at Metro Center and switched to the red line, finally exiting at Woodley Park. During the ride, I checked our food stores and discovered we needed groceries.

When we reached the zoo entrance, Joey spotted the big, concrete letters spelling "ZOO" and wanted to climb on them. I allowed both boys to sit inside one of the Os and took their picture. "Can we see the pandas first?" Joey asked, pointing to the tall, flag-like posters that flapped in the wind, greeting visitors.

"Let's find a picnic table first," I said.

"Finally. I'm starving," said Pete. "What do we have to eat?"

"Well, there's a little peanut butter, some raisins and…"

"Can't we go inside that building? I'm cold," Joey said. He was pointing to the visitor's center.

"Jump up and down," I said. "It'll warm you."

"I can't. I'm too hungry. I smell hotdogs. Can we have hotdogs?"

"Yeah, hotdogs!" said Pete. "I'll bet that smell is coming from over there." He was pointing to the Panda Café.

"Come on, guys. You know we can't eat in restaurants." Those hotdogs did smell heavenly, though. "Sit on that bench over there, and I'll fix you a peanut butter cracker with raisins." They argued with me, trying to get me to give in about the hotdogs. Pete said I was mean. Joey agreed and added that I never let them do anything and they were "the only kids in the whole world who didn't get to eat hotdogs." I stood my ground, threatening to let them starve. By the time they realized I meant business, they were forced to give in to hunger. I thought they would complain about the meager meal, but they gobbled their crackers in two bites, and asked for more. There wasn't enough food for me, so I pretended not to be hungry. I had no idea where our next meal would come from, but for now the boys had full stomachs. They topped off their lunch with generous swigs of water.

After warning the boys to stay in sight, I said, "Come on. Let's check out the animals."

Under normal circumstances, I would have delighted in watching my brothers enjoy the animals and their behaviors, but all I could think about was where we'd spend the night and how I'd keep them fed... possibly until April.

Most of the animals were inside their shelters trying to stay warm. I wondered if I had made a mistake bringing the boys to the zoo... until they spotted the seals and otters. For at least thirty minutes, they were mesmerized by the playful creatures.

As I stood near the seal habitat, guarding our suitcases and worrying, I recalled some familiar words, "Cast all your cares on me." Like my experience during our last night at the motel, I sensed a comforting presence.

"Do not be afraid. Cast all your cares on me." There it was again. I wished I could remember the entire passage.

I closed my eyes and tried to pray, but I wasn't an experienced pray-er. Our family had said grace at most meals, and we participated in the prayers at church, but speaking directly to God was not a habit I had cultivated. I wasn't sure I even believed in God. Thinking I had nothing to lose, I murmured, "Help me."

"Are you okay, Miss?" I opened my eyes to see the concerned face of a middle-aged, round woman. She was bundled in one of those quilted coats that makes even the skinniest person look fat. She wore a purple ski hat, a muli-colored scarf, and boots with fur around the top.

"What?" I said, startled.

"You seem upset. Are you okay?"

"I'm fine. I just need to find a grocery store. My sons and I are new in town, and we don't know our way around yet."

"Well, dearie, you're in luck. I've lived here all my born days. There're two stores thata way on Mt. Pleasant," she said, pointing through the trees. "It's a long walk, but you can catch a bus at the corner. If you're worried about gettin' lost, there's a supermarket on Wisconsin. It's about a mile over there." This time, she pointed in the opposite direction. "Here. Let me jot down the directions for you."

As I thanked her, she reached into her over-sized handbag and pulled out a note-pad and pen. "Andrew don't climb on that fence!" she yelled at a boy who seemed about four years old. "Did you hear me? I said get down! Just 'cause we're at the zoo don't mean you need to act like a monkey."

"Is that your son?" I asked.

"No, thank God. I'm his nanny."

"Oh. Well, boys can be a handful."

"Especially when their parents spoil 'em rotten. I raised three o' my own—by myself—and I was strict. Didn't give 'em every little thing they asked for, neither. They turned out real fine, too. I raised 'em to be genamen."

Pete and Joey came running toward us. By their expressions, I could tell there had been a scuffle.

"Stop right there, you two," I said, holding up my palm. I tried to sound stern, like a bona fide mother. "This nice lady is giving me directions to a grocery store. Now, if you want to eat supper tonight, you'd best sit on that bench and be quiet till she finishes."

"But Pete pushed me and made me..." Joey started to complain, but I wouldn't let him finish. I took hold of their arms firmly and led them to opposite ends of a bench, whispering, "Stop fighting and remember to call me 'Mom'."

"Sorry about that," I said, returning to where the woman was standing.

"Now, there's two boys knowin' who's in charge," she said, adjusting her hat to cover her ears. "And you lookin' so young, too. Here, I drew you a map. This here is the zoo entrance. You turn right at Connecticut and left onto Macomb. You'll cross over thirty-fourth and thirty-sixth. Then, turn right onto Wisconsin. You'll see the market just ahead."

"Thank you," I said, relieved. "You've been very helpful."

"No problem, dearie. Glad ta help. Andrew, what did I say?" She reached in her purse and pulled out a five-dollar bill. "Here," she said pushing it into my hand. "Seems like you could use this."

"Oh, no. I couldn't. I have mon..."

"Jes' take it, dearie. It ain't much. Buy yerself and them boys some treats."

"Come on, boys," I called. When I turned to thank the woman, she and Andrew were nowhere in sight.

"But we didn't see the big cats," Joey said.

"We'll have to come back another day. Come on. Let's go."

Chapter 25

As we walked the mile or so to the store, the boys complained and bickered the whole way. At one point, Pete pushed Joey so hard he fell onto a fire hydrant. Joey called his brother a "stinky turd" and regaining his balance, punched Pete who declared it didn't hurt because Joey was "a weakling." As I pulled them apart, I remember thinking this mom-stuff with its endless series of decisions, lessons, and referreeing was exhausting.

We parked our suitcases just inside the front entrance. Wedging them behind the rows of shopping carts, we hoped no one would find them interesting enough to steal.

After the obligatory restroom-stop, I selected our grocery items carefully, trying to be frugal with what money we had left. The boys squabbled and shoved each other until I considered abandoning them in the bread aisle. I remembered how frustrated Mom would get with their constant skirmishes. Our pre-alcoholic mom would sit them down and patiently moderate their disputes. After addiction seized her and turned her into an unrecognizable version of our mother, all her parenting skills drowned in the booze.

I remembered the five-dollar bill. If ever there was a time for bribing children, that was it. I told Pete and Joey they could each choose a treat if they stopped arguing and helped me finish the shopping. They looked at me like I had sprouted antennae and purple hair, but soon we were headed for the check-out counter.

I recall every item we placed in our shopping cart: three apples, three string cheese, a loaf of bread, a package of breakfast bars, two pints of milk, a container of wet wipes, also some beef jerky and a jar of Nutella. By unanimous vote, we had agreed to take a break from peanut butter. Three candy bars never made it into the cart.

C380

I needed to locate the nearest Metro station. The store clerk had told me to head back toward the zoo and turn left onto Connecticut where we would find the Cleveland Park Metro entrance. At five o'clock, it was already getting dark and the temperature was dropping. I wondered if it were possible to spend the night on the subway.

When we reached Cleveland Park, we were exhausted and ready to sit, but I hadn't anticipated the rush-hour crowds. We squeezed our bodies, backpacks, and suitcases onto the red-line train, only to find all seats taken and many passengers standing in the aisles. I helped Pete and Joey grab a pole, so they wouldn't go flying every time the car jerked.

"Can't we sit down?" Joey whined. "My legs hurt." I estimated we had walked a good eight to ten miles that day, and I didn't doubt his legs hurt. Mine did, too.

We could either get off at the next stop and wait a couple hours for the crowd to disburse or stick it out and hope to find empty seats. After weighing the options, I decided it wouldn't be safe to wander around a strange city after dark.

With my foot, I wedged one suitcase against the metal pole and lifted Joey on top where he could sit while holding onto me. Pete complained, of course, but there was no way I could hold three suitcases and two boys without causing a major Humpty-Dumpty incident.

At the next stop, a seat at the back became available, and I urged Pete to claim it quickly. A few minutes later, another seat opened on the opposite side of the aisle, but it was several rows ahead of Pete's. At that point, I had no idea where we were or where we were going. My only concerns were maintaining my balance and keeping a watchful eye on my brothers. Hungry and ready to collapse, I decided it wouldn't be wise for me to sit, even if I could.

Pete stood and started to approach me. "No, don't get up. You'll lose your spot," I said, with a combination of words and awkward sign language. With an angry scowl on his face, he threw his arms in the air, sat again and pointed to his mouth to mime, "I'm hungry."

I considered motioning to my backpack as if to say, "You have food in your backpack," but I had seen a sign that said food and drink on the subway were prohibited. So, I shrugged my shoulders to indicate there was nothing I could do. If that car didn't clear out soon, I'd have two hungry, grumpy, rebellious little boys on my hands. Thankfully, when I glanced at Joey again, he was leaning against the window, asleep.

It was after seven o'clock before I finally got to sit. My legs and back were stiff, and I had a throbbing headache. I woke Joey and walked him to the rear of the car where, at last, Pete and I had secured three seats together—two on one side and one on the opposite side of the car. Looking around to make sure no guards were in sight, we washed our hands with wet wipes and I asked the boys what they wanted to eat.

"Can I have a Nutella sandwich?" Joey asked sleepily.

"Yeah, me too," said Pete.

Using the knife that I had lifted from our motel room in Williamsburg, I made three sandwiches. That first bite of creamy chocolate goo made my mouth water. The soft, white bread forming gobs of dough on my tongue invoked powerful images from childhood. Occasionally, Mom would buy the unhealthy, white stuff, trim off the crust and let me roll a slice into a ball. I'd dip it in peanut butter and dry, instant cocoa, and enjoy it as an after-school snack.

After we finished our sandwiches, I explained we'd have to sleep on the subway.

"I already did that," said Joey. "I wanna sleep in a bed."

"I'm sorry, guys. I've tried to find a shelter, but they're all full. I did get us on a waiting list, though." Somehow, I had to keep them from losing faith in me and giving up hope.

"We can pull our blankets out to make our seats more comfortable." At the time, I didn't know it was unlawful for homeless people to sleep on the subway. To this day, I wonder what would have happened if we had been caught just then. Would we have been arrested, sent to a shelter, turned over to social services, sent back to Williamsburg?

"Are you sure it's okay?" Pete asked, looking in all directions like he had just robbed a bank.

"Well, we paid to get on, and we don't have to use our tickets again unless we change lines. I don't see why anybody would care." As Joey gulped a huge swig of water, I warned him there wouldn't be any place to go to the bathroom.

"I'm really tired," Pete said. "Can I go to sleep now?"

"It's may I go to sleep," I corrected him. As soon as the words left my mouth, I realized how ridiculous it was to care about proper English at that moment. I let it drop.

Unzipping our suitcases, I pulled out the blankets. Only one passenger remained in our car. Old and bedraggled, with a dirty beard, and tattered, filthy clothes, he seemed harmless, looked homeless, like us, and had already fallen asleep. We made our coats into pillows as we had done at Union Station and settled in for the night.

At midnight, we were awakened brusquely by a man in uniform. "Everybody up!" he shouted, tapping our feet with a stick. "Come on. Time to leave!"

"What? Why?" I asked, trying to wake from my death-like trance.

"End of the line. Service is suspended at midnight for Safe Track Maintenance. Not s'pposed to sleep here anyway."

"But we don't have any place to go," I pleaded.

"Not my problem. Let's move."

"Okay, okay," I said, my anger and frustration swelling toward an explosion. "Just give us a minute to gather our stuff!"

"What's wrong, sissy?" Joey asked, sitting up and rubbing his eyes.

"We have to leave."

"Why?"

"Some rule about stopping service at midnight. Grab your things."

"Where're we going?" Pete asked as we stepped onto the platform, dragging our blankets, coats, and suitcases behind us.

"I don't know. I just don't know." Like the last survivors of an apocalypse, we stood on the platform that stretched before us into black shadows. As the train pulled away, the old man threw his bag over his shoulder, and with weary eyes, glanced back at us before shuffling into the darkness. Without the bustling crowds and moving trains, the partially covered platform was silent and ghostly.

As I let my arms drop, the suitcase, blanket, and backpack slid to the tiled floor and I sank to my knees in the middle of the pile. I lost control and wept... for us, for the old man, for every homeless wanderer.

"Don't cry, sissy, I mean Mommy," Joey said, taking my hand in his.

"I'm sorry I ever brought us here," I sobbed. "I don't know what I was thinking."

"We'll be okay, Abby," Pete said, patting my back. "Cause we're together. We couldn't stay in Williamsburg. Remember? Those ladies were gonna send us away to live with strangers."

"Maybe we'd be better off," I said, wiping my nose on my sleeve. "Maybe we should go back."

"No," they both said, hugging me.

"Don't be sad, sissy," said Joey. "We'll be okay." I released my arms from my backpack strap and wrapped them around my brothers— the little boys who could drive me crazier and make me angrier than any other humans on the planet. As we huddled, I realized I also loved them more than anyone else in the world. I must not let them down. In my heart, I prayed that God—if there was a God—would give me the strength to go on.

Chapter 26

I sat up, inhaled putrid city air, and wiping my tears and my brothers', said, "Come on. Let's find a place to sleep." Now we were above ground, and it seemed like the temperature had dropped. The curved roof of a long, open walkway did nothing to keep us warm. The adjoining ticket booth was dark and deserted.

"How about over there?" Pete sniffed. He was pointing to a concrete bench beside a large column. Surrounded by a plastic shield, like a bus stop, it might be enough to shelter us from the elements.

"It could work." I picked up my stuff, determined to regain control of my frayed emotions. "You two can stretch out there, and I'll sleep on the ground."

We gathered our belongings and approached the bench. Joey looked up at me sheepishly and asked, "Sissy, do they got bathrooms here?"

"Why?" I sighed, knowing why he was asking.

"Cause I hafta pee."

"No. Just no." I threw up my hands, searching the expanse, first one direction, then the other, trying to figure out what to do. "You're going to have to go over there," I said, pointing at the idle, silent tracks.

"Really?"

"Really, but don't get too close." I held the back of his jacket and he leaned forward. "Pete, keep watch to make sure nobody sees your brother um... defiling the tracks." There were no witnesses.

"What's defiling?" Joey asked, unzipping his fly.

"Never mind. Just go. And make it quick."

"Me, too?" asked Pete.

"Why not?" I needed to relieve myself as much as they did, but I knew we couldn't enter the station at that hour. It was probably locked anyway. Without their convenient anatomy, I had no choice but to hold it until morning.

After the boys finished their business, I wrapped them in blankets and settled them, with their coat-pillows, on the hard bench. The seat wasn't long enough to accommodate both of their growing bodies, but they managed to squeeze onto it by overlapping their legs and bending their knees. Wondering who would be first to push the other off, I crawled underneath, lay on the hard, filthy tile, and positioned our suitcases in front of the bench to give the boys a soft landing. I didn't expect to sleep. I was too nervous and scared to relax. Besides, somebody had to guard our stuff. I couldn't risk having our money stolen or losing the food I had just bought. I feared being mugged and robbed, or worse yet, raped.

Never again would I look at a dirty, homeless person with disgust. Now, I understood that homelessness could happen to anyone. I had always thought of people on the street or in shelters as bums or deadbeats. Now I understood they were people like me; humans with unique histories and common emotions. They once had dreams, goals and families. That night I realized the worst part of living on the street was the relentless fear, the overwhelming vulnerability.

In one shoe, I had hidden Mom's driver's license. Divided among the other shoe, my bra and various pockets, I had stowed a couple hundred dollars and Mom's Social Security card. After checking the time, I stuffed my phone and charger in the pockets of my hoodie. If anyone tried to take our valuables, they would surely wake me. As tired as I was, I lay awake for what seemed like hours, staring at the wing-like curve of the roof that did nothing to protect us from the cold.

I must have slept intermittently because I woke at some point needing desperately to use the restroom. As my bladder continued to expand beyond its capacity, I started to panic. Surely there must be restrooms somewhere. I walked along the platform, one direction, then the other, keeping the boys in sight. Nothing! I tried the door to the station. It was locked.

Pete and Joey slept on. Then an idea struck me. I had saved the plastic bags from our groceries and accumulated extra napkins from McDonald's. Careful not to wake the boys, I pulled a grocery bag, napkins, wet wipes and a Tampon from my backpack. Keeping a look-out toward the station, I moved to the track side of the column and awkwardly took care of business. With no trash bin in sight, I tied the bag and left it on the ground next to the column.

If anyone had joined us at that moment, they would have gotten an eyeful, but there was no one. The area remained as deserted and eerie as when we had exited the subway. As the whole city slept, I felt lonely, frightened, and humiliated.

It wasn't until I returned to my makeshift den that I realized one of the backpacks was missing. Apparently, we hadn't been as alone as I thought. Someone had pilfered my backpack. Frantically, I searched the area, trying to remember what was in it. Food. Mostly food, and a map of DC and the boy's old scarves. Had I hidden any money in it? No. I began to search my pockets. Had the robber gotten close enough to pick my pockets while I slept? My phone and charger were where I had put them, and my various hiding places were intact, but my nerves weren't. I was too frightened to sleep. What if he came back? What if he tried to hurt my brothers? From somewhere in the distance, a tom cat's screeching competed with the screams inside my head.

I wasn't sure what time the Metro service would resume but thought it best to be ready when it did. I pulled out my phone to check the time and discovered the phone was dead. I knew it must be past five a.m. because I had checked it at four-thirty and, against my will, had fallen asleep.

A sign on the station wall indicated we had exited the train at

Takoma. Studying the map, I discovered we had ridden the subway almost to Maryland. To get back to the center of town where most of the shelters were located, we'd need to re-board the red line and switch to the orange line at Metro Center. I woke the boys and, determined not to share the night's frightening episode, helped them stuff their blankets into the suitcases. "Where're we going now?" Pete asked.

"I'm not sure, but I think the subway'll be starting up again soon. If you need to pee you'd better do it now. I'll stand watch." No sooner had they zipped their jeans than a light switched on inside the building and people began arriving for their morning commutes. Maybe it was closer to six o'clock.

"Can I have some milk?" asked Joey.

"May I have... oh, forget it," I said. "We can't eat until we leave the Metro. It's not allowed."

"But I'm hungry."

"You'll live." I knew the milk had been stolen, along with my water bottle and some other items.

Other passengers now occupied "our" bench, so we stood on the platform waiting for the train. I asked someone for the time and learned it was six-fifteen. Apparently, I had slept on that hard, filthy floor longer than I thought. "Let's see if we can stuff our coats into our suitcases so we don't have to carry them," I suggested. But we were too late. The floor lights flashed to warn of the approaching train.

"Where's your backpack?" Pete asked.

"I must have left it on the train last night." He had enough to worry about without adding the fear of being mugged or abducted.

Chapter 27

Exiting the Metro at L'Enfant Plaza, it felt like the temperature had plummeted overnight, bringing with it a frigid wind that blasted our faces as we walked along Maryland Avenue.

I was relieved to be back in familiar territory, where I'd stand a better chance of finding my way around the city. The boys would enjoy the American Indian Museum or the Air and Space Museum. More importantly, we'd be sheltered from the cold for a few hours.

From my field trip, I remembered we weren't allowed to take suitcases beyond the museums' checkpoints. When we entered the American Indian Museum, I asked the security guard if there were lockers available. She said "no" and suggested we try the Natural History or American History buildings. "Union Station has storage lockers," she added as we turned to leave.

"It's freezing out here," Pete said. "Can't we go inside?"

I explained that we couldn't take our belongings inside and we couldn't leave them outside. The security guard had given me an idea. We'd return to Union Station, where we could either store our belongings and head back out or spend the day inside. At least we'd stay warm and, most importantly, the station had restrooms.

It seemed I had exhausted every option for long-term shelter. We had been on the run only a few days, but it felt like months had passed since we'd left Williamsburg.

We headed back to the subway and returned to Metro Center where we again entered the city's subterranean world. Though crowded with people, the platform was as lonely as the silent, empty passageway where we had slept the previous night. We switched to the red line and finally got off at Union Station.

"Are we ever gonna find a place to live, Ab... Mom?" Pete asked. "I sure am tired of this."

"Yeah, me too."

"Can we eat at McDonald's again?" Joey asked.

"No. We have to save our money. Let's find out about the lockers."

Dragging our suitcases everywhere wore us down. An employee, who eyed us suspiciously, directed us to Gate A. As we walked away, I thought I could feel her eyes drilling into my back. I didn't turn around, but I remember wondering what she was thinking. Perhaps it was imagination that fed my paranoia. Perhaps I misinterpreted her glare as judgment. Maybe she was simply having a bad day. In my mind, she was disgusted, seeing us as inferior beings.

We followed the signs and found the gate, but it was bustling with travelers about to board a train to Boston. Waiting for the crowd to thin, we stood, eating cereal bars until we could ask the ticket agent about renting a locker. He said the locker service was operated by an independent company and sent us to another window. In the end, I decided it would take too much of our dwindling cash to rent three lockers. I opted for one space where we could at least store our outerwear for the day. It felt liberating to shed our coats, hats, gloves, and scarves.

As soon as Gate A emptied of its waiting passengers, I found an electrical outlet and plugged in my phone. "Let's sit here for a while," I suggested.

"What are we gonna do today?" asked Joey.

"It's so cold outside. I think we should stay here."

"But what are we gonna do?"

"You two need to do some schoolwork," I said. "If we wait any longer, you'll forget everything you've learned so far."

"You had to ask, didn't you, Joey?" said Pete.

"You don't want to repeat second grade, do you?" I asked.

Not waiting for an answer, I pulled a notebook and mechanical pencil out of Pete's backpack and started creating assignments for my brothers. I made a page of addition and subtraction problems for Joey, and a page of multiplication and division problems for Pete. I located only one pencil, but I scrounged around in Joey's backpack until I found a pen. I teased Pete that his first answers would have to be correct because he couldn't erase them. He wasn't amused.

While the boys sprawled on the floor with their arithmetic assignments, I went online and continued my search for a shelter. Checking the internet once more, desperation consumed me. First one webpage, then another produced the same, disappointing results.

"Can I have a snack?" Joey asked after a while. "I'm still hungry." He had consumed two cereal bars and an apple only an hour earlier.

"May I have a snack," I said, wondering if he would ever catch on to the correct usage of those two words.

"Me, too?" asked Pete.

"We have string cheese or beef jerky." I realized I was breaking the no-snack rule, but who was there to stop me?

"Cheese!" they called out in unison. I dug in Pete's backpack for the string cheese and helped Joey open the pesky wrapper. As I peeled back the plastic, it occurred to me that with kids' incessant needs, mothers have no "down" time. I found myself wondering how they ever managed to get anything done. If kids weren't needing something, they were bickering with each other or getting into mischief. I had discovered that raising children was so much more than the obvious incessant supervision. Meeting their needs required endless stores of mental and physical energy. Even while they were at school, their mothers must focus on their needs: worrying, planning, cleaning, shopping, cooking, washing clothes and dishes, making beds, and scheduling appointments. Motherhood had never been among my aspirations, but there I was, at the age of seventeen, with the overwhelming responsibility of caring for two children.

I thought about Mom. As angry as I felt toward her, I missed her and wished I could talk to her. I wondered if I'd ever hear her voice again. I wanted our lives to return to the way they had been before Dad got sick. Never in a million years, could I have foreseen our circumstances. I wanted to turn the clock back magically. I hadn't reached adulthood yet, at least in the eyes of the law, and already I needed a do-over.

Immersed in my pity-party, I scarcely noticed my phone ringing. Pete jumped up, unplugged it, and brought it to me.

"Abby, your mom's awake," Mindy said. "She came out of the coma this morning." It was the news I had been waiting for. I should have been ecstatic. Instead, I felt strangely numb.

"Abby are you there?"

"What is it?" asked Pete, who must have noticed my shocked expression.

My raised palm said, "I'll tell you in a minute."

"Yes, I'm here. She's awake? Is she talking?" I couldn't seem to make my voice sound excited.

"I haven't seen her, but a nurse called my mom and told her."

"Are you going to see her? No, wait. You're at school."

"It's a teacher workday," Mindy said. "Mom said we can go later this afternoon. What am I going to tell her about you? She'll want to know where you are. She'll wonder why you're not coming to see her."

"I don't know. I just don't know." I couldn't think. My brain played tug-of-war inside my head, trying to protect me from the weight of Mindy's news. I should have been thrilled but I felt nothing. It seemed like my whole body had been injected with Novocain.

"Don't worry," she said. "I'll think of something." By Mindy's tone, I could tell she was confused by my underwhelming reaction. She promised to call back later, and we ended the call.

"Is it Mommy?" asked Joey.

"She woke up this morning." Ignoring my dour response, the boys stood and grabbed me around the neck. As they hugged me, I allowed myself a cautious glimmer of hope.

"Can we go see her?" Pete asked.

"No, but as soon as she's well, we can go home."

"Yes!" Joey shouted, pumping his arm.

"Shh. Not so loud." I needn't have worried about attracting attention. Glancing around the noisy hall, I realized the passengers barely noticed Joey's excitement. They all went about their business, some glued to their phones, others checking the electronic screens that listed arrivals and departures. Some waited in long lines, inching their luggage forward with each step while others rushed about frantically like so many ants toward a sugar bowl. Those nearest us sat talking and laughing as if we weren't even there. I wondered if we had become invisible.

Our three-way hug brought something else to my attention, too, something that went unnoticed when we were outside in the fresh air. "We stink," I said.

"Hey, speak for yourself," said Pete.

"I'm including myself. As soon as you finish your work, we're going to the restroom to wash up and change clothes."

"Not the ladies' room again," Pete moaned.

"I'm afraid so."

"I can take Joey to the..."

"No way. I'm not letting you two out of my sight."

"You don't trust us," Joey said.

"It's not you, Joey. It's other people. We're not in Williamsburg, remember? We're in a big city where there could be pedophiles or kidnappers or..."

"Okay, okay," said Pete.

"What's pedophiles?" asked Joey.

"That's people who like to hurt little kids," Pete answered.

"Why?" asked Joey.

I regretted bringing up the subject and tried to distract him. "Finish your work so I can check it. I have spelling words for you."

"Noooo," they whined on cue.

Finally, we had gotten some good news. Mom was conscious. I thought about going home, seeing her and talking with her. But soon the nagging concerns surfaced once more. If she started drinking again we'd be no better off than before. Suppose she had intended to kill herself? Would she try again? My moment of guarded optimism gave way to the same old concerns about where we'd live, how I'd pay the rent, and how I'd finish high school.

Survival wore us down slowly, especially when there didn't seem to be a future for us anywhere. Please, God, I prayed. I can't do this. I need your help.

"Trust in the Lord with all your heart." It was that quiet voice again.

My phone rang once more. This time, the boys fell over each other scrambling to bring it to me. I reached and grabbed it out of their hands.

"Is this Elizabeth?" the caller asked.

"Who? Oh, yes. This is Elizabeth Jordan."

"This is Selima Evans from Harmony House. Do you and your sons still need shelter?"

"Yes. Oh, yes. Do you have space for us?"

"I will tomorrow. A family of three is moving to an apartment, and I'll have a room available by ten a.m."

I stood so quickly, my notebook and pen slid to the floor. "That's wonderful news, amazing news! Thank you so much!" The boys were standing, and, with wide, inquiring eyes, they jumped up and down in anticipation of the "wonderful, amazing news." I wanted to interrupt Miss Evans to share it with them, but I needed to get directions.

"Can you give me the address and some directions from Union Station? Write this down, Pete." He grabbed his math sheet and turned it over, so I could dictate the information to him. The shelter was only a few blocks away. By the next day, we'd have a place to stay. I collapsed in my seat with relief.

As I relayed the news to Pete and Joey, they grabbed my hands, pulled me up, and compelled me to dance in a circle with them. In that moment, we didn't care who saw us or what they thought of our crazy antics. We had a place to stay, and, in the dead of winter, that was worth celebrating.

"We'll have to spend one more night here," I whispered, "but tomorrow we'll be sleeping in real beds." I felt like I could sleep for weeks.

"Can't we go now?" asked Joey.

"No. Another family has to move out first. But they'll be gone tomorrow." Thank you, Lord, I whispered toward the ceiling. Truly, it was an answer to prayer. Maybe there was a God. Maybe the God of the universe did care about us.

"Okay, you two, as soon as you finish your spelling, we can eat lunch."

"Good. I'm starved," Pete said.

"Me, too," said Joey.

"Surprise, surprise," I said, allowing myself to laugh at their predictability.

I reflected on mealtimes before all the chaos entered our lives. Meals were about so much more than eating. Mom and Dad thought it was important for our family to gather around the table, at least for dinner, and share the events of the day. We ate breakfast in the kitchen, but Mom, a good cook, insisted we eat dinner in the dining room. Often, Pete and Joey argued and talked over each other, vying for attention. With Mom acting as referee and Dad trying to engage us in academic or philosophical conversations, often I resented having to be home for dinner at six p.m. Now, after observing my brothers lying on the floor of Union Station, eating their string cheese, I decided I would give anything for one more family dinner.

☙❧

I had noticed a scruffy-looking man sitting in a corner of the main lobby, his arms wrapped around a large, black trash bag. He wore a denim coat that was a couple sizes too big and khaki pants caked with grime. Long, greasy hair blended into a long, matted beard, but surprisingly the sneakers on his sockless feet looked new. What's that about? I wondered.

Joey stopped and took my hand. "Look," he said, pointing at the man. "He must be homeless."

Pete pulled down his brother's arm. "Don't look at him," he said.

Under different circumstances, I would have agreed with Pete. Weeks earlier, I would have reacted to the filthy, disheveled creature with discomfort, even fear. I would have rushed past him, deliberately averting my gaze. Instead, I searched his sad eyes and smiled. It was not pity that drove me to acknowledge him. Rather, it was an awareness that we shared a common humanity; a perspective that the hundreds of other humans surrounding us couldn't possibly comprehend. It was a gift.

Before I could stop him, Joey approached the man and handed him a cereal bar from his pocket. I thought he had eaten both bars earlier. Without waiting for a response (there was none), Joey rejoined us and slipped his hand into mine.

A station official walked up to the man and told him to move along. His tone was firm but not unkind. "Come on, Joe. Let's find you a place to sleep." He took the man by the arm and helped him up.

As they moved away, Joey exclaimed, "Did you hear that? His name is Joe, like me!" Briefly, Joe turned his head in our direction, and with dirty, decayed teeth, he smiled at Joey.

Watching the homeless man being escorted away, I decided it would be less likely for someone to identify us as indigent if we shifted from place to place. So, after lunch, we moved to another area. We needed only one more night, a few more hours. We're going to make it, I thought. We're going to be okay.

Chapter 28

We strolled through the Great Hall for what I hoped would be the last time until the day came that we could return to Williamsburg. We considered going outside, but, remembering how cold it was, decided against it. As the hours crawled by, the boys grew impatient about having a place to live. I couldn't help but wonder if it were too good to be true.

"Do you think there'll be other kids in the shelter?" asked Joey.

"I don't know what to expect any more than you do. I'll bet you and Pete will find lots of new friends."

"I liked my old friends," Pete grumbled. A good mother would have said something encouraging, but I was fresh out of empathy. Who was there to take care of me, to encourage me?

That night, again I set the boys up in a corner, a different corner, surrounding them with suitcases. I had planned to keep watch all night, but finally couldn't keep my eyes open. I think it was close to midnight when a fracas woke me. Startled, I sat up forgetting for a moment where I was. Rubbing my eyes, I tried to follow the sound to its source.

"You can't stay here," a guard said. He was talking to a ratty-looking, young man wearing a camouflage jacket and ripped, soiled jeans. His hair and beard were long, dirty and tangled."

"I ain' got no place ta go."

"You shoulda thought about that before you..." I couldn't make out the end of the sentence. "You're done!"

As my eyes focused, I spotted the uniformed guard who seemed ten feet tall. With a pot belly that hung over his belt and a handlebar moustache, he made an imposing figure standing over the man who was obviously homeless and either high on drugs or extremely drunk.

They continued to argue, their sentences interrupted by public announcements. I heard the guard say something about taking the man into custody. He mentioned calling the DC Police Department. "No more chances," he said. That's when I sprang into action. I couldn't risk being arrested, not when we were so close to having a place to live. I had to get us out of there before the guard spotted us. Since that night, I've learned that Union Station's security personnel are sympathetic to the homeless population. They get to know the "regulars" and allow them to spend an occasional night, especially in the winter. But at the time, I perceived them as the enemy.

"You know the rules. No dealing! Gather your stuff." That's when the man released a string of slurred obscenities, drawing everyone's attention to him, and, thankfully, away from us. I had no idea where we'd go or how we'd stay warm, but I woke the boys. Grabbing their blankets, I rolled them into balls and stuffed them in their suitcases.

"Put your coats on. We have to go." I was terrified, and I'm sure it showed on my face and in my voice.

"Where're we going?" asked Joey, half-awake.

"Is it morning already?" asked Pete. "I'm still tired."

"Don't ask questions. Just put on your coats." I grabbed our backpacks and ushered my bewildered brothers to the front entrance. While the guard was still engaged with the cursing, inebriated man, we made our escape.

When the doors opened, Pete and Joey looked up at me like I had lost my mind. They could see it was still dark outside. I pushed them out onto the sidewalk. A gust of frigid wind met our bare faces, nearly knocking us to the ground.

As the doors closed behind us, the three of us stood there in the cold night wondering what to do next. Where could we go at that hour? Joey started to cry, and it wasn't just a whimper. It was a loud, wracking, mouth-open wail. Pete joined in and began punching me. Initially, the shock of their extreme response paralyzed me. I couldn't stop them or hush them. I gave up trying. In my heart, I knew they had every right to boil with rage, and I let them express the depth of their frustration.

"I wanna go home!" Joey screeched at full volume.

"I hate you!" Pete yelled, shaking his fists and stomping his feet. "I hate everybody!" As my brothers continued to scream and cry into the night, I pulled them to me, trying to comfort them, but they pushed me away. I thought my heart would break, but I had no more tears. At that moment, I could have murdered anyone who crossed our path. But there was no one. The sidewalks were empty.

The end of our nightmare had been within reach. We needed only a few more hours. I plopped on the stone-cold sidewalk, pulled my hat over my ears and waited.

At last, with the boys' tantrums spent, I pressed their quivering bodies against the building, knelt in front of them, and wiped their tears on their hand-knitted scarves. They were tired, confused, and overwhelmed. Soon they would be cold. Realizing there was nothing I could say to comfort them, I focused on finding us some shelter from the wind. Zipping the boys' jackets, I pulled their hoods over their hats for extra warmth, then wrapped their beautiful, hand-knitted scarves twice around their necks, covering the lower portion of their faces. With no alternative but to keep moving, we strapped on our backpacks, grabbed the suitcase handles and started walking.

We headed toward Massachusetts Avenue and turned onto F Street NW, hoping the tall buildings bordering the sidewalks would shelter us from the wind. I searched for a doorway or any sort of alcove that might serve as a refuge until morning. Expecting Pete and Joey to give up and sit on the cold, wet sidewalk in protest, I urged them forward with promises of "just one more block." I thought I could feel their anger and dejection jabbing into my back. It was my own guilt filling me with regret.

"How much farther, Mom?" For the first time, Pete called me

Mom without hesitating.

Joey followed suit. "I'm cold, Mommy," he said through his scarf. Just ahead, I spotted a metal railing protruding from the side of a concrete building. As we drew closer, I saw that it surrounded a shallow stairwell leading down to the lower level of the structure. I reminded myself that in a few more hours we would be warm and safe from harm.

"Come on, boys," I said. "We can hide down there till morning." We descended four steps to the floor of the well. I laid our suitcases on the concrete, and pulled out our blankets, leaving the suitcases open. "Climb in," I said. Each of us hunkered down in our open suitcase with me in the middle. Pete and I couldn't stretch out our legs, but at least the suitcases and their contents provided a softer, warmer surface than bare concrete. I wrapped the boys in their blankets and pulled the third blanket around my legs. Then, I drew my brothers close, so we could share each other's body heat.

After a while, Joey dropped off to sleep with his head leaning against me. Because Pete and I didn't fit in our suitcase-cocoons, it was hard for us to get comfortable. "I'm cold, sissy... I mean Mom," he said, through chattering teeth.

"I know, buddy. Me too. Wrap the blanket around your legs and feet. We only have to make it through the night. One night. Then we'll have a nice, warm place to live. Try to sleep." I helped him wrap up and made sure Joey was completely covered. Then, Pete and I rested against each other and finally slept.

⊂ℨ৵⊃

While it was still dark outside, Joey's coughing woke me. "Mommy, Mommy," he cried, and I could tell he wanted his real Mommy.

"You're okay. You had a nightmare."

"I don't feel good," he said, his voice weak and pitiful. I noticed his body was radiating heat. I removed my glove and felt his forehead. It was hot with fever.

I lifted him out of his suitcase and drew him onto my lap. Pete, now leaning against the concrete wall, looked like he couldn't be comfortable, but he slept on. I swaddled Joey in his blanket, cradling him like a baby. I rocked him and, through my frosty breath, hummed a made-up lullaby until he fell asleep again. With the heat from his feverish body warming mine, we dozed for a couple of hours.

Pete and I were awakened by garbage trucks making their early-morning rounds. I felt so stiff and cold, I wasn't sure I'd be able to stand. I tried to wake Joey, whose head was resting on my chest. He moaned and stirred, but his eyes remained closed. He was burning up, and I could tell he was seriously ill.

"Oh," Pete groaned. "I can't move. My feet are frozen. I hate this."

"I know," I said. "Rub them a little before you try to stand." Then to Joey, I said, "Come on, Joey, wake up. We need to move." Rubbing his forehead, I tried to wake him. Again, he just moaned, refusing to open his eyes.

"What's wrong with Joey?" Pete asked, as he succeeded finally in straightening his aching body.

"He's sick. We need to get him inside where it's warm."

"But where?"

"Let's see if we can find a restaurant, someplace we can stay until it's time to go to the shelter. Do you remember passing any restaurants last night?"

"No. Ow! My back!"

"I hear you, buddy. Take your brother off me so I can stand up." Pete sat opposite me on the bottom step and pulled his limp brother backward onto his lap. My legs and back were so stiff it took several tries before I could straighten. "Can you hold him while I clean up?"

"Yeah, but hurry. He's heavy." Without bothering to fold them, I stuffed the blankets into our luggage. Then, with wooden fingers, I managed to zip the suitcases shut.

"Okay, lay him down here," I said, motioning to the suitcase-bed I had created. "I have an idea." I pulled my phone out of my pocket and prayed that one of the buildings had free Wi-Fi access.

"I thought you said we were going to a restaurant," Pete said, shivering.

"First I need to find one. I'll have to carry Joey, and I don't want to lug him any farther than I have to." I logged onto my phone and checked the Wi-Fi sources. There were three nearby. "Yes!" I exclaimed, choosing the one that didn't require a pass code. I brought up Google Maps for Washington, DC and searched "F Street NW/ Nearby Restaurants." Per the map, we had passed a couple of Irish Pubs the previous night, but I knew they wouldn't be open. If we could make it a block and a half in the other direction, there was a hotel with a bistro. That sounded promising. Surely it would have restrooms and a lobby where we could hang out for a few hours.

"Hurry, Ab... Mom. It's starting to rain."

"Okay, I found a place. Hold Joey while I pull the suitcases up to the street." I stuffed my phone into my coat pocket.

"I can't."

"Yes, you can." I dragged three suitcases up the steps, one at a time, then returned for the boys and their backpacks. So far, it was only sprinkling, but it was sleet, not rain. I feared we might be soaked and frozen by the time we reached our destination.

"Peter Jordan, you are tough!" I proclaimed.

"I used to be, but I'm not so sure anymore," he said, whining like a deflating balloon.

"Well, I need you to be tough one more time." He groaned. "I'll have to carry Joey. I can manage two backpacks, but you'll need to bring the rest."

"I don't think I can pull three suitcases."

"You're probably right. Let's ditch one." I opened Joey's suitcase and threw his blanket in the stairwell. Then I opened Pete's suitcase enough to stuff most of Joey's clothes inside. The spare bag tumbled down the steps.

After helping Pete with his load, I strapped Pete's backpack on my chest, wrapped the straps of Joey's backpack over my arm, and lifted my six-year-old brother onto my back. It would take supernatural strength and determination to reach our destination. "Help me" had become my mantra. I was getting used to asking God for help, and I was starting to realize that no matter how difficult the challenge, God had provided a way for me to meet it.

As we trudged along, F Street began to fill with traffic and, gradually, a few pedestrians with umbrellas joined us on the sidewalk.

When we reached the intersection where we needed to turn, I felt like my arms were made of whipped cream. "Are you okay, Pete?" I called behind me.

"No. Are we almost there?"

"Only a block to go. We turn here."

"You kids look like you could use a hand," a male voice said. A young man in a running suit pulled up beside us, jogging in place as he talked.

"We sure could." I didn't care if he turned out to be an axe murderer. I wouldn't have declined his offer.

"Where're you headed?"

"The hotel on New Jersey," I answered.

"It's just around the corner. Here, let me help." Without waiting for permission, he took the extra backpack from me and one suitcase from Pete.

"You're very kind."

"Hey. No problem. I'll count it as part of my work-out. By the looks of those clouds, I think we'd better pick up the pace, though." I was convinced this stranger was suggesting the impossible, but somehow, Pete and I managed to keep up.

Every time I thought I was about to drop Joey, I prayed, "God, help me," and a new surge of strength flowed through my frozen limbs. Finally, with the hotel in sight, I knew we'd make it.

The generous, young man deposited his load under the hotel's awning and wished us well. Then, he took off, and without looking back, he waved. He was out of sight when I realized I hadn't thanked him.

"We made it, Pete." I turned and looked down to find Pete sprawled on the large mat that covered the hotel's concrete entry.

"Speak for yourself," he whined, making me chuckle despite the anguish of our situation. Joey whimpered as it began to sleet, in earnest.

"Pete, help me walk Joey inside. I'll come back for our stuff."

Pete grunted as he flipped over on all-fours and stood, heaving. Together, we walked Joey through the automatic doors and laid him on a sofa in the impeccably furnished lobby. People glared at us like we had leprosy, but I didn't care. My immediate concern was my poor, sick brother. "Stay with Joey," I said to Pete. "I'll be right back." I returned to our pile and dragged our luggage inside. Then I unzipped and removed Joey's damp coat. His face was pale, his limbs as floppy as cooked spaghetti.

I looked around for a restroom and spotted the sign down a long corridor. "Pete. There's a restroom over there," I said pointing. "Go to the men's room and get a bunch of wet paper towels. Bring them to me."

"Not the ladies' room?"

"Not this time."

"Can I pee first?" he asked. "I really need to go."

"Yes, but hurry, and make sure the towels are cold." Although I had worked up quite a sweat, the lobby and its balmy temperature bathed me in its welcoming warmth. After spending two freezing winter nights outside, never again would I take shelter for granted. I shed my coat, and basked in the balminess, but my feet were still icy. Removing Joey's gloves and shoes, I began to rub his feet and hands gently. When Pete returned, I placed the wet paper towels on Joey's forehead.

"What's that for?" asked Pete.

"It'll bring his fever down," I said.

"Can we eat here?" he asked. "I'm hungry."

"There's supposed to be a restaurant in the hotel." I didn't care if I spent our last nickel. We had earned a proper, hot breakfast.

A woman wearing a hotel employee tag approached us. She had kind, brown eyes, a nice figure, enhanced by her gray blazer and navy-blue pencil skirt. She wore her reddish-brown hair in a stylish bob. "Do you kids need some help?"

"No. We're fine," I said. Then deepening my voice to sound older, I added, "My son is sick, and I need to let him rest before we have breakfast."

"Are you checking in? I can take care of that while you wait."

Despite her friendly demeanor, I could tell she was sizing us up. I wasn't sure if she had seen us enter, but I was determined to convince her we were legitimate lodgers. There was no way anyone was going to force us back outside into the wet, icy morning. "Actually, um... we just checked out. After breakfast, we'll be on our way." I could tell she wasn't convinced. She could have kicked us out, but she didn't.

"Oh. Well. There's a comfortable lounge over there where you'll have more privacy." She pointed to a smaller area adjacent to the main lobby. "Here. Let me help you move your luggage." I could tell she knew we were homeless. Our messy, filthy hair, rumpled clothes, and scuffed, dirty suitcases gave us away. I suspected she wanted us to move so we weren't in full view of the paying customers, but she wasn't unkind. "May I get you anything?" she asked.

"No, but thanks for your help." Joey moaned as I laid him on the sectional sofa.

"How about some Tylenol for the boy? I'm not supposed to dispense..." she looked around and whispered, "I think I have some in my purse."

"That would be great." Moments later, the woman returned with a travel tube of caplets and a bottle of water. I had taken money from my shoe to pay her, but she refused it.

"Thank you," I said, with tears of relief welling despite my determination to remain in control. She knew we were homeless. I was sure of it. But she decided not to expose us. I was so grateful. I managed to get a caplet down Joey's throat, and I helped him take a few sips of water.

"Can we eat now?" Pete asked.

"Not until Joey can walk," I said. "He should start to feel better soon. I need you to stay with him while I use the restroom. Hold this paper towel on his forehead and I'll be right back."

"Is he gonna be all right?" Pete asked. Joey was sprawled along one side of the large, sectional sofa, half-asleep and moaning.

"He'll be fine. We just need to get his fever down." Truthfully, I didn't know if Joey would be fine, but I was worried enough for both of us. Scaring Pete would accomplish nothing.

When I returned with fresh, cool towels, Joey's eyes were partially open. "Mommy?" he asked and started coughing again.

"I'm here, baby," I said, placing the cool, wet sheets of paper on his head.

"I hurt all over."

"I know. You'll feel better in a little while. Just rest." He closed his eyes and went back to sleep.

"Can we eat now?" Pete asked again.

"I think there's still a cereal bar in your backpack. That'll hold you for a while. Then, why don't you stretch out and take a little nap."

"Yeah. I didn't sleep much last night. I was scared we'd freeze into icicles or some bad guys would attack us."

"But we're okay, aren't we? God sent His angels to protect us." Now, all these years later, I realize it was the beginning of a personal faith experience. Our parents were occasional church-goers. We observed some basic religious rituals, like saying grace at meals. As a young child, I attended Sunday school sporadically, but this growing awareness was a revelation for me, not just a religious awakening, but a genuine awareness of God's presence. It took many years for me to understand that I had been visited by the Holy Spirit, not once but multiple times. God had answered my pleas for help in ways that were nothing short of miraculous.

"Yeah, angels..." Pete said, his voice trailing. He had taken two bites of the cereal bar when he was already falling asleep.

"Finish chewing first, so you don't choke." He roused enough to swallow, then leaned back onto the comfortable couch and drifted off. I wanted to sleep, too, but I didn't dare. I needed to watch Joey and make sure he wasn't getting worse. I reached into Pete's backpack for something to eat and pulled out a stick of beef jerky thinking the chewing might keep me alert. Just then, the kind woman showed up with a cup of coffee, complete with packets of creamer and sugar.

"I thought you might need this," she said, setting them on the coffee table in front of me.

"You are an answer to prayer!" I exclaimed in a loud whisper.

"It's my pleasure. You seem to have your hands full."

"I sure do, but this will help more than you could know." She started to walk away, then turned back to face me.

"I don't mean to be nosey, but..." She hesitated. I appreciated what seemed like an attempt to preserve my dignity. "May I?" she asked, motioning to the adjacent chair.

"Of course," I said, as I eagerly sipped the hot, strong coffee.

"Um, you seem to have fallen on hard times, and..."

"You can say that again," I said.

"I just wanted to let you know that... well... there are a couple of shelters near here. That is, if you need shelter. I'm not kicking you out or anything."

"You've been so kind, and you can't know how much we needed some kindness. This coffee is to die for, by the way."

"It's nothing. There was a time when I needed help... after my divorce. Someone helped my daughter and me get back on our feet. So, I'm always on the lookout for ways to, you know, pay it forward."

"We have a reservation at a shelter called Harmony House, but we can't get in until ten. Have you heard of it?"

"Yes. It's about four blocks that way," she said, pointing west, "and I'm going to drive you there whenever you're ready to go."

In that moment, I was so sure of God's love, I wondered how I had ever doubted it. No matter how impossible my situation seemed or how utterly alone I felt, God had answered my desperate prayers by sending help exactly when I needed it.

"Just ask for Darla, the hotel concierge, whenever you're ready. That's me."

I opened my mouth, but I couldn't speak. Darla reached forward and covered my hand with hers, giving it a quick squeeze. Then, she stood and returned to her job, leaving me to blink away tears of gratitude and finish the most delicious coffee I had ever tasted.

I looked at my phone and saw it was nearly eight o'clock. Pete and Joey slept peacefully, and now Joey's head was cooler to the touch. I couldn't resist a short nap, myself.

CRSO

I awoke to find Joey sitting up. "Hi, Joe-Joe. How are you feeling?"

"I'm thirsty," he said.

"Good! That's a good sign." I felt his head and it was cooler. Checking the time, I saw I had slept soundly for nearly an hour. The brief nap left me surprisingly refreshed.

"Well, let's wake Pete and get some breakfast. Soon it'll soon be time to go to the shelter."

"I dreamed about angels," Joey said.

"What?"

"There were angels and they helped us."

"I know, Joey. I know about the angels."

We woke Pete and, after stowing our suitcases in an out-of-the-way corner, we found the bistro and slid into a comfortable booth.

While we waited for our food to arrive, I gathered our money from various hiding places and counted it. I found I had slightly more than a hundred dollars left—just enough to pay for breakfast and purchase our return tickets home, when the time came. Once we settled in the shelter, I'd have to find a job. That reminded me of something. After breakfast, I'd pull Mom's cosmetics bag out of my suitcase, pull my hair into a bun like she wore for her driver's license photo, and apply makeup the way I had seen her do.

I kept checking my phone to make sure we wouldn't be late arriving at Harmony House. By the time we revisited our "private" lounge, it was after nine. Joey was dragging, but at least he could walk. I kept tabs on his temperature and reminded myself to give him another pill at eleven.

"Pete, see the front desk right over there?"

"Yeah."

"I want you to go there and tell the clerk your mom needs to see the concierge."

"The consi-what?"

"Concierge. It's the lady who helped us before."

"Con-ci-erge, con-ci-erge." I heard him practicing as he walked away.

"Just ask for Darla," I called after him. I turned to Joey and reminded him how important it was to call me "Mom" from now on. He flashed a weak Cub-Scout-honor sign and collapsed against the back of the sofa, looking pale and worn-out.

Soon Pete returned with Darla who, with coat in hand, led us to the parking garage. "Won't you get in trouble for leaving work?" I asked.

"Don't you worry about that. My manager knows how important community service is to me, and she lets me deduct the time from my lunch break." I settled in the front passenger seat and the boys buckled themselves in the back. "Your boys are very sweet and polite," she said. "You've done a great job with them."

"Thanks, but they aren't always this quiet, I promise you."

"I have a girl, and she can be noisier and more energetic than a half-dozen boys."

"What's her name?" I asked.

"Abigail, but I call her Abby."

"Hey! That's..." Pete started to talk, and I knew exactly what he was about to say. I interrupted him before he could continue. "What a coincidence," I said, flashing Pete a don't-say-anything look. My boys have a cousin named Abigail and we call her Abby, don't we Pete?"

"Yeah."

"How old is your Abby?" I asked.

"She's ten now and in the fourth grade. Say, I don't even know your names."

"Oh. I'm Elizabeth Jordan and my sons are Pete and Joey. Pete's almost nine and Joey's six."

Only minutes later, she stopped the car. "Well, here we are, Elizabeth. I'll have to double-park while you get your bags out of the trunk. Sorry I can't go inside with you, but I don't see any parking spaces anywhere."

"It's okay. We'll be fine, and again, thank you so much! Boys, what do you say to Miss Darla?"

"Thank you."

"It was my pleasure. Just slam that trunk hard. It sticks sometimes. Bye now and God bless." We waved as she drove away, then turned to check out our new home. It was an ancient, three-story brick structure situated on a corner lot. It looked like a typical urban house from the nineteenth century. Other than a little peeling paint around the windows, it seemed to be in good condition. From our position across the side street, I could see the backyard. A chain-link fence enclosed the small area where I spotted a swing set.

We climbed the front steps onto a generous, covered porch. After again reminding the boys to call me mom, I knocked on the door. A woman came to the door and invited us in.

"You must be the Jordans," she said. I nodded and smiled. "Come in. I'm Selima. We talked on the phone, Missus Jordan." When she made eye-contact with me, her tone of voice changed slightly, and I thought she might be eyeing me with suspicion. I lowered both my eyes and my voice, but straightened my shoulders, determined to convince her I was older than my appearance indicated. I remember thinking how glad I was that my acne had begun to clear up once I turned seventeen.

⊂⊃⊷⊶

Selima was an attractive, fifty-ish, black woman who stood a little taller than my five- foot-four height. Her curly, salt-and-pepper hair was cut as short as a man's and she wore a professional-looking, gray pant suit with a light-blue blouse tied in a bow at her neck. Not her appearance, but the way she carried herself, reminded me of Mrs. Gladstone, my school's guidance counselor. She seemed sophisticated, yet warm and friendly, compelling me to trust her immediately.

"Hi, Selima," I said, in my most commanding alto. I shook hands with as much confidence as I could muster. "I'm Elizabeth and these are my sons, Pete and Joey." She shook hands with each of them and, helping us pull our suitcases through the door, told us to follow her to her office.

"Leave your luggage here in the front room for now," she said. I heard voices and other sounds of life coming from various parts of the building but didn't see anyone else. A baby cried from somewhere upstairs, and from the rear of the house, I heard pots and pans clanking together like they were being washed or stored. The smell reminded me of Mee-maw's house, old, a little dusty, and welcoming.

Selima led us past a wooden staircase with a smooth railing and carved spindles into a small office where she sat at a tidy desk, motioning us toward the loveseat and chairs. Immediately, my eyes settled on the picture above her desk. It was a copy of Renoir's famous Mother and Children. I recognized it from the art elective I had taken my junior year showing a young mother guiding two children. Now, for the first time, I stepped onto the canvas as the young mother with her long, frizzy, blonde hair like mine. The physical resemblance ended there. She and her two girls, impeccably dressed for cold weather, seemed to move both toward something and away from a group of people in the background. The trio's prominant eyes spoke of experiences their polite society couldn't comprehend.

Selima interrupted my reverie. "Well, boys, I'm sure you're ready to get settled in your room, but your mom and I have a little paperwork to complete first. Do you like pretzels?"

"Yes, ma'am," they both answered shyly.

"Please help yourselves, but there's a limit of two apiece." She indicated the large jar that set on the coffee table in front of the sofa.

"Let's make that one each," I said. "You just ate breakfast."

Pete and Joey sat on the sofa that rested against the wall opposite Selima's desk, and I took one of two wooden armchairs directly in front of her desk. "What do you say, boys?"

"Thank you," they answered, helping themselves.

"So, how long have you and your boys been homeless?"

"About a week," I said.

"Where have you been staying?"

"We lived in our car in Williamsburg."

"Williamsburg," she repeated. "Williamsburg has good services for the homeless. I've heard that the local churches started a program to feed and house folks during the winter months."

"Well... we had to leave."

"I understand. There's no need to explain," she said. I wasn't sure what she thought she understood, but I was relieved I didn't have to make up another lie.

"Then we rode the train to DC. We spent the night in Union Station."

"I see."

"We tried to sleep on the subway one night, but we got kicked off at midnight and slept on a platform until morning. Then we tried to go back to Union Station, but we had to leave there, too. Last night we slept outside."

"It was thirty-five degrees last night. How did you survive?"

"We found a stairwell to keep us out of the wind and wrapped in blankets we brought from home."

"Well, tonight you'll be sleeping in warm beds."

"I'm so grateful," I sighed. Without bursting into tears of joy, I couldn't possibly express just how grateful and relieved I felt at that moment.

"Here at Harmony House we'll do everything we can to help you get back on your feet."

I'm not sure how or if I responded. Perhaps I was too overcome to speak. Part of me wanted to jump for joy. Another part couldn't believe our good fortune.

"Tomorrow will be soon enough to tell you about our services," Selima continued. "Right now, let's take care of the paperwork so you can get settled. Your Joey seems to be ready for a nap."

"I looked behind me to see that Joey had fallen asleep with his head resting on Pete's lap.

"As I said on the telephone, Elizabeth... may I call you Elizabeth?... I'll need to see some form of identification."

"Oh, yes." I removed my shoes and handed her Mom's Social Security card and driver's license, praying there was enough of a family resemblance to keep from arousing her suspicion. Everyone said I was the spitting image of my mother with her blonde, curly hair, slim build, and round, blue eyes. Selima didn't seem to study the picture, but simply copied the license number and Mom's birthdate.

"Hmm," I heard her say. I thought she was about to question my identity, but she didn't. She turned the paper toward me and asked me to finish filling in the requested information.

"Do you have any money?"

"Yes," I answered hesitantly. "Almost ninety dollars. I'm saving it for our train fare back home someday."

"Here at Harmony House the residents share all of their assets. You'll need to turn over your money. Don't worry. Everything you need will be provided."

"What about the women who come with no money or assets?" I asked, as I pulled the bills out of my bra and various pockets.

"Eventually, with our help, they find jobs. While they stay here, they're expected to give us ten percent of their earnings to help with living expenses."

"Mom?" said Pete. I turned and gave him a secret thumbs-up for remembering to call me Mom.

"Yes?"

"Can you move Joey?" he asked. "My leg is falling asleep."

"Sure." I stood and walked to the sofa. Carefully, I shifted Joey's position, so he was leaning on the arm of the love seat, away from Pete.

"Pete, do you like puzzles?" asked Selima.

"Yes, ma'am, if they're not too easy."

"Oh, so you like a challenge, unh?"

"Yeah. I guess so." I cleared my throat and shot a mom-glance in his direction. "I mean, yes ma'am," he corrected, and I smiled my approval.

"Well, let's see if you can get this one started for me." She pulled a box from a nearby book shelf and indicated to me to pass it to Pete.

"Thanks," Pete said, as he poured the pieces onto the coffee table. I sat down again and finished filling out the application.

"Now, Elizabeth, we need to talk about some important regulations here at Harmony House."

"Of course."

"They're very simple. No drugs, no tobacco, no alcohol, and no food in the bedrooms."

"No problem. Pete, do we have any food left in our backpacks?"

"Just a couple of cheese sticks and some beef jerky." The bread and Nutella had been in my backpack that was stolen.

"If the packages have been opened, please throw them away," said Selima. "Otherwise, I'll add them to our food pantry." She continued reciting the rules. "School-age children must be in bed by nine p.m. Lights-out at eleven for adults."

"Got it."

"We ask that you keep your room tidy, help with maintaining the common areas, including the bathroom, and take care of your own laundry. There are washers and dryers in the basement."

"Absolutely."

"Okay. Please sign here that you agree to abide by the house rules."

Without hesitation, I signed the document as Elizabeth Jordan, a signature I had perfected. Finally, we had a place to live where we didn't have to worry about being mugged or kicked out on the street.

I wanted to jump up and down and shout "hooray!" but I took care to maintain my mature persona.

"Tomorrow we'll discuss how you can get back on your feet, and we'll get those boys of yours signed up for school."

"School? They can go to school?"

"Actually, they must. Did you happen to bring their birth certificates?"

"No. That is, we had to leave so quickly."

"Yes. Well, we can request copies from the Commonwealth of Virginia."

"Oh. Good."

"Well, Pete," she said. "It looks like you have a good start on that puzzle. Shall we go see your room now?"

"Yeah, I mean yes, please." He stood to follow Selima, and I lifted Joey who was still sleeping.

"Your mom has her hands full. I can take the suitcases if you bring the backpacks," she said to Pete.

"Yes, ma'am." Again, I smiled my approval at Pete.

"Wait right here," she said, as I stood at the bottom of the staircase with Joey in my arms, his head resting on my shoulder. "You'll be on the second floor." She and Pete retrieved our bags from the front room and, awkwardly we ascended the creaky stairs. With each step, Joey seemed to grow heavier, and I was relieved when, at last, we reached the landing, thankful that our room wasn't on the third floor.

"What a beautiful, old house," I said, puffing from the climb. "I love the detailed woodwork and high ceilings. There's so much character." In trying to sound like an adult, I was drawing from shows that Mom and I had watched on HGTV. Truthfully, the building's interior could've used a make-over. The mismatched rugs and furniture were worn, and the paint was peeling in places. But with its high ceilings, intricate woodwork, and huge, covered front porch, it did have architectural interest.

"It was built before nineteen hundred, and we were blessed to obtain it six years ago. The city was about to tear it down and build apartments," Selima said. "Then, someone discovered it was listed in the historic registry. So, it had to be restored. Well, as you can see, its restoration was limited to the exterior."

"We're just happy to have a place to live."

"I've learned that many famous people like Sidney Portier and Josephine Baker stayed here during its heyday, when it was a hotel."

Just beyond the landing, we passed a room where two young-looking women sat on the bed, talking as they folded clothes. They glanced up briefly, and without smiling, returned to their work. Selima led us around the well-worn railing to the right where the l-shaped landing extended toward the front of the house and a tall window overlooked the street below. "Here we are," she said, unlocking the grainy, wood door to a room across from the third-floor staircase. I noticed the key was one of those old-fashioned types like you see in the movies. "This corner room is one of my favorites. It gets lots of natural light."

"It's perfect," I said. The room was small but seemed airy because the ceiling must have been ten feet high and there were two tall windows, one on the front and another overlooking the side street. Framed with sheer curtains, the windows included pull-down shades for privacy.

Against the front wall was a twin-size bed, neatly covered with white sheets and a mint-green blanket that was tucked in, army-style. I couldn't wait to try out that inviting bed and lay my head on a pillow again.

On the opposite wall stood a set of wooden bunk beds, also covered with green blankets. Each bed included a pillow and crisp, white sheets, also a pile of clean, but thin, white towels. A small chest of drawers completed the space, except for a modern-style, plastic chair that seemed out of place. A mirror hung on the wall above the chair. None of the furniture matched; dirty smudges defaced the walls; and the floor boards were worn and gouged in spots. It was divine.

"Cool! Bunkbeds," exclaimed Pete. "Can I have the top bunk?" Joey stirred for a second, lifting his head off my shoulder, but didn't wake up. I noticed he felt hot again, reminding me it was almost time for another Tylenol.

"I'll leave that decision up to your mom," Selima said.

"Can I?"

"May I."

"Yeah, may I?"

"I don't intend to lift your brother onto the top bunk. So, yes, you may."

"Cool." He started to climb the ladder when I added, "Hold it. Let's wait until after you've had a bath."

"Oh," he said, downcast, and stepped down.

"Let me show you where the bathroom is," Selima said. "You'll be sharing it with three other families, so please be as quick as you can and leave it as clean as you found it."

"Of course," I said as I laid Joey on the bottom bunk.

"Hey, not fair. He's as dirty as I am," Pete complained.

"Good point, Pete," I said, tousling his stringy hair. "But I don't think I could've held him one minute longer."

Selima led us back around the l-shaped landing and past the stairs. "The bathroom is just down there on the right. If your boys get up at night, I'd suggest you accompany them until they get used to the layout. We don't want them toppling down the stairs."

"Right," I said, and we returned to our room.

"Well, I'll let you get settled. Lunch is at noon in the dining room downstairs. You shouldn't have any trouble finding it. I'll introduce you to some of the other residents then."

"Fine. Thanks, again. We're very grateful to have a roof over our heads."

"I'll see you at noon." She smiled, closed the door behind her, and left us to unpack and acclimate to our new surroundings. I needed to get Joey's coat off and give him his next dose of acetaminophen.

"Pete, please take one of those cups on the dresser and get some water from the bathroom."

Once I got Joey settled, I told Pete to stay with his brother while I took a shower. "What am I supposed to do? Watch him sleep?" he asked.

"Exactly. If he wakes up, tell him to stay put and I'll be right back. Hey, I noticed a case full of books in the hallway. Go see if there's anything you can read while you wait."

"They probably only have boring stuff."

"It won't hurt to look."

I had just gathered my shampoo, shower gel and washcloth,

and wrapped them in a towel when Pete came back in the room all excited.

"Guess what, Mom!" He truly seemed to be thinking of me as his mother now, and I certainly was feeling like a mother.

"Lower the volume. What?"

"They've got the whole Harry Potter series. Look. This is the one I've been wanting to read: Harry Potter and the Half-Blood Prince."

"Good. You can get started while I take a shower. Sit over there," I said, indicating the room's only chair. He had already started reading before his bottom touched the chair, and I couldn't wait to feel warm water cascading over my skin. It didn't even bother me that I'd have to put on dirty clothes.

The shower didn't disappoint. I shampooed my hair twice and covered every inch of my filthy, smelly body with lemon-scented shower gel. Quickly toweling dry, I dressed in my dirty jeans and shirt. Without a hair dryer, my hair would frizz into a wild bush, so I gathered it into a pony tail. As soon as it air-dried, I'd swirl it into the bun that I thought made me look older.

I had a hard time pulling Pete away from his book to bathe, but I didn't have to worry about him lingering in the shower. He could scarcely wait to get back to the story. After helping him brush through the tangles of his too-long hair, it was Joey's turn. I walked him to the bathroom and sat him in a tub of lukewarm water. Too weak to resist, he allowed me to wash his hair and bathe him.

As I was dressing Joey, I heard a knock at the door. "Sorry, but we need to use the bathroom," a voice announced.

"We'll be right out." I opened the door to see a young woman holding an adorable toddler with chubby cheeks and huge brown eyes. He was dressed in a tee shirt and a pull-up.

"I'm sorry, but we're potty training and he can't wait," she said.

"That's fine. I'll come back later to clean up."

I walked Joey back to our room. He said he was feeling better, but I knew the pain reliever was mostly responsible for his temporary reprieve. Whatever, the reason, my aching arm muscles were grateful he could move under his own power.

"Is this our new house?" he asked when we returned to our room.

"Yes. What do you think?"

"I like my bed." I thought he would add that he wanted the top bunk, but he just crawled in and snuggled with his stuffed rabbit and new pillow.

Pete had settled on the top bunk with his book, giving me just enough time before lunch to clean up the bathroom. "I want you to stay here while I take care of our mess down the hall. Pete, keep an eye on your brother."

"Mm-hm," he answered, without looking up. I wasn't worried about Joey going anywhere in his feeble condition. So, I left the boys and took care of my duty.

Chapter 29

At twelve-on-the-dot, we heard a bell ring and figured it must be the signal for lunch. We joined the residents exiting both floors and followed them down to the dining room. I noticed there were no children older than the toddler I had seen earlier and one baby. After my initial twinge of disappointment, I remembered it was a weekday. The older kids would be at school.

We passed the kitchen and entered the large dining room at the rear of the house where a sprawling table was set for only seven people. Five of the mismatched chairs and two high chairs were claimed quickly. Selima had told me the house was full, and I wondered where the others were. Later I learned that many of the women either had jobs or were going to school. They would return in the evening.

Selima showed us to our seats, but I noticed the others didn't sit immediately. I indicated to Pete and Joey to remain standing behind their chairs. Although the table held no food yet, an inviting array of aromas drifted in from the kitchen where I could hear the clinking of utensils against pots and serving dishes. "I'll introduce you after everyone's served," she said. "Ladies... oh, and gentlemen, she added quickly, smiling at Pete and Joey. Let us bow in prayer and thank our loving Father for His bountiful provisions."

I couldn't have felt more thankful or more relieved to be there. Harmony House was, indeed, an answer to prayer. What I didn't know then was how significantly our time at the shelter would shape our future.

CʒꙄ

In the middle of our first night sleeping in real beds, surrounded by four walls and a roof, Joey awoke crying and complaining about his ear hurting. I gave him a Tylenol, pulled him into my bed and tried to soothe him as I waited for the pain reliever to take effect. This time it didn't help at all. He continued to cry, and I didn't know what to do for him. I picked him up, wrapped him in a blanket and carried him down to Selima's office. I knew she had gone home earlier, but the night attendant would be there. Although Selima had introduced us, I couldn't remember the woman's name. "Let's see," I whispered as I lugged my sick brother down the stairs with arms still aching from the previous day's lugging, "It starts with J. Janine? No. Geraldine? No. That's not even a J-name. Justine? No." Finally, it came to me. "Josephine. Yes, that's it. Josephine."

"It seems like an ear infection," Josephine said. She was a large, masculine-looking woman with bushy eyebrows, dark, scary eyes that bulged, and the hint of a moustache, but I soon discovered she was as warmhearted and gentle as they came. "My youngin's used to get 'em all the time. I can fix him up with a good home-remedy until he can see a doctor. Poor little fella. Follow me."

Josephine led us to the kitchen, switched on the light and directed me to sit on a stool where I could watch her make what she called a "salt poultice." Helpless to comfort my whimpering brother, I held him in my arms and rocked him like a baby.

After pouring a liberal amount of salt into a piece of cheesecloth, Josephine tied it shut with some string, and heated it in the microwave. She instructed me to lay it on Joey's pillow under the affected ear.

To me, it sounded like voo-doo or witchcraft, but the child was so uncomfortable, I was willing to try anything. "Make sure you cover it with a towel so it's not too hot against his skin."

I followed Josephine's directions, and, to my amazement, Joey slept soundly for the remainder of the night. In the morning, the towel was covered with blood and pus, and Joey jumped out of bed like he had never been sick. He shook me awake at six-thirty, claiming to be "starving."

Chapter 30

By the second week in our new home, life had become somewhat routine. We had met everyone who lived at Harmony House, and, although some of the other women seemed guarded, we were starting to make a few friends. I had moved beyond the impression that I didn't belong in a place like this—that I was somehow better than the shelter's other residents because of my middle-class background. There's nothing like poverty to instill a spirit of humility. Whenever I reflect on that time in our lives, I'm grateful for Selima Evans and her amazing staff who welcomed us without judgment and encased us in their protective cocoon. I continue to be thankful for the pool of volunteers who stood ready to equip us with tools for navigating a harsh world. Selima, our loving, communal mother nurtured all of us in an atmosphere of respect.

Yet, there were challenges at Harmony House. Because many of the children found it necessary to fight for their survival, they woke up enraged. One evening, Pete came running into our room with a swollen eye. He had been playing with Damien, the only other eight-year-old in the shelter.

"What happened?" I asked, removing his hand to get a better look at the injury.

"Damien punched me. For no reason." Joey, who was working a puzzle on the floor, stood and nosed his way under my arm with curiosity.

"Cool! Yer gonna have a shiner," he said.

"Get lost. It's none of your business," Pete said to his brother.

"Finish your puzzle, Joey," I said. Then to Pete, "There must've been a reason. What were you fighting about?"

Joey chanted, "Pete's gonna have a shiner, Pete's gonna have a shiner."

Holding Pete back from trying to kick his brother, I repeated, "What were you arguing about?

"He started teasing me 'cause I don't have a dad. He visits his father every weekend. He just came back from seein' his dad and he said, 'Ha, ha! You ain't got no dad to go see.'"

"Why? Why would he say that?"

"Cause he's stupid and mean."

"He is," said Joey. "He fights with everybody."

"What did you say or do to make him punch you?"

"Nothin'."

"He punched you for no reason?"

"Yeah, no reason." Realizing I was getting nowhere with my inquiry, I dealt with the immediate issue.

"Come with me. Let's get some ice on that eye." Later I'd talk to Damien's mother.

That evening, I left the boys doing their homework and climbed to the third floor, headed to Latisha's room. Latisha was Damien's mom. Nervously, I knocked on the door. She had three kids by three different men—information to which I was not privy until many weeks later. Damien was her oldest. Like her, he wore a permanent scowl.

"Hi," I said when she came to the door. I tried to look friendly. I didn't want trouble, but I thought I should get to the bottom of Pete's and Damien's scuffle. Otherwise, how could I help Pete handle any future disagreements with kids?

"I thought we should talk," I said.

"'Bout what?" She didn't ask me to come in. By her defensive stance—arms folded, legs apart, knees locked—I could tell she was ready for me to strike. Many times, I had seen that same body language at my high school. It usually resulted in a fight.

At first, I wanted to turn and bolt down the stairs. I wondered if I should have brought a peace offering, a candy bar or cologne or something. I stammered, trying to look and sound innocuous. "Well, you know, um, our boys got in a fight today."

"Yeah. So?" Her chin jutted forward. "Boys fight."

"I just wondered if we could help them, you know, sort out their differences... in a more, you know, positive way." Latisha's dark eyes remained devoid of expression. Her pursed lips and crossed arms told me she thought I was a blathering idiot. I realized I was ill-prepared for this confrontation.

When her three-year-old appeared from behind the door, grabbing her pantleg, and her baby began to cry from somewhere inside the room, I realized my mission was both naïve and hopeless. This mother had more pressing concerns than whether her eight-year-old learned to get along with a sissy white boy he might never see again once they left the shelter. Like me, she was overwhelmed by life.

"Well..." I said, nodding toward her children, "I can see you're busy." I managed a feeble smile and made my exit. Instead of teaching Pete an important life-lesson, I advised him to stay away from Damien.

Sometime later, after Latisha returned to her husband, Damien's stepfather, I learned that Damien's biological father had beaten her and Damien. A court order required Latisha to allow visitation, and whenever Damien visited his dad, he got knocked around. I understood, then, why both he and his mom were so angry.

CR३εᴏ

It took nearly a week to register Pete and Joey for school because I had to request their birth certificates from Richmond. Then, posing as Elizabeth Jordan, I called to transfer the records from their school in Williamsburg to their new school. Throughout the wait, I worried that the Williamsburg/James City County officials would discover our whereabouts and report us to the authorities. I worried they might know the plight of the real Elizabeth Jordan; that any day, they might inform Selima that I was an imposter. In the end, I was able to register the boys for school without a problem. Pete was accepted in second grade and Joey would be finishing kindergarten.

Acquiring my records from Lafayette High School proved more challenging. According to Mindy, the principal, guidance counselor and teachers were aware that I had skipped town. But it didn't matter because I was no longer Abigail Jordan, high school senior. Now I was Elizabeth Jordan, single mother of two children, who could qualify for the GED program simply by taking a test... or so I thought.

Mindy had kept us up-to-date on Mom's condition, and, unlike her previous report, the latest news was devastating. Dr. Santos had released Mom to a rehabilitation center for "extensive therapy." A Cat Scan indicated she had suffered significant brain damage. She couldn't talk or walk. Both Mindy and Diana said she didn't seem aware of her surroundings or recognize her visitors. My mother was essentially catatonic. I cried myself to sleep that night and tried to figure out how to share the heartbreaking news with Pete and Joey. I longed to talk to Mom... the mom of my childhood. I missed her so much. It felt like she had died.

"Doctor Santos said not to give up hope," Mindy said. I could tell she was trying to offer comfort, but I wasn't convinced there was any hope. "Therapy can make a huge difference in your mom's recovery."

"Whether she improves or not, how will I ever take care of her? How will I pay for her treatment? I can't even support myself and my brothers."

"How are you and the boys? Have you found a place to live?"

"We've found a wonderful place. Pete and Joey are going to school and making friends, and..." I didn't mention we had no privacy unless we locked ourselves in our small room or that some of the other residents were churlish. I didn't tell her there were no fresh vegetables or fruit, that most of the food came from cans. I didn't mention how differently some people interpreted the word, "clean." Often, I'd go to use the bathroom and find hair and soap scum in the sink or tub or a dirty diaper on the floor.

"That sounds great," Mindy said, "but very... permanent. Are you ever coming home?"

"Of course, but you know we can't return until after I turn eighteen or CPS'll place us in foster care. I can't let that happen."

"Yeah. I know, but geez, Abby, I miss you."

"I miss you, too. It's just the way things have to be for now. I have some good news, though. I think I can test for the GED program, and I might get to graduate on time."

"GED? Why can't you just go to a high school wherever you are?"

"Because I need a job. This way, I can work during the day and take classes in the evening."

"Oh... but wait. Wouldn't it be your mom graduating from high school?" I had finally told Mindy I was impersonating Mom.

"I know. It's complicated, but I'll be able to clear up the confusion after my birthday. Anyway, while I finish my course work, I can get a job and support us."

"And come home."

"Right. And come home." But what did I have to go home for now that Mom was a vegetable? Why, Mom? I thought. Why did you do it? Part of me felt sorry for my mother and part of me was angry as hell. I didn't understand how she could do that to her children who had already lost their father. How could she abandon her two little boys? How could she leave me to raise them when I was still a child, myself? I realized I would never know the answers to my questions. In the meantime, I needed to concentrate on my own survival and help my brothers adjust to their new environment, even if it was temporary.

A few days later, I hit a roadblock concerning my GED. I discovered that a copy of my high school transcript was required to enroll in the program. Since I was living under a false identity, I would need to provide Mom's transcript. But Mom had graduated and even attended college. If I used my transcript listing my birthdate, Selima would discover my identity and actual age. I couldn't risk being evicted from Harmony House. Whatever it took, I was determined my brothers and I would never spend another night on the street. My only choice was to delay the process until April when I could apply as Abigail Jordan.

◌3❦◌

Soon I was meeting with a career counselor. Compared to the other volunteer workers at the shelter, Lori was young, maybe thirty. An attractive brunette, she was slender, and always looked professional in her suits and heels. I liked Lori instantly and wanted to get to know her, but whenever I tried to inquire about her personal life, she would divert the conversation to focus on my life and my issues. Her no-nonsense style made it clear she was there to be my advocate and counselor, not my friend.

When Lori asked why I hadn't scheduled the GED test, I explained I was having trouble acquiring my high school transcript. "That's strange," she said. "It's usually a straight-forward procedure. Why don't you let me try?"

Because I anticipated her offer, I had prepared a response. "You see, because of my situation, there's some confusion in the records. They need a copy of my birth certificate. I requested it from Richmond, but because I was born in a different state... well, there's just a lot of red tape involved. As soon as I get it all straightened out, I can start school. I was told it might take until April." It was a lie. Another lie.

"I see," said Lori. My convoluted excuse bought me some time or at least that's what I thought. As we sat in the front parlor for our weekly meeting, I assumed I had become clever at manipulating the truth. Yet, I experienced guilt about deceiving Selima and Lori because they were being so good to me. I longed for the day I could "tell the truth, the whole truth, and nothing but the truth."

I learned that Lori's paid position was in a local high school where she was a guidance counselor. Some five years earlier, Selima had convinced her to volunteer at the shelter for a few hours each week.

It was during one meeting with Lori that an idea began to ignite the kindling in my brain. It was a turning point. Out of necessity, I had been play-acting at being an adult. Adulthood had fallen into my lap against my will. Fear, deprivation, and obligation had been effective teachers, but if I allowed them sovereignty over my world view, I risked a future wrapped in selfishness, bitterness, and cynicism.

My dream of higher education became more important than ever, but it was no longer about me and what I could accomplish for myself. Now my vision became about what God could accomplish through me. I still had to figure out how to survive, how to feed and clothe my brothers, how to keep a roof over our heads, but I had learned something else, the most important lesson of all: God had my back. God had been with me every step along the difficult journey. God had answered every plea for help. I would find a way to give back, to express my gratitude.

"What would you like to do in the meantime?" Lori asked.

"I need a job."

"Okay. Let's work on that. Without a high school diploma, your options are limited, but here's a list of potential jobs in the vicinity." She pulled a document from her briefcase and handed it to me. "I assume you don't want to expand the search beyond DC?" It was more of a statement than a question.

"Right. I need to be home when my boys get out of school."

"Of course. Look over this list and start applying tomorrow. I recommend you visit three or four businesses daily." She handed me another document. "Study these potential questions and prepare your answers in advance. If you land an interview, you'll be ready. Also, be sure to wear your most presentable outfit and show up a few minutes early."

"All I have are jeans, casual shirts, and a couple of sweaters."

"I can help with that. I have connections with Dress for Success, an organization that supplies homeless women with professional clothing for job interviews."

"Depending on the job, jeans might be fine," Lori added. "Just make sure your clothes are clean and pressed and that you're well-groomed. Here's a card with the address and phone number. I'll let them know you'll be calling." Lori handed me a business card for the organization, Dress for Success. I didn't relish riding the subway across town, but I was excited about getting a new outfit... and, hopefully, a job.

"I'll see you next week, Elizabeth. I hope to hear good news."

After lunch, I went to my room and perused the two-page list of jobs that Lori provided. Most of the positions were with fast food chains, also a few entry-level positions in local retail stores. It was no surprise to see "minimum wage" listed in the pay-scale column beside each post. As I considered the options, I couldn't help remembering that only a few months earlier, I had been planning for an advanced degree and a fulfilling career. Was it possible I could anticipate nothing more rewarding than flipping burgers?

"Trust in the Lord with all your heart..." What was the rest of that verse? I remembered that Gideons International had placed a Bible in every room of Harmony House. I opened the top dresser drawer, picked up the Bible and began to read the New Testament.

Chapter 31

For the next two weeks, I filled out applications and went to interviews. I had signed my mother's name so many times I thought I was Elizabeth Jordan. I felt very much like the mother of two boys who now called me "Mom" without a moment's hesitation.

When I got up the nerve to tell Pete and Joey about the severity of Mom's condition, they had just returned from school. We went to our room, so they could do their homework. I was surprised by their lack of emotion. They seemed to take it in stride. I could tell they were sad, but neither of them cried.

"Will we ever see her again?" Joey asked. He liked to sit on the floor and spread out on the oval rag rug to do his homework.

"Yes, of course."

"Will she know us?" asked Pete, who had pulled the plastic chair up to the dresser and was unloading his books and homework folder.

"I'm not sure. She might."

"How did it happen? How did she get sick?" asked Pete.

"Do you remember when she was drinking, and she didn't act like herself?"

"Yeah, 'cause she was 'dicted," Joey said. His voice was flat, matter-of-fact, his eyes never leaving his book.

"Ad-dicted. Remember how I said it's hard for addicts to stop?"

"Yeah."

"Well, she started drinking again, and this time, she drank so much alcohol it poisoned her body and messed up her brain."

"But why? Why did she do it?" asked Pete. "I thought Miss Diana was helping her get better."

"Diana has been a good friend. She still goes to see Mom every week, but addiction is powerful. Mom didn't think she could live without the alcohol."

"Will she ever get better?" asked Joey.

"Honestly, I don't know." For once, I was telling the truth. It seemed I no longer needed to protect my brothers with half-truths and fabrications. They were growing up.

Maybe my brothers' acceptance of Mom's condition was because they were feeling safe and relatively content in their new home. They liked their school, and each had made more than one special friend there.

They had fewer friends at the shelter. Every afternoon they hurried through their homework, so they could play on the back porch. It was still too cold outside to spend more than a few minutes in the backyard, but Selima had converted the screened-in porch into a small playroom. She explained that some years before, a donor gifted money to refurbish the back porch as a play area. The Historic Society agreed to approve the project if she didn't change the footprint of the house or the outside appearance. With the grant money, Selima hired a contractor to enclose and insulate the area that was twice as large as the front porch.

A double-wide window overlooked the backyard. It was covered with wire but still let in plenty of light. A door led to the rear steps. Another wire cage protected its window. A nearby church had provided a few used tricycles and other ride-on toys for toddlers and a small basketball hoop for older kids. A collapsible basket held balls, made of soft material, in various sizes and colors.

CB 80

I completed nearly a dozen work applications. Finally, toward the end of February, I started getting calls for interviews. I worried the interviewers would question my age, investigate my background, and turn me over to the police. To appear as mature as possible, I cut my hair to shoulder-length and practiced copying Mom's hairdo and makeup. Perhaps foolishly, I was relying on the fact that I looked older than my age and Mom looked younger than her forty years, especially in her license photo which was probably ten years old.

My new friend, Gloria, was applying for jobs, too, and we planned to ride the Metro together whenever the time came for us to actually "dress for success."

Gloria was in her late twenties with two adorable girls, ages four and six. She was short—maybe five feet—with shiny, long, black hair and dark eyes with long lashes. Originally from Mexico, she told me she had escaped an abusive relationship. Her English was understandable, but she was more comfortable speaking Spanish. Since I had taken a couple years of Spanish in school, we communicated well enough to form a friendship.

We were watching our kids in the playroom after school the day Gloria finally confided in me. She told me about escaping from an abusive father, followed by a hasty romance and relocation to Texas with her American husband. Unfortunately, he also turned out to be abusive and that led to another escape when her youngest child, Isabella, was barely three. "I am afraid he will beat mis hijos—my childs—like he beats me. I not know about antecedentes criminales. Because he is mucho handsome and say sweet words to me, I fall in love."

"So, he was a criminal?"

"Si, presidiario. How you say? Yailbird."

"A convict?"

"Si. Two times, he be in prison for ah, robando... but I not know this when I marry him. I trust him because I must leave mi padre." After hearing Gloria's story, I began to think maybe my past year hadn't been so bad, after all.

"How did you end up in DC?" I asked. She responded with the sign for hitchhiking.

"You hitched all the way from Texas?"

"Si, en autobús."

"With two little kids?"

"Si. Take many weeks. I have, ah, parientes aqui... tía y tío."

"You have an aunt and uncle in DC?"

"Si, but no find."

"You came all this way, but you haven't been able to locate your relatives?"

"No. I look, but no exíto. Maybe they move."

"How awful! I'm sorry, Gloria."

"Is okay. My childs and me are safe. Now, I need work."

"Me, too. Have you gotten any calls yet?"

"Si. Burger King and mailing store."

"That's great. I have an interview at a telemarketing company." From what I had heard about telemarketing, there was no worse job, but with commissions, it paid well. "I can't turn down any offer."

The next day, Gloria and I rode the subway to the Dress-for-Success site. The women who helped us were friendly and respectful. My consultant, Anita, said she couldn't believe I was mother to six- and eight-year-olds. By this time, I had gotten used to explaining my youthful appearance. I laughed and told her I had married young.

Anita outfitted me with a black, polyester pantsuit and two blouses—one in white and one in red. She said these combinations would make me look confident. I thought they made me look frumpy. "It's perfect," I said, as I modeled in front of the full-length mirror. Yeah, perfect. I look like Mom.

I discovered I had dropped a size and now wore a six. That was fine, but I didn't plan to lose any more weight, especially if it required being homeless and hungry. When I mentioned I didn't own any shoes—other than the sneakers on my feet—Anita sent me to another room where I tried on numerous black pumps before selecting a pair that looked stylish—for a forty-year-old.

After trying on several outfits, Gloria settled on a pretty, green dress that made her dark eyes sparkle, and some brown slacks she could wear with a top of any color, whenever jeans were too informal.

The dress made her five-foot frame appear taller.

Not only did these advisers understand work-place design, but they succeeded in making their nonpaying clients feel valued, even pampered. Carefully, they wrapped our "purchases" in tissue paper, placed them in unmarked shopping bags and sent us on our way with their best wishes.

Barely a year earlier, I would have considered a two-hundred-dollar prom dress to be an absolute wardrobe-necessity. Now, I was grateful for my used, donated suit in a style I'd never gravitate toward. I couldn't wait to tell Lori about my positive experience, and I looked forward to trying out my used career outfit that made me look mature and confident.

As quickly as Joey and Pete were growing, they would need new clothes soon. I decided to step up my job-search. Surely, I could find something more appealing than telemarketing. I knew I would lose my mind if I had to sit in a cubicle all day and talk on the phone.

Only two blocks from the boys' school, a group of us "moms" walked our kids together every morning and met them each afternoon. Starting the following Monday, I decided, I would make as many follow-up visits as I could fit into a school day. Wearing my power-suit, I followed up on every application. If the business wasn't located within walking distance, I took the subway. Selima kept a supply of donated Metro passes for that purpose.

My strategy worked. By Wednesday, I had heard from six Human Resources managers who wanted to schedule interviews. Fortunately, I didn't have to accept the telemarketing offer because I landed a job with Macy's as an entry-level sales representative. For references, I provided Selima, Lori, and Mom's former supervisor at Kmart in Williamsburg. Recalling that my mother was sober then, I cherished the memories of our last Christmas together.

Macy's hired me. Starting with a brief training period, I would work in the beautiful, modern store downtown. The hours were eight a.m. to five p.m. with an hour off for lunch. I explained the need to be home for my "sons" after school and asked if I could work through lunch and leave at four. Mr. Roberts, the Human Resources manager, said it would be fine if I took my two ten-minute breaks. He asked if I could start the following Monday, adding that I would need to be available one Saturday each month. "Will that be a problem?" he asked.

"No. Not at all," I said. Of course, it would be a problem, but I couldn't afford to turn down a job, even if it had nothing to do with my career aspirations. Maybe, if I worked hard, I could advance to a better position where I could start to save for college. In the meantime, I needed to support my family.

The next time I met with Lori, I told her about my new job and asked for her advice about how to manage the hours while dealing with the boys' schedule.

"Their school offers a care program both before and after school. There are supervised activities in the gym, and they even provide help with homework. Many of the working moms take advantage of it."

"Is there a cost?" I asked.

"There's a small charge, but, now that you have a job, you should be able to afford it."

"That sounds perfect," I said. "I'll stop by the school tomorrow and register the boys. What about the one Saturday a month I'll have to work?"

"I recommend you barter services with another mother. You can offer to watch her kids on your day off in exchange for her helping you out." Lori was a wealth of information. She seemed to have the answer to any question I could pose. I hoped Gloria would be willing to swap childcare with me.

Then, there was the issue of work clothes. I had forgotten to ask Mr. Roberts if jeans were appropriate for sales reps. If so, I could do some mixing-and-matching for the first couple of weeks, but then I'd need to buy a few more outfits for work. It seemed I had spent my first minimum-wage paycheck before payday arrived.

While I dreaded the thought of uprooting my brothers again— now that they had a home, a school, and friends—I wasn't ready to give up our objective of returning to Williamsburg. I was prepared to beg Selima to let us stay at least until I earned my GED, until I could qualify for a higher paying job. I reasoned that if I maintained this ruse until I turned eighteen, we'd be able to go home, where I could land a better job, take care of Mom, and assume legal custody of my brothers.

Contrary to my moral fiber and personal integrity, living a lie went against everything I believed. Yet, I convinced myself it was the only way to assure the survival of my brothers and me. No way would I risk ending up on the street again. While Pete and Joey seemed to have settled comfortably into our false identities, I remained in a state of high-alert.

As April—and my eighteenth birthday—approached, I wondered if I dared trust Lori with the truth about my identity. It would be the only way to earn my high school diploma. Soon, Selima would ask if I had received my birth certificate from Richmond. At some point, I'd be obligated to divulge my true identity. But I worried Selima would kick us out of the shelter if she found out I lied. I worried that Mr. Roberts would fire me for falsely representing myself.

Chapter 32

My first week working full-time exhausted both me and the boys. After dropping them off at school at seven-thirty, an hour earlier than usual, and riding the subway to Metro Center, I had a short walk to Macy's building on G Street. I spent the mornings in Macy's orientation program where I learned about the store's policies and safety guidelines, the location of each department, how to use the phone system and cash registers, and how to work with customers. Each afternoon, I shadowed a different department head. Then, I returned to Metro Station and rode the subway to pick up the boys from their after-school care. I was relieved not to be scheduled for work on the weekend. That first Saturday the three of us were so tired we slept through breakfast.

Once I completed my training, Mr. Roberts assigned me to the menswear department on the second floor, which meant I still had a lot to learn. I had already shadowed Rita, the supervisor, for an afternoon, so, I knew where everything was located. But I had no concept of men's sizes or styles. Rita was a patient teacher, but I decided to do some research on my own.

Each evening, while the boys completed their homework, I went online and found Macy's website. Carefully studying the variety of clothing offered in the men's department, I learned about sportswear, suits and suit separates, jeans, shirts, pants, sweaters, underwear, outerwear, socks and belts. By the third week, I had become comfortable with Macy's selection of men's clothing, including styles, fabrics, sizes, and prices.

Something, or rather someone, made me uncomfortable, however. A young man, maybe twenty or twenty-one, started hanging around the department. He would show up a few afternoons a week and stare at me when he thought I wasn't looking. Average-looking with dark hair, he stood only a few inches taller than my five-foot-four stature and wore dark-rimmed glasses that framed his brown eyes. Occasionally he asked questions about the merchandise or purchased a pair of socks. Finally, one day he got up the nerve to ask me out for coffee. He introduced himself as Scott Campbell and said he was a student at George Washington U. He seemed nice enough, but I turned him down. I simply didn't have time for a relationship.

Hoping to buy some clothes for the boys, I was counting on my first paycheck. But, by the time the government took its share and I gave ten percent to Harmony House, little was left of my meager wages. Even with the employee discount, I couldn't afford to shop at Macy's.

Receiving that first paycheck reminded me of something else. The IRS would soon expect a tax return from the real Elizabeth Jordan. I had no idea how to fill out a tax form. Until then, I hadn't thought much about the legal ramifications of assuming my mother's identity, but now I realized that lying to the IRS could have serious consequences. Reuben had acquired disability benefits for Mom and arranged for her long-term care, but I couldn't continue to ignore the bills that Mindy said arrived daily.

As a child, I remember thinking how much easier life would be when I finally grew up. Now that I had been forced to assume grown-up responsibilities at the age of seventeen, I was beginning to appreciate those unencumbered years of childhood.

In the meantime, the boys and I needed clothes. So, we celebrated my second paycheck by finding a Salvation Army store.

Pete had already outgrown his winter coat, and his school pants looked more like knickers. Of course, Joey inherited Pete's few cast-offs, but he needed school clothes, too. After spending fifty dollars on clothes and shoes for the boys, my second paycheck was nearly gone. I promised myself I would start saving for college as soon as I could. Determined to work hard and prove myself a valuable Macy's employee, I intended to earn a raise and advance as far up the retail ladder as possible.

◌◌

I was finding it increasingly stressful to live with the guilt of deception. Not only had I assumed my mother's name, but I was using her social security number and driver's license. Some online research indicated that identity theft is a felony. A conviction could result in up to three years of incarceration. What had started as a means of preserving my family unit could end up separating us.

April third came without fanfare. Mindy called to wish me a happy birthday, but the boys were unaware that their fake mom had turned eighteen. That morning, Selima asked me to stop by her office after dinner.

Nervous about why Selima wanted to talk to me, I hardly ate my dinner. When I finally knocked on her office door, I could feel my heart pounding against my ribcage. "Give me courage to do the right thing, whatever the outcome," I prayed. At the time, I wasn't aware that the focus of my prayers had changed. I think it was the first time I asked God for something other than my own selfish needs.

"Come in," Selima called from inside her office. Working to remain calm, I opened the door.

"Have a seat." I sat stiffly on the edge of the chair in front of her desk, recalling the first time I had occupied that chair, how relieved I was to have found shelter, how scared I was that my secret might be discovered, that we might be turned away.

"How are things going?" Selima asked. "How's that job?"

"The job is fine, thanks, and living here has been wonderful for the boys and me." My insides quivered, and I hoped my fear wasn't visible. "Everyone has been friendly and helpful. I'm very grateful."

"I'm glad you and the boys have settled in nicely. I need to discuss something with you." My hands twisted in my lap and now one knee was bouncing up and down despite my efforts to control it.

"Okay," I said. Resting her forearms on the desk and entwining her fingers, Selima stared directly into my eyes. I wanted to stand and run from the room. But I knew it was time. I couldn't live a lie any longer. I decided to trust that, no matter what Selima said, I would apologize, ask for forgiveness, and accept the consequences. I was learning to place my confidence in God's will.

"Is there anything you'd like to tell me?"

"Well. Um, you see," I started. I could feel the blood rushing to my cheeks. Selima continued to wait patiently for me to speak. "Okay, here's the thing. I haven't been completely honest with you."

"In what way?"

"In every way." I lowered my eyes in shame. As the tears started to pour down my cheeks, the words poured from my mouth. Not once did Selima interrupt me. She listened as I told her about my false identity and how my "sons" were really my brothers. I told her about our father dying, and about Mom's drinking, and about losing our home and our belongings and living in a motel, and about Mom's hospitalization, and about the women from Child Protective Services, and about living in our car, and traveling to DC only to find no shelter. My story flowed faster than my tears, and I wondered if I'd drown in the burden of it. Once I got started, everything spilled out until it seemed like I couldn't breathe. "I'm sorry I lied, Selima. You've been so wonderful and caring and... all I could think about was keeping us together." As Selima's eyebrows lifted, her back straightened to meet the back of the chair, and she placed her hands in her lap.

Despite my efforts to regain control, I grew hysterical. "I know it was wrong, and I know I could go to jail. You have every right to report me and to kick us out." I was sobbing so miserably I didn't notice when Selima rose from her desk. She sat beside me, handed me a box of tissues, and gently placed her hand on my arm.

"Are you finished, Abigail?"

"Yes. I... what?" Suddenly, I stopped shuddering and looked at her in disbelief. I had never mentioned my real name.

"How did you know? I mean, how long have you known?"

"I wasn't born yesterday, Abigail. I've been around a while and heard a lot of stories. From the first day, I suspected you weren't old enough to be the mother of Pete and Joey. I always do my research. After all, I can't risk the security of the women and children in this shelter, can I?"

"No. Of course not, but..." I helped myself to a tissue, blew my nose and wiped my salty face. "So, you knew everything from the beginning?"

"Well, it took a couple weeks to confirm my suspicions, but yes, I've known for a while."

"Why didn't you tell me? Why didn't you report me?" She took hold of my shoulders and turned me toward her.

"Actually, I did. I had to, you see. Otherwise I could have lost my job. I would have risked being blackballed from getting another job. I could even have been arrested."

"But why did you let me continue..."

"By the time women make it to our shelter, most have been to hell and back. They have children to raise and no means of support. Some have survived abuse at the hands of the system and others at the hands of a man. It takes desperation, but also great courage and humility to ask for help.

"I noticed how dedicated you were to your brothers, to providing a decent life for them. I watched as you sacrificed your own well-being to make sure they were cared for, as you disciplined them with patience and fairness, teaching them manners and life skills, as you enrolled them in school and after-school care, as you worked hard to get a job and support them. I've seen how much they love, respect, and trust you. As I gathered the facts, I contacted CPS in Williamsburg."

"You did?"

"I was pretty sure you and your brothers were runaways and that someone would be looking for you. Did you know the FBI had been called in to investigate?"

"The FBI? You've got to be kidding." I couldn't believe what I was hearing. I couldn't believe I wasn't sitting in a jail cell.

As a shelter director, I'm bound by strict rules and regulations. If I got caught harboring runaways from another jurisdiction, I would be in serious trouble. Together, we formed what's called an ICPC."

"What's that?" I felt dizzy. I couldn't seem to process what she was saying.

"It stands for Interstate Compact on Placement of Children. It's a legally binding document for ensuring the safety and stability of child placements across state lines."

"Are you going to turn me in?"

"Abigail, there's no need. I've been in regular contact with CPS both in Williamsburg and in DC. I've talked to the administrators at Lafayette High School, and I've kept up with your mother's situation—the real Elizabeth Jordan, that is."

"What? You have? Why didn't you say something? Why didn't you turn me in?"

"I convinced the social workers that you are an exceptional young woman who has proven herself fully capable of caring for her brothers, even under the worst circumstances. When I reported your whereabouts to CPS and explained how well you were doing here at the shelter, they appointed me as your temporary guardian—you and your brothers—until you turned eighteen. By the way, happy birthday, Abigail."

I grabbed Selima and hugged her tighter than I had hugged anyone ever. She had saved my life. She had preserved my family. She had believed in me and advocated for me. She had risked her job for me. I realized I could never fully repay her kindness or her trust.

"Okay," she choked. "I'd like to breathe now."

"Oh. Sorry," I said, releasing her from my bear hug. "I'm just so grateful. I can never thank you enough for everything you've done. I should have trusted God from the beginning."

"You can thank me—and God—by making something of your life, by giving back to other young women who find themselves in impossible situations like your own."

"I will. I promise." I hugged her once more, less intensely this time. I started to open the door, then turned back to face Selima. "Can you give me a few weeks to find an apartment?"

"No, dear."

My heart had been floating in the clouds. Now it sank with a thud at my feet. I lowered my head in disappointment. "Oh. Okay. I'll go pack."

Selima grasped my shoulders again, her eyes locking onto mine. "Haven't you been listening?"

"What?" I didn't understand what she was saying.

"Abigail, you and your brothers are welcome to stay here as long as you need. Lori and I will do everything in our power to help you graduate, achieve financial independence, and go to college."

"Wha... What are you saying?"

"Because of your mother's condition, and because of the excellent job you've done, CPS is prepared to grant you custody of your brothers. You'll have to go to court to make it legal, but that's just a formality."

I wasn't sure I could handle any more jerking back and forth from dejection to euphoria. Selima's words seemed too amazing to comprehend. But gradually, I was learning to praise God in all conditions, to trust God's design instead of pressing forward stubbornly with my own plans. Through the hardships I never could have anticipated, God was revealing His mercy and nudging me toward a personal relationship with Him.

"We can stay?" I asked, incredulous.

"For as long as you need."

"Thank you, Lord! Thank you, Selima! I won't let you down." I started to hug her again, but she held me at arm's length.

"I don't think my ribcage can take any more of your gratitude," she said, smiling. I was so filled with gratitude, I didn't know what to do with my hands. I threw them in the air, then covered my mouth, discovering it was agape. I wrung them in front of me, then ran them through my hair, finally allowing the reality of Selima's words to sink into my overwrought brain. More than nervous energy or surprise, my response expressed overwhelming awareness of God's grace and Selima's kindness.

"I have to tell my brothers." After Selima shooed me out of her office, I climbed the creaky stairs of the incredible facility known as Harmony House, and just kept whispering, "Thank you, thank you, thank you."

Chapter 33

With some tutoring, I earned my GED by June. Then, Lori helped me find all manner of scholarships and financial aid to attend college. I was surprised to find that poor people could qualify for so much assistance. By September, I was taking online courses to prepare for college. If I earned straight As, American University would admit me in January, and I wouldn't have to set foot on the campus.

I continued to work at Macy's, but now I was Abigail Jordan, using my own Social Security number. When I asked Lori for advice on how to confess to Mr. Roberts, she suggested I write him a letter explaining my situation and asking him to give me a chance to prove myself. "That way, you can be sure to come across as mature, stable, and committed to becoming a good employee," Lori said. She also cautioned me not to mention that Selima was aware of my identity when I applied to Macy's. "Selima has stuck her neck out for you, Abigail. She could lose her job or worse."

"I know, but why? Why would she risk everything for me?"

"She saw something different, something special in you."

"But I lied. I tried to deceive her."

"Even so, she thought you were worth the gamble."

"Everyone in the shelter is worthy of a second chance," I said. "I'm learning that from my Bible-reading."

"Absolutely, but not everyone shows potential for making something of herself and contributing to society. That's what she saw in you. You owe her a lot."

"I owe her my life."

Concerned that I'd break down in front of Mr. Roberts like I had with Selima, I took Lori's advice and wrote that letter. Mr. Roberts had every right to fire me on the spot. He could also have me arrested. But I was learning to trust my future to God. Gradually, my prayers had evolved from the self-centered cry, "Help me" to a more mature, "Help me accept your will."

I had finished reading the New Testament Gospels and realized I was ready to turn my life and my will over to the Lord. Like Saul on the road to Emmaus, I had met the living Jesus on the road to Harmony House.

When Mr. Roberts called me into his office, Rita, my supervisor, had already given me an excellent review. Later, I discovered she had begged him to keep me in her department. Mr. Roberts said that while he didn't condone my dishonesty, he understood the extreme circumstances that had prompted it. To my immense relief, he gave me a month's probationary period.

CจBO

By that first November, the boys and I decided it was time to visit Mom. I had saved enough money to buy our train tickets, and I took off nearly the whole week of Thanksgiving, promising Rita I'd return in time for Black Friday. Facing our negative memories associated with Union Station, we showed up at Gate B and boarded the train for Williamsburg.

As we traveled by rail once again, the three of us talked about the events that had brought us to that point. We couldn't believe how much our lives had changed since the day we first learned of our father's illness.

I apologized to my brothers for subjecting them to the dangers of running away and asked for their forgiveness.

"But we had to leave," Pete said.

"It's okay," said Joey. "You took care of us."

Their responses were more evidence of God's grace. They had every right to hate me for what I had put them through.

After my meeting with Selima, I told Pete and Joey they could go back to calling me Abby, but they had gotten used to thinking of me as their mother. They continued to call me Mom.

"Mom?" Joey said as our train passed through Richmond. "Do you think our real mother remembers us?"

"According to Diana, she says our names sometimes."

"Do you think she'll know us?"

"I don't know, Joey. I hope so, but don't expect too much."

Then, Pete asked, "Does she look different?"

"Remember? I told you she had a couple of strokes after they moved her to the convalescent center. One side of her body is paralyzed. She can't walk, and she can't carry on a conversation. Diana sent me a picture. Would you like to see it?"

"Yeah," they both answered. I hadn't shown them the photograph because I knew it would upset them, but now it seemed important to prepare them for what they were about to face. I removed the photo from my wallet and warned them our mother looked very different, much older and maybe even a little scary.

"That's not Mommy," said Joey, turning his face away.

"Wow," was all Pete could say.

"She's been very sick," I explained. "And now the doctors are sure she won't get better."

"Not ever?" Pete asked.

"Probably not."

"So, we'll never live with her again?" Joey asked.

"I'm afraid not, buddy." I placed my hand on top of his. "You see, she needs special care."

"Like nurses and stuff?"

"Yes."

"Is it okay to feel sad about Mommy?"

"Of course. I feel sad, too. It's like our mother died, isn't it?"

"Yeah." He turned his head toward the window and stared at the trees whizzing by.

"Does that make us orphans?" Pete asked.

"Well, no because... now you have me, and I'm your legal guardian. You'll always have me. I'll never leave you. I promise."

"But you'll get married someday and have kids of your own," said Joey, rejoining the conversation. "Then you won't want us around."

"That's not going to happen for a long time. If I get married before you two are grown and on your own, you'll live with my husband and me. Hey, how about some lunch from the café car?"

"Can we afford it?" asked Pete.

"Absolutely."

"Yay! Let's go."

CRWD

Mrs. Trent had invited us to spend Thanksgiving week at her house, and she met us at the station in Williamsburg. Mindy was due to arrive from Ohio State the next day, and, although she and I had stayed in regular contact, I looked forward to seeing her for the first time in many months.

Like Union Station, the tiny train station in Williamsburg evoked unpleasant memories. As we walked to Mrs. Trent's car, I found myself scanning the parking lot for our old, blue Chevy. I wondered where it was and whether I should try to retrieve it. I recalled how cold we were and how scared we felt. I realized I had been foolish and immature to run away.

Brendan and Bella greeted us inside the Trent's front door. I noticed Brendan had grown several inches taller, but so had Pete.

Although Bella had slowed down since our last visit, she was every bit as enthusiastic to see us as we were to see her. The boys tripped over each other trying to get to her, and she allowed them to smother her with hugs and scratch her belly.

The Trents had already decorated their house for Christmas. They went all-out with lights, garlands, table and mantle decorations, and the most beautiful tree I had ever seen. The entire house smelled amazing. The inviting scent was a combination of evergreen needles, cinnamon, and whatever concoction bubbled in the crockpot.

Mrs. Trent headed for the kitchen, and the boys took off for Brendan's room to play video games. For a moment, I stood frozen in the front room, staring at the spectacular ornaments. With a warm fire glowing in the fireplace and lights twinkling everywhere, it resembled a scene from the Hallmark Christmas specials Mom and I used to binge-watch every Saturday between Halloween and Christmas.

I remembered our previous Christmas in the motel, the tiny tree from Kmart and the few, simple gifts we gave each other. Mom was sober then, and, while she must have been struggling with her demons, she did her best to make the day special for her children.

"Abby, how about giving me a hand?" Mrs. Trent called from the kitchen.

"Of course," I said, draping my coat over a chair. "You're so kind to let us stay here while we're in town."

"Not at all. You and your brothers are always welcome." She gathered ingredients from the refrigerator, handed them to me and motioned for me to place them on the counter. "And, besides, Mindy would never forgive me if you weren't here when she got home. Why don't you take her car and pick her up at the airport tomorrow?"

"Don't you want to do that? I'm not sure I even remember how to drive."

"You'll be fine. How about stirring the green beans in the crockpot?"

I took a wooden spoon from the spoon rest and a potholder from the drawer. As I lifted the lid cautiously to let the steam escape, the pleasant aroma of ham and beans floated through the air.

"Her plane arrives at four-fifteen in Richmond. I think you two need some time together without three boys hanging around."

"Well, okay. If you're sure." I stirred the beans, returned the spoon to its resting place, and re-covered the pot.

"I thought Brad and I would take the boys to Christmas Town at Busch Gardens. That is, unless you want us to wait for you girls."

"No. I'd rather catch up with Mindy. Pete and Joey'll be thrilled, though. How much are the tickets?"

"It's our treat. Brad gets a big discount, so it's quite affordable."

"Thanks so much. I don't think Joey has ever been, and Pete was pretty young the one time our family went."

In a large bowl, she mixed ground beef and eggs with bread crumbs and spices. Now her expression became serious. "Abby, when do you want to visit your mom?"

"I was thinking Tuesday or Wednesday."

"I should warn you, she's in bad shape. She may not even recognize you."

"I know. Diana has kept me informed. I've tried to prepare the boys, but I don't even trust my reaction. It's going to be hard to see her that way."

As we worked together preparing dinner, Mrs. Trent shared the details of Mom's steady decline since suffering the first stroke. She explained how Reuben had gotten Social Security Disability to cover her long-term care and how our church had rallied to help once they finally learned what happened.

"Someone from your mom's circle visits her every week, and one of the pastors goes often, too. Hand me that casserole dish, will you?"

"I'm grateful for the way the community has supported her. If only she could have reached out earlier. I realize now that shame and embarrassment kept her isolated, kept all of us isolated. Who knows, maybe she wouldn't have sunk so low if she'd allowed our friends and neighbors to get involved."

"Pride is a powerful motivator, Abby. There's a Bible verse, from Proverbs that says, 'Pride goeth before a fall.' I think it's a warning to guard against arrogance and too much self-sufficiency."

"Mom wasn't arrogant or self-sufficient. If anything, she lacked confidence in her ability to handle life."

"Shame is a form of pride. Hand me the salt and pepper, and how about setting the table?" Mrs. Trent had always amazed me with her ability to work and talk without skipping a beat of either task. She placed the aluminum-wrapped potatoes in the oven and spooned the meatloaf into a greased casserole dish. "Your Mom thought if she asked for help, she would lose her dignity and expose her shortcomings. As much as she loved you children, her fear of losing face was too strong for her to admit powerlessness."

"If she could've kept going to AA, she would've learned that lesson. She chose self-medication, instead. Sometimes I resent her for it. Is that terrible, Mrs. Trent?"

"Honey, you and your brothers have been through hell because of your mother's addiction. It's normal to feel resentful, but if you keep praying for her, you'll be able to forgive her someday."

"Shall I use the everyday dishes?"

"Yes. I'm saving the good china for Thanksgiving Day. They're in the... you know where they are."

"I hope I can forgive her," I said as I pulled a stack of dinner plates from the cabinet. "She really was a wonderful mother until... well, you know."

"I know, dear. I know. Let me pop this meatloaf in the oven. Then, we can sit by the fire with a cup of coffee." It felt so good to be in her familiar kitchen, one that I had known since kindergarten. Mindy's mom had always been like a second mother to me. She had welcomed me into her home and made me feel like a member of the family.

"That sounds great," I said. I set the table while she made the coffee.

CB&O

"Now, let's revisit the subject of pride for a minute," Mrs. Trent said, when we settled across from each other on matching, floral sofas that framed the gas fireplace. "Then, I promise not to bring it up again." As the fire bathed us in its warmth, I reveled in the happy sounds of play coming from Brendan's room upstairs. But I braced myself for what I was about to hear.

"Okay," I said, guardedly, "I'm listening." As Mrs. Trent stirred cream into her cup, I took a sip of the strong, hot coffee.

"Is it possible that false pride is hereditary, Abby?"

"What do you mean?"

"Well, it seems to me Liz wasn't the only one who let her pride stand in the way of seeking help. You could've used some help last winter, too. You could've spared yourself and your brothers unnecessary suffering if you had reached out instead of…"

"But…"

"Hear me out. Okay? You know Brad and I would've gladly welcomed the three of you into our home."

"Of course, but you had already taken Bella, and…"

"Instead of allowing others the chance to get involved, you ran away and placed yourself and your brothers in danger. You lied about your identity and swore your best friend to secrecy, even from her parents." Feeling the sting of her words, I lowered my mug to a coaster and gave in to remorseful tears. I knew she was right. I had no excuse for my actions… no viable excuse, anyway.

"I was so scared," I said. "But you're right. I didn't think it through. At the time, I couldn't see any other options."

Mrs. Trent set her mug down, walked around the coffee table, and sat beside me. She wiped my tears with the end of her apron and placed an arm around my shoulders, wrapping me in her love. "You don't need to end up like your mom, Abby. That's all I'm saying. Don't ever be too proud to ask for help. None of us is meant to walk alone through this life. If we can't share our needs with each other and help each other through the rough times, then life doesn't have much meaning. I think God designed humans with a hunger for connection."

"You're right," I sniffed. "I know you're right, and I've learned so much in the last few months. Mainly, I've learned that, through it all, God was with me. Even when I felt the most alone and afraid, God sent people—human angels—to watch over us and minister to us."

"It sounds like you've learned from your mistakes and done a whole heap of growing up. Now let's get dinner on the table before Brad walks through the door and three hungry boys descend on us."

We stood and hugged. "Thank you, Missus Trent," I said. "Thank you for everything."

"Oh, and one more thing." She held me at arm's length, her eyes smiling. "Now that you're an adult, how about calling me Lisa?"

"Thank you, Lisa." She took my hand and led me back to her beautiful kitchen with the shiny, granite countertops and sparkly backsplash, a kitchen that emanated appetizing aromas and had always been filled with enough love to share.

Chapter 34

As much as I wanted Bella to climb in bed with me, I knew the boys needed her nuzzles more than I did. I laughed when Pete, Joey and Brendan divided our visit into thirds and assigned Bella to a schedule, which they claimed was the only fair means of sharing her attention. Since I was not included on the Bella-sleep-schedule, I volunteered to walk her twice a day. Unlike when she lived with us, she was ready to turn around immediately after taking care of business. I felt sad when I multiplied her thirteen dog-years by seven and realized she was an old lady who likely wouldn't be around much longer.

After spending the night in Mindy's familiar bed with the comfortable mattress and cozy, down-filled pillows, I was more anxious than ever to see my best friend. We had a lot of catching up to do. Yet I wondered how much to share with her about the months of our separation. I was such a different person. In the brief span of a year, I had passed through some deep waters and returned transformed. Mindy still lived in her perfect, cookie-cutter world. I questioned whether she could relate to the events I had experienced.

The forty-five-minute drive to Richmond International Airport seemed endless, but with a gusty November wind and the usual high volume of traffic on the interstate, I didn't dare exceed the speed limit.

Mindy's plane landed on time, and as soon as I saw her emerge from the gate, my tension dissipated. We rushed into each other's arms, hugged and squealed with abandon. We didn't care what any onlookers might think.

"Abby, you're so thin," she exclaimed after hugging me for the third time. "Are you okay?"

"Don't worry. Your mom's cooking will have me fattened up by the end of the week."

"And you look older, more mature, somehow. Oh, Abby! It's so good to see you!" She sounded like a gushing thirteen-year-old. I hardly knew how to act with my life-long, best friend.

After we reached the parking garage and loaded Mindy's luggage into the trunk, I handed her the keys. "I'm sure you've missed Marilyn Monroe more than you've missed me, so you can drive her home." Mindy had named her Pontiac Sunfire for the sexy actress after she and I watched *Gentlemen Prefer Blondes* on Netflix. She thought the pale, yellow color reminded her of Monroe's hair.

"Just think, next semester Marilyn gets to go to college with me," she called over the roof. "It'll be good to have a car on campus."

She entered the driver's side, and clicking her seatbelt into place, asked, "So, you started school?"

"Not exactly," I said, settling into the passenger seat. "I earned my General Education Diploma, plus some extra credits during the summer. I'm in the process of applying to American University, but I need a few more courses before they'll consider my application. I'm taking two more on-line courses this fall and I hope to start in January."

"That's terrific!"

"I went for an interview and because of my situation, you know, with Mom and raising my brothers and all, I should qualify for financial assistance. Like I told you on the phone, I'm working at Macy's, but I'll need loans and grants to pay for college."

Once we were back on I-64, heading east, I said, "Mindy, I need to apologize to you for something."

"What are you talking about?"

"I never should have asked you to keep our whereabouts a secret, especially from your parents."

"You didn't, silly. You never told me where you were."

"That's right. I didn't." We laughed and finally fell into our comfortable stride. It was almost like old times—the times before Dad's illness, that is.

"Now, start at the beginning and don't leave out anything," Mindy said, and I did. We talked all the way home. I told her about living in our car at the railroad station and hiding in the bushes from the cops. We talked in the supermarket as we checked off items on her mom's grocery list. I told her about riding the train to DC and sleeping in Union Station, then spending the day outside in the cold, sleeping on the subway and getting kicked off at midnight. We talked in her room as she unpacked. That's when she heard about us sleeping on the street. She stopped what she was doing, sat on her bed, and began to weep.

"Here I was thinking you were having this great adventure," she sniffed. "You made it sound like you and your brothers were fine." I sat beside her and she laid her head on my shoulder.

"I know. I should've been honest with you, but I was afraid you'd betray my confidence if you knew the truth."

"I would have," she said, wiping her eyes on her sleeve.

"Do you want me to stop?"

"No. Go on and don't leave out anything."

"Even if it makes you cry?"

"Even if it makes me cry." We talked until three tired, happy boys returned from Busch Gardens at nine p.m. Then, after the boys were tucked in for the night, we talked in her bed until two a.m.

"Pete and Joey call you 'Mom.' What's that about?" asked Mindy at one point. I explained how I trained them to act like I was their mother, so we could get into a shelter. Then I told her about Harmony House, how I impersonated Mom, and how I lived in fear of being kicked out or even arrested. In Mindy's darkened room, I couldn't see her face, but I heard her sniffling. She rolled toward me and held me tightly.

"Oh, Abby. I'm so sorry."

"It's okay," I assured her. "We're okay now."

We fell asleep like that, wrapped in each other's arms.

⚜

The next morning, we weren't ready to get up, but that didn't stop the boys from pushing Bella into Mindy's room at seven o'clock, her paws sliding along the hardwood floor. "Time for my walk," said Pete in a high-pitched voice from outside the door.

"Wake up, Mommy," added Joey in his own version of Bella's voice. "I need to go outside." This ventriloquism act was followed by giggles, padding footsteps, and a slamming door. With a groan, Bella plopped down on the rug beside Mindy's bed and waited.

"I'll get the coffee," said Mindy.

We bundled up and strolled through her neighborhood of stately, brick homes with their columned porticos and perfectly manicured yards. The cloudy sky threatened rain or snow, and the frigid morning air made me shiver. I couldn't help but think about the many homeless people in DC and other cities who had no other option but to live on the street, whatever the conditions. Lord, please show me what I can do to relieve the suffering, I prayed quietly.

"What did you say?" asked Mindy through the scarf she had wrapped around her neck and face.

"Oh, nothing. I was just praying," I said.

"Praying? When did you start praying?"

I explained how God had revealed His loving presence to me while we were on the run. I told her how He had sent people to help us along the way; how these 'angels' had appeared just when we needed them. "I've learned to recognize God's voice," I said. "It was a gradual process that brought me to a new faith experience."

"You mean like a conversion?"

"Not exactly because we went to church and Sunday school when I was younger."

"I know. We used to go together."

"Right. We had a basic religious foundation, but this is different."

Chapter 35

The next day we went to see Mom. As Mindy pulled Marilyn Monroe into the nursing home's parking lot, I was a nervous wreck, and I could tell the boys were uneasy. Of course, we wanted to see her, but not in her current condition. Not knowing what to expect, I said a prayer, asking for courage. Would she be able to communicate with us? Would she even know who we were?

Diana met us at the front desk of the pleasant facility. The floors were shiny, and the walls looked freshly painted, but I detected a faint smell of urine. Beyond the reception area, elderly folks in wheelchairs lined the walls. I noticed a small library to my left and straight ahead was a large room with a TV blaring.

It was wonderful to see Diana after so many months. She had changed her hair color from brown to sandy blonde, which emphasized her kind, chocolate eyes. She rushed toward us like we were her own children. I couldn't have been more grateful for Diana's continued dedication to my mother. I discovered she still visited Mom weekly. She tried to prepare us for Mom's condition, but it was shocking to see our once-vibrant, attractive mother in a wheelchair, slumped to one side, her hair now completely gray. The left side of her mouth drooped from her latest stroke, and she held her limp left arm, pulling it up with a jerk whenever it slid off her lap. She didn't seem to recognize Diana, and I wondered if she knew we were her children.

"Look who's here to see you, Liz," Diana said cheerfully, motioning us into Mom's tiny, but light-filled room.

Seeing her, or what remained of her, was even more upsetting than I had imagined. My mouth went dry, and I wanted to turn and escape from the room. As I reflect on that moment, I realize it was only God's sustaining power that kept my knees from buckling.

When Mom grunted, and stared blankly at her three children, I felt like an entire lifetime had been stolen from us. But I knew it was important to set aside my feelings and help my brothers cope. Afraid to approach her, they hid behind me. I understood their fear. This creature before us didn't resemble our mother in any way. Our beautiful, stylish mom had been replaced by a withered, gray-haired skeleton of a woman, wearing a faded, blue housecoat, drool sliding down her chin.

I worked to calm my ragged nerves and hold my tears at bay. "Why don't you guys sit over there," I said, pointing to a chair in the corner of the spare, but attractive space. I knew I needed to model acceptance of this "stranger" before I could expect my brothers to approach her.

Pete took Joey's hand and led him around the bed to the room's only chair beside the window. An aide, wearing purple scrubs was milling about the tight quarters, cleaning up from the morning's routines. Not wanting to consider what those routines involved, I knelt beside Mom's wheelchair and placed a hand on her good arm. "Hi, Mom. It's Abby." She grunted but didn't raise her head. I looked to Diana for guidance. "Can she talk at all?" I asked.

"She says words sometimes, but they're random. They don't seem to have any context. She's still getting speech therapy, also physical therapy."

"Do you think they're helping?"

"Maybe a little. It's hard to say."

I turned back to Mom whose eyes remained downcast. "Do you know who I am? It's your daughter, Abigail. Your boys are here, too. Right over there. See?" I pointed to my brothers who sat like statues, looking terrified. "Pete and Joey came to see you." Her head jiggled like a bobble-doll as her eyes followed my finger. It seemed there was some comprehension of my words but no indication that she recognized her boys. She took the tissue from her lap, and with her good hand, wiped the drool from her lower lip and chin. Not knowing what else to say, I babbled, "I like your room, Mom. It's pretty, especially the yellow curtains. This seems like a nice place. Do you like it here?" She grunted, but I couldn't tell if her answer was affirmative or negative or whether it was any response at all.

I motioned for Pete and Joey to come closer. Tentatively, they stood, but didn't make any effort to move toward us. My heart broke for them. They had seen Mom in the hospital, which was hard enough, but this creature didn't resemble our mother in any way. I waved them toward me again. "It's okay," I said. "I'm right here." God is here, too, I reminded myself.

Finally, the boys approached and stood behind me. I could feel their tension as they leaned against my back. I reached behind and, pulling them beside me, held each around his waist. "Mom," I said. "These handsome young men are your sons, Pete and Joey. Look how much they've grown. They're both doing well in school, too." I looked up at Pete and nodded. "Can you say, 'hi' to our mom?"

"Hi," he said in a tiny voice that didn't sound like my brother.

"Hi, Mommy," Joey said when I signaled him.

"We've missed you, Mom," I said, trying to sound cheerful. I noticed Mindy had taken the seat vacated by the boys. Sadness distorted her pretty face. "We've been living in DC since... well, for a while," I continued. "We have a wonderful place to stay and wonderful friends. I got a job, and I'll start college soon. Isn't that wonderful?" I remember thinking, Good grief! Can't I think of any other words besides wonderful? I wanted to be anywhere else, but I was determined to set aside my heartbreak to help my brothers feel at ease with their own mother. Why can't you at least look at them? I thought. Show your little boys you recognize them; that you remember them. But the light had disappeared from her eyes.

"Can we go now?" Pete whispered in my ear.

"We need to get going, Mom," I said as I stood, "but we'll be back." Could she even tell one day from another? Did she know where she was or how she got there? "Bye, Mom. We love you." It was a strained declaration, but I thought if I said it aloud, I might find the strength to believe it. I wondered how long it would take me to forgive her. I knew I had to. I thought I should kiss her, but I couldn't bring myself to do it. So, I patted her knee, instead. Then, I tipped my head at the boys, encouraging them to say good-bye.

"Bye, Mom," Pete said weakly.

"Yeah, bye," Joey said.

"I'll stay and eat lunch with her," Diana said, moving closer. She was smiling but her eyes radiated sorrow.

"Thank you for everything you've done, Diana," I said, as I hugged her.

"This could have been me," she said. "If it hadn't been for my sponsor..." When she started to tear up, I knew I wouldn't be able to hold it together any longer. I gave her another quick hug and turned toward the door.

"Are you ready, Mindy?" I asked. She stood and approached Mom. Hesitantly she touched Mom's shoulder.

"Good-bye, Missus Jordan. It was nice to see you."

The four of us walked to the lobby in a silent daze. Mindy signed us out at the front desk, and we donned the coats and hats we had been holding. I placed my hands on my brothers' shoulders and told them how proud I was of them. Then, I guided them through the automatic doors and tried to forget the disturbing sight we had just witnessed.

Mindy and I visited Mom again Wednesday afternoon. I decided not to put the boys through the stress of seeing her again. She still seemed to have no idea who I was. I could tell she was well cared for, but she seemed unaware of her surroundings and oblivious to the severity of her condition. Maybe that was a blessing.

Thankfully, Reuben Gray had remained Mom's case worker, successfully acquiring Social Security Disability and Medicaid to cover her care. From Diana, I learned that Reuben had managed to get all of Dad's remaining medical expenses exempted and that he was continuing to work with Mom's credit card companies to reduce the exorbitant interest charges that had mounted. Both Diana and Reuben were gifts from a benevolent God.

♋

We spent a memorable Thanksgiving Day with the Trents. Throughout the day there were moments when I was tempted to resent Mindy for the ease and privilege of her life, but ultimately, I was thankful for my spiritual awakening that wouldn't have happened without my hardships.

Mindy and I spent the morning helping her mom and dad prepare the food and set the table, both of which beckoned us. The boys and I weren't accustomed to eating much fresh meat or vegetables. At the shelter, most of our food came from cans. Infrequently, we enjoyed fruits and vegetables donated by local supermarkets, but dessert was nonexistent other than the occasional Jell-O or canned pudding.

Because it rained most of the day, the boys were stuck inside, but it didn't seem to be a problem. Pete and Joey, who insisted on wearing their new outfits, had given up their video games when we moved out of our house, making Brendan's assortment that much more appealing. Also, Brendan had a ping pong table and tons of Legos in the basement. Other than a few squabbles over whose turn it was, they played contentedly all morning, moving from the second floor to the basement and back again with Bella hobbling behind.

I couldn't help but notice how much my brothers had grown both physically and emotionally. Like me, they had seen things and experienced things Brendan couldn't even imagine. While his attention focused on his upcoming basketball season and video games like Mine Craft, Pete and Joey now viewed the world from a different, more mature perspective. At first, I felt sad that some of their childhood had been robbed from them, but when I overheard them describing Harmony House to Brendan, my sorrow changed to gratitude.

"It's not fancy like your house," Pete said. "But after we tried to sleep on the hard floor in Union Station and spent a night outside in the cold, it seemed like a palace."

"Yeah, we're used to it now," said Joey. "Some of the kids are kinda mean, but we have nice friends at school and Miss Selima is great."

No, my brothers would never be the same, but maybe like the pebbles in an oyster shell, their encounters had produced just enough irritation to create the lustrous pearls they were becoming.

Dinner with Mindy's clan was filled with delicious food and happy chatter. Her family was huge, with two sets of grandparents, numerous aunts and uncles, and seven cousins. Ten chairs surrounded the children's table, alone. Yet, Mrs. Trent seemed unaffected by the chaos. She remained calm throughout the day and even appeared at-ease with additional people tramping through her pristine house.

As memories of our own family gatherings emerged, I couldn't help but compare. Most of the time, there had been just the five of us Jordans for holiday celebrations. I wondered how differently our lives might have turned out if we had been surrounded by extended family like Mindy's. But, what was the point of speculating? It wouldn't change anything.

CABO

That evening as the boys and I rode the train back to DC, I realized there was nothing we could do for our mother and nothing we could expect from her. I recalled the Serenity Prayer from Mom's AA meetings:

God, grant me the serenity to accept the things I cannot change;
courage to change the things I can;
and the wisdom to know the difference.

I had no alternative but to accept the past and move forward with the new life we had created. For me, that life now included awareness of a loving God who, I recognized, had been with us all along. The next step was to find the strength to forgive our mother for what she had put us through, to understand that she, too, was a victim. I tried to help Pete and Joey understand how God had forgiven us and now we needed to forgive Mom. Pete said he was "really mad at Mom" for loving alcohol more than she loved us. I couldn't argue with his assessment, but I wanted him to understand that she had tried to be a good mother and that, despite the alcohol dependency, she had always loved us.

"Besides, there ain't no God," Pete said.

"Isn't any God," I corrected. "Except there is, and He loves us."

"Then why did He make Daddy die and why did we lose our house and why did Mom get to be an alcoholic, and why did..." Joey sat with his eyes wide and his mouth hanging open like he thought I was going to explode with anger. I had been reading the Bible to the boys and praying with them at bedtime. They knew about my new, personal relationship with Jesus Christ. What they didn't understand yet was that the teachings of Jesus had changed my heart. My brothers weren't where I was in my faith journey, and I knew it wouldn't be wise to force my newfound faith on them.

"It's easy to blame God when things go wrong in our lives," I said. "But what I've learned from Jesus' teachings is that God doesn't cause suffering. Sin and evil are what cause suffering. We live in an imperfect world where people, including us, make bad decisions. Remember the verse from Romans that we read a few nights ago? It said, 'For all have sinned and fall short of the glory of God.' Do you remember the next verse?"

"No," they both answered. I couldn't quote it exactly, but I explained how God loves us so much that He sent His son, Jesus, to take our punishment. "All we have to do is repent and accept His gift."

"What does repent mean?" asked Joey.

"It means that when we mess up, God still loves us so much that He forgives us when we're truly sorry."

By their facial expressions, I could tell they were still confused, but I left it there. Gradually, gently I'd continue to introduce them to the Savior who had revealed Himself to me. I had made a life-changing decision, and there was no turning back.

Mindy helped me make another decision. It was true. I was drawn to Scott Campbell with his warm, brown eyes framed by those Harry Potter glasses and dark curls that fell across his forehead. What harm could come from having coffee with him and seeing if we had anything in common? I promised myself that if we got together, I'd be honest with him from the beginning. Then, if he should decide he didn't want to get involved with an eighteen-year-old guardian of two growing boys, so be it. He wouldn't have to waste one more minute with Abigail Jordan.

Epilogue – Ten Years Later

L adies and Gentlemen, it gives me great pleasure to introduce our new Director of Homeless Services, Dr. Abigail Jordan." From backstage, I hear the words resounding through the large hall filled with round tables that have been cleared by a bustling wait staff. It takes a moment for the announcement to register in my consciousness. It seems I'm the featured speaker whom three-hundred prominent Washington leaders have gathered to hear. I enter the stage and they are on their feet, smiling and applauding before I open my mouth. What if my speech flops? What if my words bring more harm than good to this important cause?

As I approach the podium, carrying the iPad on which my carefully prepared talk is saved, I look down at the large, round table positioned below the stage in front of the dais. Among those gathered there are my three most ardent supporters: my incredible, attorney-husband of two years, Scott Campbell, and our very tall, teenage "sons," Pete and Joe. Pete, a college freshman, plans to earn his MBA, and Joe will graduate from high school next year. Gratification swells in my chest when I think about the extraordinary young men they have become.

Standing next to Scott is my dear friend, colleague, and mentor, Selima Evans, the woman who changed my life. Opposite her is our friend, Gloria, with her husband, José. Beside Gloria, Grandma Jordan sits in her wheelchair. After Aunt Mavis passed away last year, Grandma moved to the east coast. Scott made the trip to Williamsburg to fetch her for this occasion. Although she can't rise from her wheelchair, the expression of pride on her face is ovation enough.

My lifelong best friend, Mindy Trent-Sage, would have aptly completed the circle, if she weren't weeks away from giving birth. According to her obstetrician, a trip to DC from Ohio is out of the question. However, both Mindy and her parents sent their congratulations and best wishes.

I'm not sure exactly when my career aspirations took a detour, but I remember the moment God nudged my heart. It happened at Harmony House the day Lori was helping me sort through the limited job opportunities available to high school drop-outs. Soon, I realized that, because I had received such abundance from God and his earthly "angels," I must one day find a way to give back to the universe. I could have accomplished nothing without those who helped me along the way, compelling me to assist others who find themselves in seemingly hopeless circumstances.

As my eyes adjust to the bright lights, connecting with one genial face after another, I can't help but remember the faces of "angels" who ministered to my brothers and me when we thought we were alone in the world. Many were total strangers whom I haven't seen since and likely never will see again. There was Officer Petronowich who drove us to the hospital in Williamsburg after Mom overdosed and Diana Manning, Mom's AA sponsor, who remained her devoted friend despite receiving not as much as a smile or a verbal response in return. We couldn't have made it without Reuben Gray, Mom's dedicated case worker, or Ellen, my online counselor through Alateen.

I remember the sweet, elderly lady at Union Station who, despite my rejection of her attention, sensed that we were in trouble and shared her own grandsons' hand-made gifts with my brothers. Then, there was the kind nanny, who appeared exactly when I needed her, providing directions to the nearest supermarket, sharing much-needed affirmation and pushing a five-dollar bill into my hand.

I'll never forget the unidentified jogger who helped my brothers and me traverse one final, impossibly long, city block to shield a feverish six-year-old from the cold, or Darla, the generous concierge who ministered to us with simple gifts of coffee and Tylenol, then insisted on driving us to the shelter. And I will always remember Josephine, the night security guard at Harmony House who, with her simple salt poultice, cured Joey's ear infection.

I'm grateful for the women at Dress for Success who treated Gloria and me with dignity and respect, and Lori Raymond, my dedicated counselor at Harmony House who advised me and equipped me with tools for the bright future that awaits me. Now I, too, volunteer at the shelter, trying to help other young women escape homelessness.

I will be forever grateful to Lisa and Brad Trent, who not only adopted our sweet Bella, but who continued to treat us like their own children, inviting us to every holiday celebration since that first Thanksgiving in their love-filled home.

Now that I've earned a doctorate in sociology and acquired a position of leadership, I stand here ready to present my detailed ten-step program, a plan for empowering indigent Americans and giving them hope for a better future. My premise is not based on pity or hand-outs. Rather, it follows the effective model of Harmony House, offering more than a temporary haven. It includes varied and valuable resources—especially education and employment—for enabling homeless citizens to get back on their feet. Step One focuses entirely on indigent citizens trapped by addiction. Other steps address the issues of nutrition, medical and dental services, mental wellness, and affordable childcare. The final aspect of my project is the pay-it-forward step. Every person who commits to the program and achieves success must agree to help others as they, too, seek to restore their self-worth and independence.

I'm about to unveil the documentary film I created for my doctoral dissertation. Following the presentation, I'll introduce my guest, the CFO of Macy's Department Stores, to announce that Macy's has awarded my non-profit project a one-million-dollar grant to underwrite Phase One.

How I wish my parents could be here to witness this proud moment. Sadly, Mom suffered a third stroke, ending her life at the age of forty-eight. Once I could afford it, my brothers and I traveled to Williamsburg monthly to visit her, though her condition failed to improve. We'll never know if her psychological demons drove her to toxicity or if she tried intentionally to commit suicide. The truth is no longer important. What matters is that, a few years before her death, with God's help, my brothers and I found the strength to forgive her.

Finally, the Jordan kids are free to reminisce about those early years when our lives were surrounded by the love and security of two devoted parents. We even talk openly about the long, lonely year after Dad's death when poverty and Mom's drinking plunged us into darkness.

Resting my iPad on the podium, I adjust the microphone and clear my throat. The guests take their seats. Now the hall grows silent, expectant. Briefly, I glance at Pete and Joe. Our eyes meet, and we share a smile. At last, my brothers and I can embrace the future with hope. We'll never forget the pain and hardship resulting from our father's untimely death or our mother's alcoholism, but through forgiveness, we have found release from the destructive power of resentment.

The Jordan kids are home.

Acknowledgments

I wish to thank the members my critique group in Williamsburg, Virginia who have provided support, friendship, and valuable counsel throughout the writing of this novel. They include Elizabeth Brown, Sharon Dillon, Barbara McClellan, Patricia Paquette, Christian Pascale, Dave Pistorese, Peter Stipe, and Susan Williamson.

I am grateful to Sharon Dorsey for her proof-reading and suggested edits. She embodies the essence of cooperative mentoring.

I thank my nineteen-year-old granddaughter, Katherine MacKenzie Tunstall (Kenzie), for her honest feedback and suggestions. Because Abby, my protagonist, was seventeen when she ran away with her brothers, Kenzie's young adult perspective helped me portray Abby authentically. Thank you, Kenzie, for loving my story as much as I do.

I am indebted to Jeanne Johansen, CEO of High Tide Publications, who transformed me from writer to published author with my first two novels, *Unrevealed* and *The Dark Room*. Through her tireless efforts to encourage her High Tide authors, Jeanne continues to accomplish her mission of promoting "literary late bloomers" like me.

Two other publishers, Dawn Brotherton of Blue Dragon Publishing and Greg Lilly of Cherokee Press have provided ongoing support and promotional opportunities for me and other local authors. I thank Dawn for her *Author Series* and *Author Academy*, and I thank Greg for his valuable *Writers' Workshops* and for establishing the annual *Williamsburg Book Festival*.

I couldn't write six hours a day without the expertise of my one-man geek squad, Carl Freeman. He maintains my laptop, rescues me from technological quandaries, reads my manuscripts even though they don't include space ships, helps with book launches, and keeps the IRS at bay (honestly). He also does the grocery shopping and most of the cooking. What a guy!

Finally, but most importantly, I thank my heavenly Father who loves me whether I succeed or fail, and who has been my source of strength and provision in every walk of life.

About the Author

After forty-five years as an educator and musician, Cindy L. Freeman began writing fiction. She relishes a good mystery, as in her novella, *Diary in the Attic* or an intriguing family secret, as in her novel, *Unrevealed*. Her second novel, *The Dark Room*, explores the difficult issues of Battered Woman Syndrome and Child Abuse.

In 2012, Freeman won a contest for her essay, "A Christmas Memory" in the online publication, wydaily.com, and in 2017 she won the Chesapeake Bay Writer's Golden Nib award for her non-fiction story about growing up during the cold war.

Cindy and her husband, Carl, live in Williamsburg, Virginia, where she directed a music school for twenty-seven years. They have two grown children and five grandchildren.

Visit her website: www.cindylfreeman.com to learn more.

Made in the USA
Middletown, DE
18 July 2019